THE ALPHABET
OF VIETNAM

The Alphabet
of Vietnam

Jonathan Chamberlain

BLACKSMITH BOOKS

The Alphabet of Vietnam

ISBN 978-988-19002-8-9

Published by Blacksmith Books
5th Floor, 24 Hollywood Road, Central, Hong Kong
Tel: (+852) 2877 7899
www.blacksmithbooks.com

Copyright © 2011 Jonathan Chamberlain

Dedication

This book is for Patrick and Christie.

Acknowledgements

I would like to thank the teachers and students I met in Vietnam who helped me translate the poems of Ho Xuan Huong.

CHAPTER 1

I'm sitting here waiting for her in the usual place, Betty's Bookshop. I check my watch. She's late. I look out the window to see if I can see her coming. I can't. Up till now she's been pretty good about the time thing. That's something I hate – people being late. But I guess it doesn't matter. I don't mind sitting here, reading. Betty has set out one corner of the shop with a few tables and a coffee machine. There's a rack of leaflets of upcoming events. And for those of us who are too mean and cheap to buy a half-way decent coffee, she also provides free coffee. It's the worst. Not much different from dirty dishwater. But hey, it's free. You get what you pay for. So here I am. Betty is behind the cash register with one of her girls. That's the way Betty swings. She may not know about coffee but she does know how to run a bookshop. And if it takes a dyke co-operative to achieve that, I have no qualms. That's just fine with me. Joe would cackle invective at the thought. 'You fucking pinko liberal shit.' I can hear him drawl out the words with mocking venom. It's almost as if he's still alive and living in the synapses of my brain. I'm not alone here. The girl at the next table is pale, no breasts, just skin and bones, face studded, spotty, shoulder tattooed, hair matted. Got a baby with her. How on earth did she get a guy to pop her cherry? (That's the way bro, Joe cackles. You tell 'em.)

I check the time again. Alice is ten minutes late. I can read from the confusions of feeling that I'm feeling about this that I've kind of fallen for her. She makes my stomach quiver in a loose bowel sort of way. This is a new feeling for me. It was never like this with Norma. And Maddie screamed into and out of my life like a blazing comet. Falling in love at fifty-five is no joke. It's crazy. Silly. I feel a fool. She used to scare me. Not because she's scary. She isn't. Not at all. It's me. I'm pathetic. Emotionally very wobbly. Vulnerable. Like jelly. Not because of her. Because of everything else. I just didn't know it until I met her. Then I saw how impossible it was to just reach out. You've got to reach out from a place. I didn't have that place. There was nothing there. And she was beautiful and pretended not to see how it was with me. And she is so strong and confident and clear eyed and everything a person should be and I am still stuck in this thing that I should have got myself out of long ago. But I'm getting out of it now. Something's happening. That's scary too. A different kind of scary. I want her to know how I'm feeling but I'm scared it's too strong. Don't worry, I tell myself. She's not going anywhere. You don't have to rush anything. Just let the way you like her seep into your words and the way you talk and the way you wave your arms and the way you smile. Let her know. But you don't have to dump it on her all at once. Let her feel it. And if she likes it she'll let you know. That's what I tell myself. I call myself 'you'. Like I'm my own father. Weird.

But I'm not sure yet what to make of her new Cadillac. 'My husband left it,' she explained when she showed it to me. 'He came to see me to sort a few things out and when he left, he gave me his Cadillac. He's gone now. He won't be back. He's gone from my life.'

'How can you be so sure?' I asked.

'I just know.' And there was a firmness about the way she said it so I know she knows something she's not telling me. Like he's got terminal cancer or something. But I don't understand about the Cadillac. But then again, why should it make sense? Some things just don't make sense.

Above the coffee machine there's a TV. The flicker of it caught my eye. The sound is off but the images are clear enough. Our soldiers in Iraq. They're coming back. Barack says so. Yippee! And then what? We still haven't learned from Vietnam. You send soldiers to fight meaningless, vicious, enemy dehumanizing wars and they come back home, they bring the war back with them. And the grand violence of our policy makers gets transmuted into little parcels – small individually wrapped little packets – of hate and rage and brutality. I know about this. I feel a surge of disgust. I can't look at the screen any more. I can't watch it. The knowledge I carry is sour in my belly. And then there she is! Alice. She's sitting right there at the table smiling at me. She must have snuck up on me. Christ! I jump with the shock of her being there suddenly.

'Ouch! I didn't see you.'

'You were a hundred miles away.'

Ten thousand more like it. Or nine thousand two hundred and fifty to be a little more precise.

'Was I?' I smiled sheepishly and nodded. 'I guess I was.'

'Like you were in a trance.'

'I must have been.'

She glanced over at the TV.

'It's good they're coming home.'

For them. Not for those who have gone to replace them. Note of caution – look at the statistics, not the pretty pictures.

'Yeah,' I said dutifully, looking into her gray-blue eyes. And I am quivering in my soul that this woman is in front of me, is my friend, is the object of my soul's desired connection.

'What were you thinking?'

I shook my head.

'You were thinking something,' she persevered, half question half statement.

I nod. She waits. I'll tell her or not. Up to me. No pressure. I want to tell her. I've already told her some. But the words won't come.

'Are you thinking about your brother, about Joe? Do you mind if I call him Joe?'

I nod and shake my head all at the same time. Why should I object?

'It's the same thing over again.'

Alice shakes her head and smooths back a strand of hair. 'It doesn't have to be like that.'

'Doesn't have to be. But it will.'

'We're wiser now,' she persists.

If only. 'You give poor boys the tools and the attitudes to wreak ungodly violence, they're suddenly going to let it all just drop away? It's all going to magically disappear? Hmm?'

'People…' she started to speak but I was into my rap. 'When we lost Vietnam everyone just turned their heads away. Ignored it. Froze it out. And the whole world went along with us because we're the power on the block. We learnt nothing. So Iraq comes along and it's the same thing all over again. And it may not be the disaster that Vietnam was but…'

'We've done some good!' she protested.

'Have we? Maybe we have. I don't know.' What else was there to say? You read stuff in the papers, you see stuff on TV. But is it true? You know it isn't. You know it's what someone somewhere wants you to think, wants you to believe in. There's always an agenda. It makes me sick. Just give me the truth. Whatever that is! And would I know it if they did? Jesus, the whole thing stinks.

'Why don't you..?' she paused. Perhaps she wasn't sure how I was going to take it. Maybe she didn't want another rap laid on her. But she decided to go ahead anyway and say it. 'Why don't you write it all out?'

'How do you mean?'

'Write a book about the lessons we should have learned from Vietnam. You know, like writing therapy. Write it all out. Get it out of your system.'

This was a new idea. Something to think about. The truth. The reality. The basic building blocks to understanding. The alphabet. Yes, that was it! I suddenly had a glimpse of how it might be. The alphabet of Vietnam. It was a good idea. Not quite how she meant it, maybe. But maybe if I tell the story. Joe's story, Maddie's story, Wash's story. Maybe then people will understand. Maybe in time Benjy will come to understand. Vietnam. The alpha-beta-gamma of the whole damn thing. Christ yes! Why hadn't I thought of that before? Just throw the whole thing down and see how it all comes together in its own way. If it does.

CHAPTER 2

For me it all started that day when Joe... What was he thinking that day? A normal day like any other, according to one of the only two men to see anything of what happened. Some sun. White clouds flecking the pale distant blue of the sky. The gorge itself rich with the colors of fall. Topton was the name of the place, the junction where highway 19, having climbed up the side of the mountain, ends in a T junction right at the head of Nahantala Gorge. A left turn takes you down the gorge with the stream beside you and the railway line on the far side. But here at Topton the railway track swings in towards the road and goes under the bridge that is the end of the highway. Then road and railway run parallel for a short way. According to the man who was painting his cabin a hundred yards or so away, standing on a ladder, he had taken little notice when he saw the car stop by the bridge and guessed it had come up the hill behind him. He heard the whistle of the train and it made sense why the man would want to stop his car at that point and watch. Trains! There was something nostalgic about a train – now just for freight and a day out with the family to see something of the countryside, but in the old days... Yessir. Trains brought back memories. When going places was a high adventure. Here, the Great Smoky Railroad, did a trip or two most days. Goes from Andrews to Bryson City and on to Dillsboro. Excepting only that this wasn't the scenic train with its carriages filled with day-trippers but an unscheduled freight train hauling what-all-ever out of Andrews. That was all he saw: the man stopping and getting out of his car, the sound of the train and the man scurrying over the bridge. Nothing there to detain a man's mind and he'd flicked his eyes back to the job of putting a layer of enamel white paint on the woodwork of his cabin. And had it not been for the sudden metallic screech of the train whistle and brakes it would have sunk plumb to the bottom of the still well of his thoughts and disappeared without a trace. But when he heard the train come screeching – no other word for it – that high pitched whine of metal wheel scraping against metal rail, he guessed there might be something amiss and he'd stepped carefully down off of his ladder and put his paint down carefully and hurried best as he could, had to be careful of his hip that was troubling him some, to the bridge. When he got to the far side he couldn't at first see anything that might have caused the problem. But then he saw it and he had to turn away at the sight. God help him.

According to the train driver, they had just come out of the dark of the tunnel into the momentary dazzle at the far side. Something caught his eye. A movement he guessed. He turned to look back and saw this... this... (listening to him in the witness stand at the coroner's court you guessed he was struggling not to say idiot or some such descriptive word that summed up his true feelings)... yessir, the victim. Saw him scramble down the steep embankment.

It wasn't too far down. Just tall grass and low bushes at that point. He'd made it down to the trackside and for a few seconds seemed just to be running alongside the slow moving train but then he'd suddenly dived towards the train. God knows what he'd been trying to do. It didn't seem as if he'd tripped and stumbled. No sir. It had looked like a deliberate act. No, he couldn't say it was a clear-cut suicide attempt. Could be he'd wanted to catch himself a free ride. Maybe he just missed, misjudged the speed or the distance or his strength and he'd fallen across the track and the wheels had gone over him and well... sliced him in two. Messy business.

An accident. That was the eventual judgment of the court. Chrissie could cash in the modest insurance policy. There were no kids to think about. It was all hers. She could move on with her life.

And that day as I listened to the witnesses make their statements under oath it never occurred to me that suicide was a possibility.

I understood the train thing, the excitement, the sense of moving, going someplace, the adventure of it. I have a memory of trains and Joe. I guess it was when we were living in Lumberton, in Crescent Street – a small detail I remember because it was a strange name for a short straight street – just two lines of clapboard houses and trees and rubber tire swings that all merged one with the other without any fences between one yard and the next – a seamless stretch of grass and feelings. It was as if each section of the road had its own special shade of mood and smells. We lived there a year or two after dad died. Ma had a friend who lived there who helped us awhile. Crescent Street! Why's it called Crescent Street when it's dead straight? I kept asking until every time I asked they'd hit me on the arm, specially Joe.

On days when we weren't doing anything much in particular we'd saunter down to the rail yards where they loaded the tobacco. The air would be sodden with the heavy smell of the tobacco leaves. It is still the smell of my boyhood. We'd squat by the track and from time to time a train would go by. The V and CS. The veeunseeyess. That's how I saw it in my mind. It was just a sound. It was the sound of all trains, that odd hiccuping rhythm of a moving train tee-dum tee-dum (pause) tee-dum tee-dum (pause) tee-dum tee-dum (pause) the veeunseeyess (pause) the veeunseeyess. It didn't have any referent outside of that that I knew of. Later I found it stood for the Virginia and Carolina Southern Railroad Company. The track ran 100 miles in a straight line from the coast inland to Charlotte. We didn't know that. We'd see a train rolling by and we'd start shouting out the names of places we wanted to go to, maybe just because we liked the sound of the names.

'Kansas City.'

'Texas.'

'Nashville.'

'Santa Fe.'

'New Orleans.'

'San Francisco.'

Just any old name that sounded like it might be a neat place to travel to. Not discriminating between cities and states. And it didn't matter which names we called out because it wasn't any particular place but the whole wide world out there. I still have a sleeper pin, one of those eight inch nails of rusting raw shaped iron they'd hammer into the wooden sleepers and the rails to keep it all in place. There were lots of them lying in the gravel bank by the side of the track. One day I picked one up and decided it was my lucky token. But it was too heavy for my pants, kept pulling them down. I soon got tired of it and left it at home. I use it as a paper weight.

*

A is for arrival. It is hazy. There is hardly any color at all to the landscape. I had expected bright sharp colors but all I can see from the window is dull brown, a sort of gray-green, mottled concrete. Then a crunch as we hit dirt. A heavy landing and the roar of jets as we brake. We have been warned not to take any photographs in the vicinity of the airport. What are they frightened of? I remember the story of the American general inspecting Chinese troop emplacements. 'If the Russians come they will die!' the Chinese general proudly boasted. 'Yes, they'll die,' the American general agreed. 'They'll die laughing.' That's how it seems here. There is nothing here to hide. A few ancient aircraft sit on the apron. Some concrete loops, like huge pipes cut in half, run parallel to the landing strip. What on earth can they be for?

Disembarking, we are taken to a hall where we are given forms to fill in. They look like forms I have already filled in except that some of the questions are different. Along with nationality and religion they ask for details of my cultural level. I ponder this. Would 'American' be sufficient? Given that I am American should I write 'high' or 'low'? I don't know what value to give to my cultural level. If I prefer jazz to classical music is this a minus? The room is organized so that immigration counters are set up on two sides of a square. The queues that form inevitably get entangled. There is some laughter at this. But perhaps the problem lies in the idea of queues. Maybe the arrangement is designed for huddles. The immigration officers work in pairs, a man and a woman. As ritualized as marriage. The woman at my counter is slim and delicately featured and very, very attractive. I am fortunately near the front of my huddle and it takes only twenty minutes or so to emerge into the freedom of the airport hall. I have now officially arrived. It's a strange feeling finally being here in Vietnam. I was too young to go myself – go to that Vietnam that was a war waging way over there on the other side of the globe. This Vietnam is not a war. It is just a place, a country. 'I'm here!' I think to myself wondering why on earth I think this is somehow significant. But it is.

*

Back to Joe. It all started with that parcel, that letter. The funeral had been on the Friday. Now it was Monday lunchtime. I was in the college staffroom having sandwiches when Paulette from the office downstairs came in carrying a box.

'I'm sorry. I should have given you this earlier. It arrived last week when you were away, at your…' she hesitated, not knowing how to say it. I noted that she seemed slightly flushed, out of breath.

'The funeral, yes, yes,' I said to reassure her. 'That's fine.' I took it from her hands. I looked at the address and saw it was in Joe's handwriting and nodded to her that yes it was for me. He'd scrawled 'urgent' across the top. Why had he sent it here? I remember asking myself. Then I thought it must be Norma. He hadn't wanted Norma to open it. I was slowly puzzling it out wondering whether or not to open it here or to wait till I got home. I took out my pocket knife and cut through the brown tape holding the box together. Inside there was a letter and below that some notebooks. I opened the letter reluctantly. I might easily not have opened it at all. I shiver when I think that I might not have read it at all. But I unfolded the sheets of paper and began to read.

Dear Fucking Brother,

I need someone to talk to. Guess you drew the short straw. This is buddy-buddy stuff OK? Strictly Confidential. Just you and me. And a bottle of Jack Daniels and my tortured dreams. Oh fuck Jack!!!! Shit! Why can't I keep my head in shape? I want to blow my fucking brains out. Jesus. For once I'm not cursing. Jesus save me. I wish I believed that crap. God and forgiveness. How can you forgive the unforgivable? I am beyond redemption. I've committed great evil and it won't go away. It sticks to me. I've tried scraping it off but the evil is in my very core. In my bones. In my fucking marrow. You're the literary bastard. Isn't there a phrase about that in Shakespeare? And if there isn't by God there ought to be. Jesus, this is hard. This is going to take much longer than I expected.

Will you forgive me? Why am I asking you? Jack, fucking brother Jack, you are reading this because I have decided to go ahead and kill myself. Truth is I'm already dead. When did I die? Didn't happen in one day. It wasn't like I was alive one day and dead the next. Guess I just took a long time dying. Now it's done and I am dead and Wash couldn't save me. Not this time. I fragged my insides and no-one can see except me. I'm leaving you these words so as you'll understand why I'm not coming back.

But you've got to do something for me. You've got to save my kid. Promise me you'll do that. Oh fuck. The kid's been driving me crazy. I've been talking to it – remember how I told you our Pa used to talk to you while you were still in Ma's belly. Well, that's how it's been with me. And the kid has judged me, Jack. Those wide open eyes of innocence. They see the truth of me. And the kid has to live – this kid is my future. This kid is the whole world to me. I really don't know how to explain it. But Maddie is the mother and if Wash has his way she'll be dead in a matter of weeks and the kid with her. But Wash is my brother and I cannot do him harm. Just cannot do it. I can kill myself but I cannot kill Wash. I thought about it. Believe me. Tried to psyche myself to do the deed. But although I am an evil bastard, I just could not do it. I am in a wild blue funk. You have no idea. I can't stop the whirl of thoughts in my sick head. Going mental. There's a look in her eye, a kind of knowing. I can feel it comprehending me. Did you ever feel that, Jack? The eye of wisdom and all knowledge? The look that sees right through you, and sees the worst and forgives. That's right. She's scared. She knows the score. And I don't want it to happen but what's the choice? I can't let her go. Jesus, what else can I do? Christ!!!!! Wash is my brother! Fucking brothers, man. That's the mantra. There ain't no other truth. Oh God! Oh God! And she's the suffering Virgin Mary. Can't explain it better than that. She's the very principle of goddamn everything that's true – it's her beauty, the beauty of trampled innocence. Jesus! What am I trying to say? She's what I yearned for when I was 17, when I was 18 and 19 and when I came back from Nam I was too ugly for it. And now she says she's having my baby. A baby. Oh Jesus. I can see the eyes looking at me right now, big round and innocent as judgment itself. Oh Jesus! Oh God! What do I do? What do I do? This can't go on. I can't go on feeling this way. We got to stop what we're doing but Wash ain't going to stop. I know him. It ain't his fault. He's been fucked up by life same as me. But I want to stop and he ain't going to stop. And she's going to die if I don't do something. And I feel she has in her something that can heal me. But I'm way past healing. I'm too far gone. I know that. Got to go. Time to do the deed. The least of ten thousand evils. Damn I wish I could save the girl. Jack? Could you be a fucking hero? You read these notebooks of mine you'll understand. Jack, do what I'm too chicken to do. Please Jack. It's the last thing I'll ever ask of you. Ha! That's a joke man – Sick joke, I know. Time to move. Don't think too badly of me, Jack, OK? I ain't all bad. Oh God! How do I say this? Jack. This is Goodbye. See you when you get to Hell! No. Shit. Can't leave it there. I'm just meandering again. Let's get back on track. You got to go to the cabin (I've drawn you some maps) and you have got to rescue Maddie and the kid that's growing in her belly and if you can do this without killing Wash I would be very much obliged. But he's a mean fuck and if you have to do it, then do it. And maybe you need to do it anyway. You'll be doing the world a favor. Fuck! You don't know what I'm asking. You have no idea. And maybe I'm setting you up to be killed yourself. So you got to be careful now. You got to have a weapon. I'm trusting that you with your brains can find a way out of this mess. And I want you to know that much as I have abused you in my thoughts I have always respected you for your intelligence and stubborn persistence. You are the salt of the earth and if you were here I would hug you. I want you to know I am proud of you. Proud to have had you as a brother. Proud to have been your brother. Understand? I wish you good luck, brother. Bring the next generation of Gausses home and bring him up as if he was yours. For me. For my sake and for the sake of the kid you and Norma never had.

> *Your ever loving brother,*
> *Joe.*

I looked at the following pages that contained a number of maps – each one narrowing me in on a remote cabin deep in the Appalachians. The final one gave me a detailed layout of the cabin itself and the outhouses.

I had to read the letter several times. The truth refused to sink in. What's he trying to say? I asked myself, refusing to take in the simple truth. And then at last I got it. There was a pregnant woman up in the Appalachians who might already be dead – but if she wasn't, it was my job to rescue her. And my first thought was just to hand this over to the cops and let them deal with it. But I thought of Waco, Ruby Ridge. The last thing I wanted to be responsible for was a shoot-out that ended in a tragedy. I just didn't trust them. Dammit, why couldn't I trust them? Why did I have to do it? And what exactly was it I had to do?

'You OK? You look as if you've seen a ghost,' Harland Fullilove commented. But the buzzer went for the start of afternoon classes and I was saved from having to respond. Fortunately, I had a free lesson. I was going to have to do some hard thinking.

*

A is for Ao Dai. This is the national costume for girls and women. It consists of a top with a tight neck, that is taut down to the bottom of the rib cage, then flows like streamers separately front and back down to just below the knees. Under this they wear a pair of trousers that are tight round the buttocks and then the leggings billow out wide. It is a beautiful sight. Every time I saw an ao dai I turned to watch. It was only towards the end of my stay that I realized that I was eyeing up schoolgirls. The pure white ao dai is the national school uniform for secondary students. The young girls let their hair grow long. It flows down their backs to their waists. Some wear conical bamboo hats to keep off the sun. It is the very image of innocence to see a bevy of beautiful girls on their bicycles, shimmering white against the dust and green of the landscape. Curiously, the girls not wearing ao dais are not spectacularly beautiful. I understand a little more Joe's terrible compulsion. I look at these girls. Breasts firmly outlined. White underpants clearly visible. I am aware of the sexual tautening in my groin. I try to put it out of my mind. 'They're schoolgirls for Chrissakes!' I tell myself sternly. I feel like a rampant ape in Eden. Even at my age! I force myself to look elsewhere. 'Jesus, Jack!' I tell myself again, 'They're only schoolgirls!'

CHAPTER 3

There's a picture of Joe on the mantelpiece in the sitting room. A photo taken at his passing out parade. His hair is a tight brush of blond bristles – a vestige of hair. The rest of the scalp is shaven. His face is taut with a smile – a real smile, a smile that hides devilry proudly – held tight between clenched lips. His uniform is buttoned down. This is the photo that every family with a son in the army has on its mantelpiece; the photo that appears in the obituary columns of the hometown newspapers.

Elsewhere, in albums, in a large box of stuff of his that I've kept, there are other wartime photographs. The gangling soldier with helmet strap dangling, cigarette hanging from the edge of the mouth – the very image of Vietnam cool. Giving the V sign from a hammock. Sitting in the back of a pedal-cab. Arm draped round a girl in a bar. Lying against a levee in a paddy field. Joe, is this all that's left of you? That and our memories. The strange details one remembers. The volumes that have been forgot. We lived together some eleven years by my calculation. He was six years older than me. He left when he went into the army when he was seventeen, one month short of eighteen. So from the time my permanent memory started to kick in at around the age of four, say, until he left home when I was twelve, there would have been eight years about when things happened that I would have remembered. But my hoard of memories is pitifully small. I remember once we had a fight and he threw a cactus at me and I spent an afternoon on the couch having cactus bristles plucked out of the back of my neck. We were always fighting. I tried to hang around him when he was hanging around with his friends Paul Baxley and Spencer Bullard. They were always trying to shoo me off. It was just a game for a while until I had friends of my own to hang out with: Lonnie Linkhaw, and Kevin Oxendine and the Rancke twins. I never took it personally that he didn't want to play with me. It was just the way things were. As far as he was concerned I was just an annoying brat who got on better than he did at school. He hated the fact that he had to walk me to school and then back home again in the afternoon. He always walked ten feet ahead of me, as if he weren't really with me, that it was just a coincidence. I remember the time he had to be taken to hospital after he fell out of the tree in Mrs Kelly's yard and had to have his hand put in plaster. And he looked funny with his broken front tooth until they fixed it. Then there was the time he played an April fool joke on me that I fell for: told me our dog Jake had been run over by a car and it was lying crippled two doors down in Sally Avery's kitchen. Well, I ran over there fast as I could and was no doubt incoherent in the agony of my anticipation. Well, they all had a good laugh about that. I wanted to get my own back but I never could think of a good enough story and he would laugh in my face. Fact is I was never a good liar. And then, for most of my teens, he was away at the war, then at college somewhere in California, courses that seemed to change and that he never seemed to quite complete, then there were jobs and girls that never quite stuck to him – and I had my own teen years to grapple with. He'd come home for Christmas. We had moved to Oxford, Virginia by then. Those were good times. We'd throw snowballs at each other and build snowmen and wrestle and choose different teams to support. And then he seemed to grow up. The years passed. Chrissie came on the scene. For a long while he was happy. Then something changed. Maybe ten years ago. He became distant in a strange hard way I never could fathom. Harder even than that emptied out hardness he came back from the war with. At least that's how I remember it. Not a lot. Now he's gone. Oh God! Once he put a king snake in my bed and I leapt as high as the ceiling it seemed to me when I pulled back my sheet and blanket and saw it. Yikes! And he nearly keeled over screeching and squawking with laughter. I was sure glad when he left and joined the army. That way I got to have our room to myself. I was getting self-conscious about being seen naked, growing my first sparse crop of pubic hair, getting my first wayward erections. If we live on in the memory of others then Joe's is an impoverished immortality. I want to change that, write things down, try to remember the details. But where do I start? As soon as I grab hold of one idea, other thoughts start tumbling in until I have something like a ball of tangled wires in my head – a tangle of ideas. I can't do it all at once, teasing out these tangled thoughts.

*

In the evenings at home, I sit over Benjy's sleeping form and when it gets too much – the thoughts, the memories: one sparking several that fly off in different directions – I pour myself another whiskey. And then it occurs to me that Joe wrote down something that... where was it? I dig into the box he sent me and pull out an exercise book. Here. I leaf through it, already fearfully familiar with the contents of this and all the other exercise books filled with his thoughts, his writings, until I come to the passage I'm looking for.

> *Why is it, when you're reading a book, it's all clear and simple and leads on from line to line so natural it takes you with it? But with me, old buddy, I can't barely get a thought out when it doesn't explode on me in all directions – I can smell the noise of the explosion. (Yeah! That's right. Funny ain't it. I can smell the noise of an explosion. It smells of wet mud up your nose and the shit-smelling gas of a paddy field)...*

That puts it as well as anyone ever could: ideas exploding in all directions. But then, as I think of it, it seems to me our experiences are not as similar as I first thought. For Joe, it seemed, ideas generated new ideas, and the momentum of thought was outwards and upwards and away from the center – but with me the ideas do not come from a single source, instead they are many and various, moving inwards, coming together from different directions. A slow, very slow, implosion.

Now that the box is open, I pull out a handful of the exercise books that Joe wrote in – he was always writing, even up to the morning of his dying. Like I'm doing now, it seems, he was trying to remember the details, get some sense of coherence, yes, just make some simple sense of it, explain himself to himself. It came as a shock to me when I first started to read them. They were like arrows to my soul. They traveled at the speed of bullets, hitting me in my chest and guts, into my innermost being. You see, when Joe wrote, he always wrote in the form of a letter, and they were all, every single one of the letters, addressed to me. For years he was talking to me, describing his deepest thoughts and feelings and I never knew. I didn't know because he never sent them. He had a lot of papers: rambling thoughts and memories that he couldn't tell anyone but himself and posterity. And they were all addressed to me. I opened one of the books at random, then leafed through a few pages until I came to this one:

Jack

You're the man with the brains. Have you figured it out? A man kills another man and he fries as they shove 20,000 volts through the bastard. Another man sends 60,000 guys to their death in Nam, and he's a fucking hero. He's a great man. Lyndon B Bloody Johnson. How does that make sense? Can governments do what the fuck they like: kill, rape and pillage and all that crap but we have to toe the line? Why for Chrissakes? What gives governments the goddamn right? Because they got the guns? Is that it? Might is right? Huh? Is that it? Is that all there fucking is to say about it? I have to do it or my ass will get busted? I just don't know. You grow up believing everything's for the best, everything's just the way it ought to be. God's up there smiling down on us. Mom and Pop are happy and content. The government wants what's best for us. Teachers are doing everything they can to make you into a good citizen so you can step into your pappy's footsteps. The news you read in the news magazines and watch on TV – that's the truth. You grow up believing it all. And so you join up for the righteous war and next thing you know you're crapping your pants up to your eyes in some fucking muck of a rice field on the other side of the world and the fucking guys you're supposed to be fighting for and with are sitting somewhere else nice and cozy and all bunkered down because you're the patsy and shells are blasting craters all around you – and you realize it's your own fucking side that's shelling you because some ignorant fuckhead has got his co-ordinates wrong indubitably (that's your kind of word, Jack, right?) because his fucking brains are addled with various kinds of hallucinogenic chemicals. And does that make sense? No, hell it does. Then you realize NOTHING makes sense. Two and two make sixty three and a half. Nine minus four means you're totally screwed. That's what I learned out there in the paddy fields of Nam in the cold crystal moonlight of terror. Might fucking is right man. You take what you want and spit out what you don't. There are no rules man – excepting the rules you make for yourself, the rules you choose to live by. All the rest is a mere mess of dogshit – the coincidence of accidents. And it's a choice. It's your choice. You can go on believing God is good – or you can wise up. That way you may get to live a little longer – or live, goddam it. Just live.

Get what I'm saying kid brother? I guess what I'm saying is
I've lived my life pretty much as I want to and it may not
look pretty but it's mine. I done things that I know would just
disgust you. But I ain't got any regrets. Everyone's the enemy
so everything you do is justified. That's right brother, let your
mind dream up horrors. I dare say you couldn't dream up
something so horrible I haven't done it. That's the truth. And
I say it again. I got no regrets. Yeah. You got the pretty, pretty
life. The flower beds, the two story house with carport and
lawn. You got the wife and you teach your students and you
go to church – in one of those snooty red brick colonial clean
and neuter baptist churches – and you got it all made man.
You're a decent citizen. Hell, you're up to your eyeballs in the
crap. And maybe that's how I would have been if I hadn't
gone off to war for flag and country, to defend the American
way of life.

Now, I'll tell you Jack...

But what it was he intended to tell me ended there. Maybe he'd
got up to pour himself another whiskey – he liked his whiskey –
and happened to catch a baseball game on the box and when he
came back to the letter he couldn't figure out what it was he was
going to tell me. Or he'd fallen asleep or had had a pressing need
to piss. One minute he'd had a message so urgent it had demanded
its own entry point to the page; the next minute it was gone. He
was left with the butterflies of the mind, the momentary flicker
of evanescent truths, a glimpse of the inexpressible absolute. But
Joe had written and written and written. Bits and scraps. Over the

years. A whole treasury of pain. A testament to horror. Because Joe was one hundred percent right. There was no horror I could imagine that he didn't claim to have perpetrated – that I fully believe he did perpetrate.

*

A is for Agent Orange. Chemical defoliant. It kills the vegetation. It deforms babies. It gives people cancer. There is no scientific proof that Agent Orange causes genetic deformities or causes cancer, say the American administration. Sure. Just as there is no evidence that cigarettes cause lung cancer. At the American War Crimes Museum, there is a horribly deformed fetus preserved in formaldehyde. I was horrified. I peered at the bottle wondering what it was. Realization grew with terrible slowness. 'Oh no!' I said out loud in the empty room: 'No! No!' The words tore themselves from me. I had to turn away and look elsewhere. For a moment I was embarrassed. Then I wondered at my embarrassment. Why should I be embarrassed at the raw horror I felt at the awful consequences of chemical war? Should I not be more embarrassed to admit that I could look at a photograph of a man being stabbed in the guts by a G.I. and not feel much emotion? There were pictures of other deformities. Not merely ugly. Monsters. A face with no openings for eyes. Another with only a mouth and a single eye – no nose. These are not normal defects. Propaganda! I can hear people say. Commie Propaganda! Maybe so. But it is very effective propaganda. As someone once said in other circumstances: 'Why is it always their propaganda. Why can't it be ours?'

I read somewhere of a poll in which 82% of Vietnam veterans said they would be prepared to fight again in Vietnam if all constraints were lifted. I wonder what that would mean. No constraints at all? Joe, how would you feel about that? No constraints Joe? I ask. I can almost see him licking his lips. No constraints at all?

Agent Orange was not alone. Before Orange there were Agents White, Blue, Pink, Purple and Green. After Orange, scientists developed Agent Super Orange. Many scientists must have worked very hard on this project. I think of these scientists. They must have been proud of what they did for the war effort. All dedicated men. Were there any women among them? Should they not be made to work with pictures on the walls of their laboratories of deformed babies, genetically deformed, twisted mockeries of human flesh containing little human beings? It might give them a sense of their true purpose.

A is for Apocalypse Now. This is the name of a girlie bar in Saigon. It has the reputation of being the raunchiest place in town. Compared to many bars back home it is tame. A dark, dimly, pinkly lit interior. I walked past it one evening. There was a young American lad inside. He was in his early twenties. He had a bandanna round his head. He stomped from the front to the back and said in a deliberately twangy voice: 'Hot Shit!' It was clear he was, in the interior videos of his mind, playing a part, re-enacting a moment, the moment of orgiastic amoral violence – like that depicted in the film. This was a text. I analyzed it. War had been translated into an attitude, a style. Some enterprising Vietnamese was making money by providing a set for these infantile desires to be expressed. Appropriate, in the context, that violence and sex go hand in hand.

A is for *An Autumn Scene*. A poem by Ho Xuan Huong.

> *The sound of rain*
> *Dripping on banana leaves*
> *Slow and monotonous*
> *Gloomy and sad*
> *No artist's magic can capture its beauty*
> *Far away a tree spreads its branches*
> *A large green umbrella.*
> *Weed on the surface of a placid river glitters*
> *I am drunk drinking in this view*
> *I am filled with wind and the moon*
> *I grow heavy with poetry.*
> *I tell you, the world has its feelings*
> *And people have their weather*
> *Oh sight! You speak to my heart.*
> *We are at one with one another.*
> *How can I not feel a most profound wonder.*

*

Here's something else Joe wrote:

> *Jesus! Wash's right. Go to ground. Let the madness swirl*
> *around you. Stay still. Get dug in. The whole thing is going*

*to blow. You can't trust the newspapers or radio or television –
definitely not that old propaganda whore television. You can
only trust your senses. We're dug in. Can last a year I reckon.
Conventional warfare. No-one's going to nuke Compton. Gas,
germs, fallout? You can only do your best. Food, guns and a
fuck. That's all you need. One day they'll turn the guns on you.
And the incoming is your own side trying to blast the hell out
of you cos they don't like what you're saying.*

*I've been hard places. I envy you, Jack, and Mom for your
basic, simple, fucking decency. You live, you have lived, your
simple decent lives without it seems any moral qualms. You
have nothing to have qualms about. A little petty meanness
here, a dirty, little moral turpitude there. I spit on it. Nature
is grand. It is absolute. What do I really think? If I could
change places with you tomorrow would I do it? You. Fat,
ugly Jack and your shovel-faced bitch wife Norma? Shit. I'd
be bored to tears. I keep myself in good shape. I can still fuck
three times a night. Still got it in me. I can still go out and get
any piece of ass I want and I can make her do what I want
and then... Sure! I can do it! Maybe not now. Not right now.
But it'll come back.*

*Jack, you've dug yourself deep into your books because
you're scared of what life is like. You haven't dared set foot
outside our home town. OK. You went to Chicago but then
you came scurrying back. You choose to live with an ugly
woman because she is no threat to you. She won't leave you.
Never. Ugly as you are Jack with your shit-scared jelly fat that*

you've covered your body with to escape from having to... Oh shit! Why am I trying to hurt you? Forget it.

Maybe this is for you. I never was good at saying what I wanted. I wanted to tell Wash but he's gone into deep paranoia. He's shot the roof a couple of times. It's the silence. It's the shagged out girls. We thought it would be paradise up here among the trees and the mountains. But it's not working. We thought it would be a gas. Pull in the girls and then dump them when we'd used them up. It was fun at first, a real high. Yeah. I used to laugh at you. You've never known that electric buzz thrill of going over the edge, way over the edge and then coming back again. Whhoooeee! To do the outrageous, the unforgivable. That's a real high. But then comes the low. It's an adrenalin kick. You get withdrawal symptoms. I thought of you as dead. I despised you. You'll never know what it's like to lick the razor's edge and relish the bitter taste of blood. You're kind of bunkered in nice and comfy. Yeah. You haven't done any evil like I have. You haven't roamed the lonely streets of night looking for action. Looking for euphoria. Let me tell you something. It's not out there. It's just mean and hard. You know that, don't you? You don't need me to tell you. I felt superior to you. I just want you to know that I don't feel that way any more. I envy you, man. I envy your simple orderly existence. But I got shipped out to Nam and when I came back there was no way I could infiltrate back into normality. I was too way out. Church and red-brick houses and lawns shaded by oak and chestnut. Shit! I was cut off from that. I went to church but inside I sniggered. Can't get much worse than that. At judgment day they'll line us all up and when my turn comes they'll say to me: 'You killed some babies and you tortured some women and you sniggered in church.' It's going to be real bad when I come face to face with my maker. Just joking. I belong to the school of thought that says I'm just dust and I'll go back to dust and my energy will zip round the cosmos for an aeon or two until I get wrapped up in a new living being. What will I be? A sea slug? A snail? Something slimy, something that stinks.

I'm saying a lot of things that don't make much sense maybe. I never did tell you about Nam and I never will. I've written some of it up but frankly I'd rather you didn't know what I did. Just take it from me, it was bad. Or maybe one day I'll let you — no, I'll make you — read what I've written and I'll watch your face screw up in disgust. Yeah. Then I'll beat your fucking brains out.

You know it's funny. I thought I had a lot of things I wanted to say to you. But it turns out I don't. Whoo Whoo! There's an owl out there. It sounds like a train in the distance whistling away. Only thing I ever loved was the trains. Remember? We used to go to the tracks and say to each other: That one's going to Pittsburgh. That one's going to Philadelphia. That one's going to Kansas City. That one's going all the way to New Orleans. That one's going to New York city. Buffalo, Chicago, Illinois, Wherever. I didn't know. I was just inventing destinations. Names I'd heard of but didn't know where they were. That's how I feel right now. I feel I'm looking down from a great height on a lot of tracks. Each one is heading in a different direction. All I know is I've got to take one of those tracks. I just don't know which one. But I got to choose now else I'sa gonna 'splode. Private joke.

I suddenly realize, re-reading this epistle that you don't know who Wash is. That's how distant you and I are. You don't know who my very best friend is. Wash's my war buddy. We killed Cong together and they did their fucking best to kill us. And who's Jack Daniels? A good question. I'm looking into it.

I should start at the beginning, shouldn't I? Like all good story tellers. But I don't know where that was. In the beginning...I was sent off to the war. Before that I was just a clear-eyed blond kid. A high-school jock. Then I went off to the war. Nam. I didn't even know where it was on the maps. Jesus I was dumb. I thought it was the whole fucking blob of land. I didn't realize it was just a skinny strip of territory hugging the coast most of the way. So that was the beginning. Weapons training. Oiling the black metal. Taking it apart and putting it back again blindfolded. I loved the cold feel of the gun metal, loved getting blasted on every one of the vicious concoctions that came my way. I did everything. Horse, coke, whatever. Then I quit. Frank Zevich bawled me out. He was my number two amigo for a while – Wash was always number one. You don't know Wash. That's another story. Frank said he'd personally take great pleasure in fragging me if I didn't straighten out. I was a liability to the team. Fear. Fear's as good as any drug. The adrenalin rush. I got addicted to that. I quit. I even quit smokes. Quit everything for a while. Really cleaned up my act. If Zevich hadn't been messed up real bad by a mine – one of ours – God bless you Mr Claymore – I'd be on the straight and narrow, gospel thumping road to Heaven. As it is... I love the fear. The edge. Did you ever walk close to the edge? And stay there? I got to savor the fear. I liked to analyze its components: the quaking emptiness in the stomach, the dryness in the mouth, the asshole tightening, the breath. That's what you had to control. Fast breathing was the first sign of panic. You had to relax. Breathe slow and easy. That was the trick of it. I guess you don't get to panic too much in that dinky colonial campus of yours. You ever get cornered by a horny co-ed? Just joking. I can see you panicking already at the thought of what Norma would say to you. You and Norma? I never did see the attraction. And how is it you got so fat and I stayed slim as a weasel? Life's funny, ain't it? Ha Ha! I was telling you about fear. The edge. And then it started that you didn't give a damn. You got used to that fear. You needed more. You needed to get closer. And then you're so damn close you don't even dare breathe. I been there, Jack. Many times.

I was OK for a while after I came back from Nam. I thought I'd left all that behind. The swamp stink. The fear sweat. The fuck urge. The desire to explode. The need to inflict pain, to destroy, to obliterate. I said to myself: that's all in the past. It's over. It's done with. I had come to see the maggots in my soul. I identified that with Nam. I said: I'm going home. If not to Mom, poor Mom, if not to blueberry pie, still I'm going home to green lawns and manicured flower beds and a decent job and a wife who smells fresh and white. Yeah, the whole dream. I was young, Jack. That's what I thought I wanted. And it started out all right too. Tina. Remember Tina? Blonde Tina? I thought I loved her. I really did. The whole American dream. She was the living image. Know what? I couldn't get it up for her. It was humiliating. And she was so nice about it. Six months of humiliation. That's why I ran. That's why I disappeared. I couldn't stand all that crisp cleanness, and the virginal blueberry pies, and the homey twitterings of Thanksgiving and the suffocating warmth of Christmas. I didn't belong any more. I had to split. I had to go where it was dirty like my soul was dirty. I needed to talk to someone who understood. I packed my bags one day and lit out. I headed for Wash. In my hour of need he was the only one I could turn to.

Let me tell you about Wash. He was and is and always will be my true brother. My black brother. We went to the war together and we survived together and we came back home again together. He's a truer brother to me than you could ever be. I don't say that to hurt you. I wish we were closer. I wish we could have gone fishing together. Fishing is just a metaphor you understand for the great game of life. How would you have liked to fuck a girl at one end while I fucked her at the other — like Wash and I do when the mood takes us? Ah fishing! It was a joke that only I could laugh at. Hunting and fishing. I guess you understand now what I mean. I've hunted a lot of girls. And that's not just a metaphor. I've hunted them with real guns and real bullets. Yes, Jack. I can only guess at the growing horror on your face. I've killed a lot of women that I used and abused and then disposed of in the abattoirs of the forest. The killing ground. Then dug their flaccid flesh and bones into the ground. Why am I telling you this? I don't know. But you will never read this. I've been writing a lot of things. Writing my life out. The fun's gone out of it. Something new is happening. But I'm cut off from it. I don't know. I don't know anything. I'm feeling as lost as I did when I came home from 'Nam but this time there's no place to run. Oh shit. I need a whiskey. I need a whole lot of whiskey to addle my brains.

He needed to talk to someone and he only had me. But he couldn't tell me really. Not while he was alive. So he wrote me these letters in exercise books and put them in a box. And now and again I dip into the pile. I should burn them maybe. Maybe we don't need to know the truth. Maybe the truth won't help anyone. Maybe we have to keep on inflicting violence. Maybe it's our nature. Maybe… shit!

*

So I did what he asked me to do. I went up to the cabin. It was for Joe's sake. I wanted to tell Norma and I didn't want to. In the end I didn't have the words for it. Funny how neither Joe nor I ever had kids. A genetic sterility passed on from generation to generation, Joe had joked once. I guess I figured (if I did any figuring at all) that if anything happened to me Norma too – like Chrissie – would just move on with her life. We'd become a prematurely old middle-aged couple. So I took a week off work to deal with, as I explained to the Head, urgent, but vague, family matters; a request that, in the light of Joe's recent death, was sympathetically received. I felt a stir in the sludge of adrenaline I hadn't felt in a long time. It's a strange thing to say now but I was looking forward to the trip. I just told Norma I needed a break, to get away by myself. To go fishing. She must have thought this strange as I didn't have a rod and had never done any fishing. But I guess she figured I was still shaken up by Joe's death. Which I was.

It was a two day drive away. Long days on the interstate. Then, coming off the main highway, following a series of side roads that got progressively narrower until... I had just passed a barn, I remember there was a man plowing a field holding the plow down as he followed his horse. A lean man with a long straight shaggy beard, his baggy, shapeless pants held up with suspenders. There was something of the biblical fundamentalist about him. I had thought for a moment of consulting him, checking I was on the right road, but something dissuaded me. And then I saw the road ahead suddenly begin to climb up into the trees round a bend. And, there, at the bottom, at the side of the road, was a sign, hand painted but very clear. The sign said: 'Caution! Your safety beyond this point cannot be guaranteed.' What did that mean? I had been driving slowly in any case but when I read the sign I braked to a standstill. Cannot be guaranteed? Was it warning me of falling rocks or some other natural hazard? It seemed not. I didn't see any sign of authorship. This had not been put there by any department or forestry commission that I could see. And the more I puzzled it out, the more I could see that it could only mean one thing. If I continued along this road there was a fair chance I'd be shot at.

I checked the maps again and I thought perhaps I should retrace my steps to the farm a mile or so back. But that again did not seem to be smart. This was a part of the country where outsiders were not welcomed. He was as likely to mislead me as help me. I paused to consider my situation. Here I was. A little stream ahead of me was my Rubicon. The slight hump of the road as it bridged the stream was the way ahead. I had no choice. Either I braved the unknown hazard or I went home. It had taken me two days to get here. What the hell. Life is short. I gunned the engine and began the long climb up the track that soon ceased to have a hard top but became instead a dirt track of two rutted tire lanes. If the map was correct I was about eight miles from the cabin.

CHAPTER 4

Alice. We met first late last August. Brushed past each other as we did all the other parents as we brought our little darlings and angels to their first shock of education. For me all the faces were a blur, the daily contacts, the phatic exchanges of amicability, an agony to be endured, then, quick as I could, slipped away from. Oxford, Virginia is not such a big town and they all would have known my story. Not straight away perhaps but, you know, eventually. Benjy of course would have stood out – his connection to me not obvious. People would have asked, politely no doubt, tentatively. What's the score here? But gradually it was Alice's face that I came to focus on, her face that seemed most often to be turned towards mine, that smiled friendliness at first and then conspiracy and then, one day, we found ourselves (Hah! Joe's voice cackling. Found yourselves? She cornered you, bro! Yes, perhaps that's how it was.)

'Hello,' she had said that morning before I was even aware of her presence. The woman with the sophisticated look and the immaculate make up was all I knew about her. And then, bending down, she smiled into Benjy's face.

'And you're Benjy, aren't you?'

But Benjy didn't hang around for conversation. He wriggled his hand out of mine and started to run towards the other kids in the room. I had to hurriedly catch up with him to coax his coat off and mittens.

'Bye bye, Benjy!'

But he took no notice of me as he made for the box of toys in the corner.

'I guess that means he likes it here.'

I turned to the voice, nodding. 'I guess so.'

'My girl, Kathy, is the same. The minute she gets here she's off. And she doesn't look back.'

I managed to force my eyes up from her mouth, which I had been watching with as much concentration as if I read lips, to her eyes. I had to force myself to meet her gaze. But when I had managed the feat, I registered a slight shock. Her eyes were a surprising color – a deep water blue, the color of the ocean. Warm. I wanted to run, but I knew I had to deal with it.

'You're Jack Gauss, aren't you?'

She held out her hand.

'I'm Alice Baker.'

'Oh yes... yes.' I shuffled Benjy's coat to my left arm and shook her hand. There was the momentary shock of touch.

'Now, I have to um...' indicating the jacket.

'Oh here, let me help you,' she said taking the jacket from my arm and walking over to the hooks.

'There!'

'Um. Thanks.'

Clearly she was in charge of this exchange so I resigned myself to taking my cues from her.

'Maybe we could get together for a coffee sometime?' she suggested.

'Oh, yes, sure.' My heart plummeted at the thought of it.

'Maybe, after we've dropped the kids off one day?'

'Yes, yes.' (Stop saying 'yes' for Chrissakes! I yelled at myself. A silent scream.)

'Why don't we make it tomorrow? I'd really like that.'

Tomorrow? The word rose like a black curtain of storm clouds obliterating the horizon. Oh God. She must have seen the panic.

'Or the next day. Whenever.'

'Um...' (Make a decision! Dammit! Might as well get it over and done with) 'Tomorrow?' I was about to agree to it but then changed my mind. 'Perhaps Monday or Tuesday next week?'

'OK. Let's make it Monday.' She said decisively. So Monday it was.

'Great,' she beamed a nice friendly smile, 'I'll look forward to it.'

She put her hand out again and once again I shook it, feeling again the cool shock of touch.

'Well, got to run. Bye!'

'Yes... yes... um... Bye!' (Now what?)

Now what indeed. And Monday could not be put off forever. Taking Benjy into the school building, I was already aware of palpitations in the chest. Just keep calm, I told myself. Everything's going to be just fine. Just fine. Just fine. I caught hold of the

repetition as a mocking echo clanging around in my brain. And –
Oh God! – there she was, as if waiting in ambush.

'So, Good morning!' Alice Baker smiled, 'How are you today?'

(Just fine! Just fine! went the mocking echo).

'OK!' I finally managed to say after a pause, as if I had fully
considered the question and was making my best call at the
truth.

'Where shall we go for our coffee?'

Her smile and direct gaze disconcerted me anew. Her eyes
gleamed a clear, healthy, glistening white. It was unsettling to be
the recipient of this attention. I was a little awed by her eager
energy. She positively radiated. I could not force myself to meet
her gaze for more than a few seconds at a time and I felt a powerful
sense of relief when we turned to walk, she a little in front of me,
down the hall to the entrance and the world of light outside. The
morning air had a sharp cool edge to it.

'Come,' she hooked her hand in my arm. 'Let's walk downtown.
We'll find somewhere.' And I could feel something inside me
shrink into myself, away from her, away from the easy familiarity
of her touch, until it felt like a hard knot in the brain. Oh God.
Please just let me cope! I thought.

We found a booth at Mario's (The Italian Coffee House as it
subtitled itself) and we both ordered cappuccinos. And everything
was all right until I lifted my cup and my hand started to shake
and white suds of foam slopped over the side. I hastily replaced the
cup in the saucer.

'Oh God!' I said and felt like I wanted to vomit but couldn't.

Alice reached across the table and took hold of my hand.

'Please. It's all right.' Her voice had a sudden husky caring quality.

'Is it?' I wanted to run, to hide somewhere and wait till it all disappeared.

'I know something of what you're going through.'

'Yes?' Disbelieving.

'Yes, I do. I had a breakdown myself a few years ago.'

'You did?' I heard the victim in my voice reach out towards this understanding, like a dog eager to be petted and open suddenly to the possibility of abuse. I wanted immediately to withdraw it and go back into my hole but it was out there hanging in the air between us. But how did she know? It was a small town.

"There's life after Hell, believe me.' A certain sardonic note had entered her voice, flavoring her words with self-knowledge. At this moment, I knew this was a person I could talk to.

'Yeah?' Suddenly hopeful, desperate to believe.

'Yeah!' Smiling.

And for the first time I looked up to meet her gaze without fear and I found I had it in me to smile back. 'Honest!'

It was like being a kid again sealing a promise. I felt the heady, lifting, dizzying, stomach stirring sensation of release, of cares ascending, of them being taken away from me. It felt like a healing. Her eyes offered me the promise of new life. I gave myself up to her willingly. Perhaps this was too evident, too raw.

'Now tell me about Benjy and you. I want to hear the whole story.'

I laughed.

'That's what someone I knew once called a six-dinner story.'

'I'm not going anywhere.'

'No? What about Mr Baker? Mightn't he have other ideas?'

It was her turn to laugh.

'There ain't no Mr Baker in my life – not any more. That's a two or three dinner story in its own right.'

And so we got down to the business of telling each other our life stories. Alice started.

'Rich, that's what he liked to be called, but I used to think of him as the Big Dick. He'd get drunk most weekends. Then he'd beat the shit out of me. I took it for Kathy's sake. She was daddy's girl. But one day he hit her too and I was out of there. I didn't want him anywhere near the girl. I've made a new life for myself here in Oxford. I guess I was lucky. My Dad died, left me some money so I can live. Poor Dad. I didn't mean it that way.'

'You still use his name?'

She laughed.

'Oh yeah! The name thing. I tell you I married the man for his name. I married the first man who had a normal name who asked me out. I didn't think about whether I even liked the guy, I loved his name. Richard Charles Baker. You don't get more normal than that. When you're brought up as Alice Lipschitz believe me you don't want to know about it. I guess that's part of why I hated my Dad, you know, that white hot, livid hatred that only teenagers have the energy for. Giving me that name. It just wasn't fair. Shitlips is what the guys called me at school. No prizes for guessing that. Sometimes it was Licky Shitlips, say that when you're drunk. You bet I'm a Baker. I deserve this name.'

As she spoke, her brittle impeccability dissolved a little and I was relieved to see she was frail and vulnerable and human beneath it all.

And then it was my turn. I told her something of Benjy. The present I could talk about but the past was another place. I edged towards it then veered away, then back again nudging the story back even more, ever so slightly. Then, after a while, the words went dead on me. I was talked out. Drained. There's just so much you can say at one sitting. My mood slumped. I felt exhausted as if I had been running or swimming or climbing a mountain for hours at a time. Alice saw it and nodded.

'Hey! We had a good talk!'

'Yes, we sure did.'

'Let's make a habit of it.'

'OK.' (What was I letting myself in for?) 'Sure.' That sounded too distant. 'I'd like that,' I added.

We stood for an awkward moment in the street before Alice stuck her hand out to shake mine.

'I'm going this way,' she said indicating the direction of the shops. I elected to pretend I was heading in another direction.

'See you later,' she said and punched the air. And then she was walking away and I watched her for a while liking what I saw immensely.

*

B is for baguette. Everywhere you go, on every street corner, it seems, there is a stall selling long French loaves with tomatoes, onions, pate, cheese. They will make you up a submarine sandwich for twenty cents. Now, there is one thing you must note about this baguette and this pate. It is a common fate of things that they are taken from one place to another and on the way they change. 'Improvements' are made. The French left in 1954 after the battle of Dien Bien Phu. Almost 40 years have passed. But the bread is as good as any bread you will find in France and the Pate is, well, it's pate – what else can I say. It has not changed. The Vietnamese have taken it on unchanged. I commented on this to someone at the embassy.

'You're right,' he said, 'In Cambodia too. French baguettes. But even more interesting. When the Khmer Rouge took over in 1975 and started their mass killings and purges they wished to reduce Cambodia to a state of original innocence. They killed millions of people! Everything that had the slightest foreign connotation was cut out, exorcised, expunged. But the baguette stayed. It never occurred to anyone that the baguette was not from the very beginnings of time fundamentally Cambodian.'

'And we Americans didn't even leave behind the hamburger,' I said.

B is for belly. I waddle down to flop in the clear waters of the South China Sea. But once I am in the water I am curiously like an animal that has found its element. I used to swim for the school. I was the butterfly man. I find I can still do it and it feels that I am doing it with at least some grace because the beach kids are copying my action, or trying to. They flop and splash. They don't see the hidden movements of this most satisfying of swim strokes.

I dig deep into the water and arch and fly and dive and kick my way to the blue water beyond. The water is clean. Some occasional coconuts. They have no packaging to dispose of. I can see that with development the beach will soon be awash with plastic bags. But I was telling you about my belly. The fact is, it is excruciatingly funny for everyone here except me. People mime huge pregnant stomachs as I pass by on the way to the beach. I soon came to realize something. I was the only fat man on the beach. Even the other tourists are young, wiry. As for the Vietnamese they are uniformly hard, lean. Skinny agile boys do acrobatic backward somersaults on the sand. There isn't an ounce of fat on anyone. They eat rice and vegetables I suppose. They eat baguettes and pate. But they don't eat in the quantities that I eat in and they don't guzzle beer as I do. A beer now and then of course and the local beer is good. It has taste, body. I wonder who the Vietnamese copied their beer from.

*

Jack

I got to tell you how it is and was and maybe ever will be. I have to tell someone. Sometimes I think it'll kill me, or drive me mad. I know you don't want to know but to hell with that brother, I am going to tell you.

You try tell people what it was like, really like, and you have to stop. You see them saying to themselves: 'This is gross. This is disgusting. I don't have to listen to this.' Men. Women. It's the same. But what about me? I've got all these memories and thoughts inside me. Where did they come from? I went out to fight for God and America and God and America turned their backs on me and walked away. I'm left with the slime. Fuck you God. Fuck you America! Fuck you clean and pretty blonde prissy America! You came and dumped the collective trash can into my soul. Emptied the communal sewer filth into my heart and guts. Fuck you! You got to listen. You got to know how bad it hurts!

Wash says I know now how a black man thinks. He says I'm thinking niggah thoughts. Wash's my brother. He knows how I think. I know he thinks the same way. We're brothers.

God and America said to me one day: Joe! You've got to do your duty now, hear me? Got to go to Veee-etnahm. I said Yessuh! Yes Maaam! I got to go and kill a few Cong for God and America. Kill me a few Cong. Wear nice clean underwear. Wipe my bottom when I shit with good ole American Kleenex. Come home and marry a purty gal with a nice flowing frock and have crew-cut clean kids and get a job, go sell some 'surance and go to church every Sunday and think clean thoughts.

Wash cracks up every time I do this skit.

'Yo. You got it!'

'Yessuh, Mr Washington Thomas, suh!'

Oh Wash and I go back a long way. I saved his life. He saved mine. We fucked together. Still do. Brothers. How can I tell the world the truth about Wash and me? No way. No-one wants to listen. People want pretty thoughts, nice ideals. No-one wants to see the truth of the world. No-one wants to see the ugliness. But God and America shoved my head in the shitcan till I couldn't hardly breathe and the only way out was to eat my way out to the other side. No-one wants to know. That's a fact. Wash says it's been like that ever since he knew anything. But I saw Veee-etnahm get to him. Wasn't no re-run of normal everyday existence even for a nigguh.

Wash and I have this way of talking. It's the voice we use with each other. It's the voice I hear inside me when the darkness comes and I'm scared. I've got my good old Middle-America, white, suit and tie and barbecue in the back yard voice. I've got that too. Funny isn't it? And this voice would go into the rap at the click of a finger: 'Craziest war there ever was. The President had this dream thing. This dream said to him: America is golden. America can do no wrong. American is powerful. Got to show off this power man. People got to respect me. Goddam it those Russkies got to respect me. And the people around the President said: Yessuh! That's how it is. And their assistants said yessuh! That's how it is. And all the Generals and Admirals and Air-fleet Commanders said Yessuh! That's how it is. And all the brigadiers and colonels and majors and Captains said Yessuh! That's how it is. And all the Grunts said: Hey man! What the fuck's happening down here? This ain't what they said it was going to be. Shit man. Reality is different. These guys ain't never going to stop coming at us. This thing you're asking us to do is likely to end up in me being killed. Know what I mean? And a lot of other people besides. And it's dumb, can't you see that? And then some sergeant comes along and says 'Hey! You a soldier or not?

You best not question the truth. What do you know anyway? You ain't seen the cables. Cables contain the whole truth to which you ain't privy. And anyway since when did God give grunts brains?' Fact was no-one was listening. No-one. They were all doped up on this dream thing. More addictive than coke or heroin. Reality is not what you see, it is what we tell you it is. Not one fucker was listening and then we go and lose the war because hallucinations are a fine thing and all but they don't scratch hard facts.'

And Wash would grin his devil grin: 'Yo! You got it. Yessuh! Got it in one!'

*

B is for boat. It leaves the small fishing village at the end of Nha Trang beach under the shadow of the villas that the last Vietnamese Emperor Bao Dai built for himself on the headland. Mediterranean villas in peach and blue. The boat takes us to islands. The water is clear down to forty or fifty feet. I worry about sharks like a typical greenhorn. 'Are there sharks here?' I ask. 'Sure!' the crew answer and laugh.

There are fishermen splashing in the water, playing, pulling a rattan coracle which holds their nets. They are wizened and toothless and strong. They laugh at my belly. I have learnt to laugh too. Not uproariously. Quietly.

One of the crew is a shaven headed, tattooed seventeen year old whose stomach muscles are sharply outlined. He wields a knife with ease as he peels the potatoes and onions. He has a madman's grin and from time to time he leaps around fooling around. Knives flash. I have an image of pirates and the men who became pirates. We spend a few hours over lunch of prawns and crab and fish, floating in the crystal waters of a beach that shimmers gold. The water is shallow. Paradise.

After lunch I swim to the beach and go exploring. At the far end, hidden behind coconut palms there is a village that stretches back. A young man sees me and greets me and pats my belly and leads me through the village like a curator. The last house is concrete and substantial. There are young men working on a net. A girl is there looking at me in shy amusement. She is plump and pretty. My guide points at me, makes a half grab for my cock and then points at the girl. He makes a piston-like movement of his arm. He understands the need to communicate graphically. I decline with a laugh and wave and turn and go. The girl too seems doubtful.

*

I guess I was fifteen or sixteen and I just had the urge to do something crazy. Guess it was them hormones. Yessiree. All that testosterone coursing through my brains and my blood. A young man's fuck-need, but he don't know it. Or he knows it but he doesn't know how to do it, or if he dare. He'd have to jump someone and do it. And this time at night there was nobody to jump out on the street. And, anyhow, if he tried any of that nonsense he'd certainly get caught. But maybe it was worth it. Anyway, this night, I snuck out of the house with the car keys round about eleven, maybe twelve, after Ma had gone to bed and you were fast asleep – you always did sleep like a fucking pig, Jack, I could have played bongos all night and you'd never wake up – and drove off not knowing what I wanted to do or where I wanted to go – but just the need to thrill. I knew I had to find the heart of the moment and complete it. I drove off into the darkness of the countryside – down near Scuffletown – then headed off down a dirt track. And there was no moon at all that night. I know cos I stopped the car and turned off the headlights and I had the window rolled down and it was just me and nature out there, raw nature. At first I thought it was silent but then as I listened more I could here this low high pitched zinging of insects – a hissing and zzzzinging and behind it all a soft sound like the sound of breathing. Can't really describe it – like an infinite barely audible breathing. It was still, almost windless. It must have been one of those breathless hot days. I can't remember that kind of detail. Then I got out of the car. I was shitting myself man. I was thinking about all the snakes and bugs and spiders and so on. But my eyes had got accustomed to the dark and it was like a dare. It was something I had to do. And then I started to undress. It wasn't something I had decided to do, it was just something I did, as if it was the most natural thing to do. I took off my shirt and then my shoes and socks and trousers and pants until I was standing in the open air buck jack naked. I could feel the mud at my feet cool and damp. And then I got this great hard on – the biggest, strongest hard on there has ever been, like an iron peg. I grabbed hold of it and began to pump myself in a frenzy. Wow! What a great feeling that was when I finally came. Wowwee! Then, soon as it was over, I stood feeling emptied out and surprised at myself, and maybe a bit disgusted and ashamed of myself. Then it came to me that someone could come along at any moment and they'd catch me without a stitch of clothes on. I scrabbled back into my clothes. It was as though I had just been returned to sanity. I don't know what I would have done if anyone had driven up right then but they didn't. I climbed back into the car and gave a real whoop. It was like I'd done something really wild, crazy and now I was sane again and nervous and shameful and amused. Hormones man. They really make us crazy. Maybe that's the answer. That's why we're all goddam crazy. It's just hormones. It's just the way God made us. The more I think on it, the more I think that is the ultimate truth. Fucking hormones.

*

B is for bookshop.

Going into that bookshop – another bookshop half a world away – was to escape from one world to another; one glare-bright, sticky, sweat-sodden world of clanging, honking, screeching cars and motorcycles and pedicabs, a world of dull women clutching, of children pestering and demanding, of limbless men standing dumb and sullen, of limbless and deformed children; a world of dust and the intense, oppressive and burdensome heat of early afternoon; from that world into another, a world of cool shade and orderly peace. Reflective. The sounds of the outside world carried into the shop along the filtering space of the short corridor – but it was a distant clamor. Here was sanctuary. The books were old, mostly out of print. Cloth covers, leather. The titles suggested another time. 'Is China Mad?', 'The Hudson Report on Vietnam', 'The Quiet American'. Others were photocopies of popular paperbacks. Fingers touched the books lightly, here and there paused, drew a volume out to browse it, placed it back on the shelf, moved on, coming, at last, to a slim volume entitled 'Know Your Enemy!' Ah yes. We should all know that. The book taken out proved to be in good condition. The title page gave more information: 'An historical novel about ancient China by renowned French scholar, Marcel Jean de Boinville'. The copyright page showed it had been written in 1932 and translated two years later. I momentarily wavered. Did I really need this book? But if not me, then who? It might, for all I knew, be the last copy left in the whole world. Books dissolve, disintegrate, disappear, die. Pieces of the past disappear and die. Some money changed hands and the book was placed in a paper bag.

Know Your Enemy! As good an epitaph as any for Joe. Oh Joe! I look for you everywhere in this city that you also knew once, that was part of that crucible that formed you – deformed you.

But just as yesterday's river is not today's, the eternal molecules of time spinning forever their webs of infinite change, so this Saigon was not Joe's – even though I was here looking for the fragments that might explain the sudden implosion of his life.

This is Mr Hung's bookshop. Mr Hung worked for an American press agency before 'Liberation'. When the war ended all the embassies closed up. Libraries were thrown out on to the streets. Huge piles of books. So much rubbish. Mr Hung is 73 but looks 53. His cheeks are smooth, nut brown. His cheeks gleam. His eyes gleam. It is a good story. He beams round his bookshop. Crusty books.

'I haven't read them all. How can I? I have over ten thousand books. But I can say that there is something of me in every book. There is something of my spirit in each one. I chose every one of them. It wasn't so easy. I only had a bicycle with a basket. There were so many books. I had to choose carefully to make sure the books I was taking home were worth keeping. I had to thumb through them. They knew what I was doing but they left me alone. I was followed of course. But otherwise...' he shrugged. 'I would take three or four books each trip and I would make six trips a day. No-one else dared to pick up the books. But I did. I did it because I love books. I love culture. I love history. Without culture, without values, what do you have? My father wanted me to be a hero. My name 'Hung' means hero. But I am just a man who likes books. I am not a hero. All I want is to survive and to be comfortable. Is that too much?'

Mr Hung is clever. No-one buys these old decaying books, but they make a good backdrop for his main business which is selling photocopies of perhaps fifty titles. When Vietnam comes to recognize intellectual rights he will be in trouble, but that is a few years off. He also has done something valuable. He has made compilations from various sources and bound them together: a history of Cholon, a history of Vietnam. He has added illustrations.

He is now doing very well. His books are not cheap. I wish him luck.

It is here in the bookshop that I first encountered the Vietnamese poetess, Ho Xuan Huong. I was browsing in an anthology of Vietnamese literature when I came to pause at a page. There was this poem:

> The Swing
> *A swing has four supports, God be praised!*
> *He stoops over, swinging back and forth*
> *She lies back and watches, bracing wide her haunches*
> *Four peach-pink trouser legs flutter in the breeze.*
> *Two pairs of legs jerk sweetly taut.*
> *Playing Springtime.*
> *You know the games of Springtime, don't you?*
> *When the swing's support is taken out*
> *It leaves behind an empty hole.*

I had to laugh. It was very prettily done.

'This is marvelous!'

Mr Hung looked at the page.

'Ah! Our dear, dear poet. She is everyone's favorite. She is so clever. Impossible to translate.'

'But here is a translation,' I protested.

'All you have is the idea. But her ideas are often sharp and hidden. People may disagree over the meaning. And the games she plays with words, with sounds, with combinations. When it comes to poetry English is a clumsy language. Even French, though French is better. But Vietnamese. You can do many things in Vietnamese that you cannot do in English.'

*

B is for bus. I took a bus from Dalat to Nha Trang. It was supposed to take six hours for the 200 kilometer journey, and it cost around two dollars. Bus is a rather grand name for the vehicle I climbed into at 4.30 in the darkness before dawn. It was a minivan that, when full, carried twenty-six people and their luggage. Leg-space was the problem, tight even by local standards. My knees were jammed sideways. Still, we managed to get five people side by side in each row. Behind me a woman was carrying a cake with elaborate icing that she had to hold with great care to avoid damaging. She propped it into the upturned bamboo hat she had with her and rested this on the seat in front. The motion of the bus kept the hat's rim jabbing into my spine. We smiled at each other. Sweat rolled off me. The bus took an hour to fill up and as we left Dalat a bleak, watery dawn illuminated the sky. Six hours became seven, nearly eight as we punctured twice along the way. We all seemed to welcome these pauses in the journey. They allowed us to stretch our legs. It was well past midday as we rolled into Nha Trang.

B is for breadfruit.

> *My body is like a breadfruit in a tree*
> *The peel is rough and the cloves are thick*
> *Young man, if you love this breadfruit,*
> *Come here, drive in your peg.*

> *But please take care*
> *Don't touch the oozing juices with your fingers*
> *Or you will get them sticky.*

Mr. Le, a teacher I met, discussing this poem, provided the following piece of information. The breadfruit, when it is fully ripe, will fall off the tree and smash open on the ground below. For that reason, sensible gardeners will take the fruit down while it is still unripe. The fruit can then be ripened by forcing a wooden peg down the stem into the fruit.

'But some uneducated people only see a cruder meaning in the poem. Cloves have a clear sexual significance in Vietnamese,' he shook his head sadly.

B is for beggars. Children, young women with babies at the breast, cripples. The children are sharp, savvy. They speak French, then English. I heard one speaking Chinese or maybe it was Japanese. The cripples I give money to. They do well enough that others emulate them. I saw one man pretending he had no arms. Definitely he had one, probably he had both. One arm sleeve was closed with a clip. The other shoulder was artfully built out and his arm disguised within the shirt. He went from restaurant to restaurant singing Vietnamese folk ballads – one assumes the appalling sound had some traditional virtues. There are shoe shine boys. Old men and children hustle to sell maps, stamps, drawings. I never felt threatened, as I thought I would be, by pickpockets until one day an overly aggressive man trying to sell a map made me instinctively feel for my money belt. Under cover of the map his hand was unzipping it. I brushed him off. I was lucky. From that time on I was wary of the map sellers.

As I said, I give to the cripples. I think of it as a tourist tax. I keep my small change handy. They won't get rich from me. I hand out five cents, ten cents, sometimes as much as fifty cents. I saw a drunken sailor give ten dollars US to a girl who was dragging her brother around. He was blind. One eye bulged out and had a growth on it. A disgusting, pitiable sight. Ten dollars. She stared at it, dumbfounded. Ten dollars. They would remember that for the rest of their lives. I felt guilty then with my mean handouts. There was a woman with a baby at the breast and a hat held out. I put in a one thousand dong note. She kept her eyes mutely on me. I was in a shop. I got a further two thousand dong in change for some transaction. Impulsively I handed that to her as well. Three thousand dong! Enough for food for a day. Thirty cents American. Inside me a voice said: 'Go on. Give her ten thousand, twenty thousand. It's only a dollar, two dollars. I imagined myself heaping money into her hat. Ten dollars, twenty dollars. Why not? I had the money and wouldn't miss it. For her it might possibly change her whole way of life. But would it? Would I not simply be confirming in her the value of begging as a way of making money. Maybe if I gave her a lot she would be attacked and beaten by, who? Someone passing by who saw, perhaps, or her husband who needed it for gambling. Would I not be giving incentives to others to beg instead of work? The moral issues weren't clear. I could sense the evil of the grand gesture. So emotively pure. So riddled with contradiction and paradox. The great solution exacerbating the problem. Here! Take ten bucks. Get lost! Another problem solved.

Express your gratitude and never complain again. Oh America, where is your humility? And the young girl stood in the street with her blind brother and stared at the money in the palm. She was too stunned for gratitude. It was too munificent. The restaurant owner had to wave them off. They were lost. I thought about this a lot that evening. The way I saw it, the girl was faced with a dilemma. Should she report this to her mother? How could she hide it? But perhaps the mother would now demand that she bring back more the next day, now that she showed she was capable of getting more. It is a whirligig of conundrums, this grand gesture business.

*

Chrissie has been good for me. But she hasn't cured me. I thought she had. For a long time I didn't feel the urge. I just felt released. It was a good feeling. Not the best, maybe, but I'll admit it was good. But then Wash turned up- after all those years! And I was reminded of my true nature. Wash had been kicked out by his old woman, Carmen. She'd caught him cozying up to her thirteen year old daughter by a previous husband. Wash laughed to tell the story. He'd already fucked the kid. Forced her on the bed one morning and took her virginity. It's a simple truth. Every man is a rapist. Not every man has raped but every man wants to do it with violence. The idea of rape is exciting. Sex and violence. The words go together like peanut butter and jelly. Fuck is not a word of love but of hate. Fuck off! Fuck you! Go fuck yourself! Mother-fucker! To fuck a girl is not to give her love but to take the red

hot poker of lust and plunge it in her waters to cool. Women
exist to take the edge off man's hatred and violence. They're
there to swallow up all that hatred and turn it into babies.
You know something? When a woman knows she's going to
be raped and she's scared, you know what? She lubricates her
cunt. It's like she wants to be raped. That's the truth. That's
nature's way of saying that's the normal thing. Our nature is
made from violence and is composed of violence. Goddamn
it, that's the truth!

*

C is for cyclo. a tricycle with a chair in front and a cyclist driver
behind. 'Where do you come from?' 'Do you like Vietnam?'
'How long in Vietnam?' etcetera. The small talk of barbers and
cyclo drivers. But they are persistent. I asked them back: 'Are you
married?' 'How many children?' They want to talk. 'How long have
you been learning English?' I ask. Three months, four months.
They speak well. They should do well. It is hot work cycling
around, faces and shoulders are burnt. I tried to think of a word to
describe a deep brown that suggested also sweat and pain but all
the words that came to mind suggested ease and luxury: tanned,
bronzed, burnished. Chocolate brown, nut brown. `Sunblasted'
was the nearest I could come to it. I felt slightly concerned about
the weight I am forcing these drivers to pedal around until I saw
women going to market with huge sacks of produce, which they
perch on top of. I once saw a cyclo seat filled with eight children.
I didn't feel so bad then.

C is for Cholon. Chinatown. It is a suburb of Saigon. I did not look at my guidebook with close enough attention. I had it fixed in my head from what Joe had said about the place that it was a sister city. But there is nothing between the two places. No gap. One moves from quiet avenues to, a few blocks later, a throbbing, pulsating stream of humanity going about its busy business. The streets are crammed full of cyclos, cycles, cars, buses, minibuses, every kind of vehicle. The shops along the side are all open and bulging with goods. As one progresses along the avenue one passes elaborate Chinese temples.

Joe wrote to me several times about Cholon. It was a stinking stew of a place. It was evil. People disappeared here. This is where the deserters came. This is where the drugs were. The source. The Chinese whores tottered back wearily on clattering high-heel shoes with the approaching dawn. Cholon. The name breathed corruption, danger, slippery realities close under the surface. But for me, here, now, new and innocent, I had to smile. Certainly, it was crowded. The streets were narrow. But the people were people. Girls selling cigarettes at small street stalls caught my eye and smiled fresh, open, shy, somewhat surprised, smiles. People went about their lives in a simple, functional way. Everything was reduced to a basic functional simplicity. Clothes? A cotton shift over cotton pants and sandals. Food? Rice, vegetables, pork. Home? A room with a bed, a basin, a toilet, a cooker, a small, low bench to set food out on and diminutive stools to crouch on, chopsticks to eat with. What else did you need? Everything exactly what was needed and not one elaboration more.

But this seemingly endless, seething flow of humanity excludes. One cannot imagine entering this world as one can consider entering the world of Saigon. It is utterly foreign, that's all. And no doubt it is corrupt as it always, no doubt, was and always, no doubt, will be. Corruption is a very human disease. It inhabits the heart of every city in America. Why should it not be here too?

C is for camera. Walking in a backstreet in Cholon I saw a handsome young man. He was lean, bronzed, taut. He was shirtless and wore graceful, baggy, very fashionable (I guessed) trousers which were tight at the ankles. He was riding a bicycle with one hand and in the other he held a fighting cock. He was a proud young man. When I saw him first I thought to myself: 'Damn. There goes another fine shot I've missed.' But I came across him again a few minutes later, when I turned a corner and found him chatting with friends. As I passed I smiled and pointed at my camera and expressed with a show of hands that I would like to take a photograph. He seemed happy with the idea and immediately set the cock down on the ground. I wasn't sure what was happening but I gestured to him that I wanted to photograph him with the cock. When he realized what I wanted he pointed to himself and shook his head violently. Only then did I realize he had thought I had wanted to photograph the cock! He was so proud of his bird! This was the first experience I had of that old Chinese fear that photographs steal the soul. At least I guess that was it. Leaving him I followed the road down to a canal. There was a small shack with walls of straw mats and some rickety tables and chairs outside.

'Hey!' a man shouted and waved to me. A crowd of laborers gathered as I paused and bobbed my head and smiled. The man saw the camera. He made an obvious gesture inviting me to take his photograph. Instead I selected a man in the crowd to press the button and posed myself in the center of the crowd. Not everyone, it seemed, was bothered with the question of souls.

*

The dirt road was still slick from rain and badly rutted. I had the window down and my elbow out ready to wave to anyone I saw. The trail switched and turned round the edge of the mountain and then crossed over a saddle into gentler country. The driving was made more treacherous by the light, going from bright sun into the deep shadows of the overhanging trees and then back into the blazing light again. I had a sense that I had left civilization. Out here I was on my own and God help me if ... But what ifs awaited me I didn't dare conceive. I must have driven like this maybe forty minutes or so when, finally, bouncing over a metal bridge that spanned a swift flowing stream, I rounded a bend and saw below me the cabin. It was set against a forested hillside. There were outhouses and beyond it the land fell away, plunging into a deep valley. The track I was on turned abruptly to the right, climbing away. I stopped at the turn off to consult the map. There was no doubt about it. This was it. Oh Jesus.

I had a hand gun – one of Joe's that Chrissie had given me after the funeral (she'd wanted it out of her house) – in the passenger glove compartment. Instinctively, I checked it was still there, wrapped in a cloth. I had some provisions and some whiskey in the back. My peace offerings. Best not linger up here too long. I released the brake and started to roll down the trail towards the cabin. I pressed the horn. I didn't want to surprise anyone. Surprise, definitely, would not be a good thing. I pressed the horn again. Still no sign of anyone. I waved my arm out the window to anyone watching and then came to a halt about 50 feet from the cabin. Anything nearer seemed overly familiar. I switched off the engine. I thought I saw a face behind one of the windows and waved again. I opened the door and got out. The silence hummed with taut threat. No place to run to, I thought.

'Wash!'

My voice seemed to fall flat in the still air. I tried again.

'Wash!'

Again silence. I shouted a third time but my voice was thin. I felt exposed, trapped – like an ant caught in amber. The silence buzzed with the low distant hum of insects. Should I walk to the cabin or stay close to the car? What the hell was I to do?

'I'm Joe's brother.' I called again. 'Joe sent me.'

This was the abracadabra that opened the door. A man stepped out on to the porch. This was Wash alright but different from what I had expected. Perhaps it was watching too many basketball games, or some ancestral fear sweat of the psyche, but I had thought of Wash as big, muscled, deep black and glistening but the man in front of me was maybe five foot nine, medium brown. Maybe he'd once been lean but he had filled out a bit. His ears stuck out prominently and the front of his face seemed pushed in. But what I mainly paid attention to was what he was holding. He had an automatic gun hanging casually in his right hand. One quick movement was all it would take to bring it up. A little pressure on the trigger. That's all it would take to end this adventure right here.

'Wash?' I tried to make it casual.

'Who wants to know?' He drawled.

'I'm Jack, Joe's brother.'

'That right?'

I nodded.

'He said I should come up and bring you some provisions.'

'Did he now?'

He let the words drop unhurriedly into the pool of stillness in which I was beginning to flounder. What now? A voice screamed inside me. What do I do now? I was aware of the dryness in my throat as I attempted to swallow. All I could do was nod my head and seem harmless, open-eyed, without guile.

'Where's Joe? Why he don't come hisself?'

'He had an accident,' I lied. 'Had a car crash. Broke his leg bad. He's laid up. Can't move.'

We surveyed each other across the short space that separated us. He cold eyed me, hard and suspicious. Later I guessed he had just slowed down. Not talking to anyone except Maddie for weeks and months on end. Smoking too much dope. Joe the only distraction. But I didn't know that then. I watched him, uneasy, sweat forming around my eyes. There was a movement behind him but my eyes were glued on the man in front of me who had the gun in his hand. I had a glimpse only of a woman in a cotton shift in the doorway.

'Get inside!' he growled and she disappeared. But somehow the tension between us had been broken.

'Provisions you say?'

I nodded and cleared my throat.

'Just some cans, some steak and whiskey and stuff. Didn't know what you wanted. Thought maybe, we'd sort that out when I got here. You could give me a shopping list…'

Too eager, I thought. I slowed down.

'You say whiskey?'

I nodded.

'Hell, bring that in. Let's have us a party.'

I pulled two bottles of Wild Turkey from the back seat and held them up. Wash's face lightened. A grin spread across his face but I didn't see much humor in it. More a grimace. I approached the porch slowly with a bottle in each hand and climbed up the steps. Wash nodded for me to enter the cabin.

The girl, who I assumed was the girl Joe called Maddie, was a shock. Pale, thin, her dress ripped and torn, her hair matted. She gave me a quick piercing look before turning away in the face of my horror.

'Jesus!'

'Get some glasses, girl.'

Maddie turned and shuffled across the room. That's when I noticed she had been hobbled.

'Joe tell you about the girl?'

I decided on caution and shook my head.

Wash, I saw with relief, had set the gun down on the floor beside him. He picked up the whiskey and smiled with appreciation as he fondled it.

'Just the thing for...' but he didn't finish the sentence.

A quick twist of his hands and the bottle was open. He filled the two glasses and passing one to me lifted his own to his nose.

'Oh yes. Just what the doctor ordered.' He lifted his glass for a toast.

I raised my glass.

'To finally getting to meet you,' I said and gasped as the whiskey hit the back of my throat.

'Joe tell you about me?' Wash asked, eyes half open.

Again I sensed Wash was not to be played with.

'Not a lot,' I improvised. 'Just said you were his number one Vietnam buddy. Didn't tell me anything about you and him and this cabin up here. Not until he had to. You know, the accident...' I ended lamely.

Wash nodded slowly, weighing the words in the obscure scales of probability, finally accepting them.

'So, now what?'

'How do you mean?'

'You being up here. Now what?'

I saw what he was asking.

'I guess he wanted me to help get you what you needed.'

'Sure. Sure. And then what?'

'I don't know.'

'You planning on chilling up here?'

I let the thought hang there for a moment before answering.

'Would that be a problem?

'No. No problem man.' He was clearly still trying to puzzle out what it meant for me to be there.

'Hey Joe's brother. Fancy that. Let's drink to that.'

He poured out another drink and we clinked glasses.

'Yeah,' Wash grinned 'Joe told me about you. Told me a lot about you, in fact. That he did.'

And what Joe had told him I could only guess was not too complimentary. I sipped my whiskey slowly. I wasn't used to drinking much and I guessed Wash could hold his drink a hell of a sight better than I could. And there was Maddie. I couldn't avoid that forever. Best deal with it now.

'What about her?'

'What *about* her?' Wash grinned and winked. He was thawing out fast.

'What's the situation?'

'The situation?' Wash nodded his head up and down as if he was bouncing on a trampoline. His big grin was as cold as an iceberg.

'The situation?'

He pulled some tobacco out of his pocket and started to roll himself a cigarette. Still he was rocking backwards and forwards, vibrating with hidden truths.

'Well, Jack,' he paused. 'The situation ...' He added some extra stress to the word, mocking it. 'The situation is this. This here is the girl. She don't have a name as such. It's not important, anyways. You just say to her: Girl, do this. Girl, do that. She gonna do it.' I nodded slowly. 'That's right, Jack. She's the house fuck. You want to fuck her, Jack? Go on. Fuck her. That's what she there for.' He surveyed me coolly across the room. 'That a problem? It shock you, Jack?'

What could I say? I knew it but to hear the facts stated so bluntly was a shock. I couldn't hide it. The shock was spread across my face.

'Yeah. I guess.'

And I could feel shame too crimsoning my cheeks as I realized I had felt a twinge of excitement in my loins.

'Joe done tell me you a college professor.'

'Well, not really. High School. I'm a teacher.'

'So, what is your take on all this, Jack?'

His constant repetition of my name was getting to me. I wasn't sure what he meant by it. On the other hand I didn't want to confront him in any way. Not yet. I needed to feel my way, find his point of weakness. I was going to have to keep my wits very firmly about me if the girl, if Maddie, and I were going to get out of this alive.

'I guess it would get lonely up here all on your own.'

'That's right, Jack. It sure do get real lonely. A man has need of company. That is the truth of it. Yessir. That the truth.'

I looked across at Maddie and our eyes met but I could feel Wash's eyes on me. I kept my face impassive.

'Anytime, Jack. Just say the word. That girl getting down on her knees.'

His expression mocked me.

'What's the matter, Jack? You don't like this girl? You queer or something?'

'Sure. I like her...'

'Yo, just kidding, man, just kidding. Go on. You want. Just go fuck the bitch.'

'Maybe, later.'

'Sure. If you got the balls for it, man.'

'Yeah. Maybe later.'

CHAPTER 5

Joe's isn't the only voice in my head. There's Maddie too. I remember one night. It was three in the morning, I guessed, my head heavy with sleep. It was pitch dark. I was aware of her stale breath as she pushed herself into bed with me, I could feel the heat of her face inches from mine. I groaned and tried to roll away.

'You bastard,' she whispered fiercely. 'You bastard.'

'What is it now?'

I backed away to give her room. I wanted to turn over, turn away, sink back into sleep.

'You fucked me too, you know that.'

I mumbled something that was supposed to be a yes.

'They fucked me, I could understand that, you know, but you...!'

'I know.' I moaned the word out. I didn't want to go through this again. It was just too much. Over and over. The scene replayed in her head. I could understand that. Trauma does that. You wake sweating from the nightmare that never lets you be, never lets go. Oh God! Oh God! And I am in her nightmares. I am one of the bad guys. I'm also one of the good guys. Like a yo-yo I bounce

back and forth. Good guy... bad guy... good guy... Bad Guy...
Good guy... I understand that.

'Why, oh why?'

'I'm sorry,' I told her. 'I'm sorry.'

What else could I say? That if I hadn't, maybe we'd both be
dead? And Benjy too. Another truth to sink into the hurt. Doesn't
lessen the pain.

'I know. You were sorry even when you were doing it. I could
feel it. But I hated you for it. I despised you.'

'I know.'

We've been through this so many times but I still have no
answer for the shame.

'I hate men!' she says.

'Yes.'

'What do you know about it?'

'Nothing. I'm just agreeing.'

'I need you to hug me.'

'Sure.'

I put my arms round her and pulled her close to me. She was so
slight she was almost weightless. One of her hands curled around
my testicles and began to squeeze. It was not a friendly gesture. It
was a hard threat. I woke up at once.

'Now tell me about it.'

'Again?'

'Yes, again and again until it makes sense to me, until I can
goddamn accept it, alright? Now fucking tell me buster.'

'OK, OK,' calmly. One day she'll go too far. I think of the
drone whose job it is to inseminate the queen in flight. As he

ejaculates all his innards are ripped out of him. This is a simple truth: Nature is cruel. I moved my hand to disengage hers. 'Come on, be a good girl.'

There was a brief spasm of tension as she clung to her fierce resolve. One day, I think, one day, she'll do it. But not this time. She relaxed, let go and nestled closer to me. And maybe that's the big, unsayable answer: nature is cruel and we are of nature.

'Where do you want me to start?'

'I saw you first,' she said and I let her carry the story on from its beginning.

'That's right.'

'You got out of your car.'

'That's right.'

'I was peeling potatoes at the sink. I heard the sound of the engine. I thought it was Joe. Joe hadn't been to the cabin in a coupla weeks. I guess I was kinda looking forward to seeing Joe. Not looking forward to seeing him as if I liked him. Jus' hoping it was him 'cos we had a kind of understanding. I sure hoped we had an understanding. 'Cos if we didn't... I was dead meat. They was going to kill me soon. Couldn't go on forever. I could feel it every time Wash touched me. Guess he didn't know either way himself. Was he going to kill me or was he jus' going to get his rocks off. And then what was he going to do? He was jus' mean, mean, mean. I can still see his yellow eyes and feel his hot heavy stink all over my face as he leered and panted. Huh! Huh! Huh! Oh Jesus! Jesus! I don't want to keep seeing his face. I swear to you I can smell his stink right now, like it's all over me. I want to puke.'

I tried to hold her tight to my chest. I wanted to say let it go, forget it, leave it be. But I was the enemy and she started to writhe, tried to hammer me with her tight little fists.

'Hey! Hey! I'm on your side remember.'

She froze into a tight ball. I breathed in and out slowly, deeply, let her know I was relaxed. Then she let go of the tension and it was OK again.

'I'll get you some water.'

'No, don't move. I'm OK. OK?'

'OK.' I rubbed my thumb against the smoothness of her shoulder and gently stroked her hair as I waited for her to take the initiative again.

'I'm OK,' she muttered more to herself than to me. 'I'm OK.'

For a few minutes neither of us spoke. Then she said: 'You talk. Tell me your side of things.' So I started to talk.

'I was in bed with Norma. It was about eleven going on twelve...'

Maddie interrupted.

'You miss Norma?'

'Now?'

'Yeah. You miss her at all?'

'No. That's dead.'

'You don't blame me? Think it's my fault or anything like that?'

'No. Really. We were a middle-aged couple going on ninety-three. I'm glad it's over. I'm glad I got out. I'm glad, more than glad, that I'm with you.'

'Yeah?' Doubtful. 'But you're not really with me. Don't put that one on me. I'm a free agent.'

'Sure.'

'I made that clear. That was the condition. Right?'

'Sure.'

'So you was loving up old Norma when the phone rings...'

'I'd just given her a goodnight peck on the cheek when the phone rang. It was Chrissie. She was hysterical. I think she'd just been to the morgue to identify the body.'

'What was left of him.'

'There wasn't much damage to the front of the face. Chrissie just said she took one look and it was him, just like he always looked but he was just so cold and empty. Later, she told me how they took her into where all the bodies were in drawers like a huge filing cabinet and he'd been in one of the bottom drawers and she'd got down on her hands and knees and when she saw it was him she just took his head in her hands and kissed him.'

'Yuk!'

'Anyway, she was crying all over the phone and it took me a few minutes to get out of her what had happened.

'How would you do it, if you was going to?' Maddie interrupted.

'Do what?'

'Kill yourself.'

'I've never thought of it. Have you?'

'Sure. Every other day, it seems. It's one of those thoughts that I play with. You know, would I jump off the Empire State Building or O.D. on sleeping pills or what?'

'Do you ever come to a decision?'

'No. Sometimes I'd like to do something really violent like blow my head off with some great big gun. Then I think I don't want to do that 'cos I'd want to leave behind a beautiful corpse so everyone could look at me in my casket and say: 'Poor girl. Ain't she beautiful now she's at peace and with the Lord.' Or some such shit like that. But it wouldn't be sleeping pills.'

'No?'

'No. I'd want to be in control. Seems like with sleeping pills I wouldn't.'

'And when is this going to happen?'

'Oh Lord knows,' she laughed. 'It's jus' a game. Now go on. Keep talking.'

'Would you jump in front of a train?'

'Lord no. Something would stop me for sure. I wouldn't have the guts for it. I'd think about maybe falling on the tracks and being cut in two. It don't bear thinking about.'

Yes. Joe had the guts for it. Knew what he was going to do. Did it. Maybe he'd tried to do it other times and failed. Or maybe he succeeded at the first try. We'd never know.

'Tell me about you and Joe. You said you had an understanding?'

'It was just a feeling.' She stopped speaking. She was thinking back, seeing it again. Then, after a long pause, she started to talk about him.

'It was Joe picked us up at the bar. Said sure, why don't you come up to my cabin for the weekend, just laze around in the middle of nowhere, get a feeling for nature and all that crap. Tina didn't want to. I kinda twisted her arm: said I was going to go up there even if she didn't. I knew she didn't want to be left alone so, finally, she said Oh OK let's go.'

She sniffed and I could feel the tears streaming off her cheek on to my arm. She caught hold of a corner of the sheet and wiped her eyes.

'I know.' I whispered.

'How the hell can you know anything, Mr. fat-ass fucker?'

'Ssh!' I said softly.

'No. Don't tell me to shush! Don't treat me like a child. Tina's dead and I'm to blame.'

'You didn't know.'

'How could I know?'

'You couldn't.'

'Yes, I could. I could have had the sense not to go off in the middle of the night with a man I didn't know from Adam.'

'Yep!'

'What's this? Yep? Yep?' satirizing my voice with wild mimicry

'What do you know about it?'

'Go on. Tell me about Joe.'

'Well, first thing we didn't know anything about Wash being up there. As far as we knew it was just us two and Joe. And Joe seemed like an OK kinda guy. So, we drive up to the cabin and Tina's feeling a bit ill by the time we get there. Too much to drink and her mood gone sour. So I'm helping her get out of the pickup truck when this man just looms out of the dark. I can hear his voice even now a kind of rasping, dry leathery voice saying something like 'Weeeell nahoww. What we got here?' I nearly jumped out of my skin. Joe jus' laughed and said this here is ma buddy, Wash. Jus' call him Wash. Like it was all OK and friendly. But Wash was jus' through and through mean as a pit viper and I could feel it and my skin jus' crawled. And everything was so dark and there was nothing we could do about it, so I says: my girl friend here is feeling a bit sick, I think maybe I need to take her home.' I wanted to get the hell out of there but Joe said flatly he wasn't going to drive no-one nowhere. So I helped Tina walk to the cabin and she washed her face at the sink and when she was feeling a bit better we sat around the cabin and Joe says, matter of factly, as if it's all been discussed and agreed: 'OK this one's mine for the night,' pointing at me. 'That's yours,' pointing at Tina. `That'. That's what he said. Not 'She' or 'Tina': jus' `that'. I wanted to say something but I knew then that I'd made a big mistake. Biggest mistake in my whole life and I thought better of saying anything that might make the whole thing a lot worse. So I pretend I'm happy with the whole thing and say: 'OK let's get it on.' as if I'm into it. Tina jus' looked kinda stunned.

'Carry on without me,' she said. 'I'll just lie here on the sofa.' and she made to lie down.

'The heeeell!' Wash had this way of stretching words out real long. He jus' grabbed her and pulled her into the bedroom. Tina was shouting and screaming and I could hear she was being knocked about. I wanted to do something but Joe just grabbed my hand and pulled me into his room...' Maddie's voice dropped to a whisper, 'And that was that!'

She was trembling and shivering now and sweating as if she was there again.

'Oh God! Oh God! Oh God!' a litany of pain oozing out of the dark well of memory.

'I got to go pay my respects to Tina, lay some flowers on her grave and pray to her to forgive me. Please Tina, forgive me,' and I tasted the salt of her tears on my lips.

*

C is for Cu Chi. About sixty kilometers north-west of Saigon is Cu Chi. All I knew to begin with was that there were some tunnels there. Big deal! But it was on the way to the Caodaist complex in Tay Ninh, up near the Cambodian border, that I wanted to see. Joe had described them once in a terse phrase: Fucking ice-cream churches. An ice-cream church? I wanted to see that. We turned off the main road and followed a narrower road. We came to a wooded area. Suddenly there were remains of rusting tanks, helicopters. There was a small parking area. It was empty. This was it. I paid three dollars and a military officer lead me to a room with a map and a television screen.

'Please watch this video for ten minutes. It will explain something about Cu Chi,' he said. I sat back and watched.

Cu Chi, the narrator informed me, was an area of rubber plantations. The peasants were happy and worked their fields. There were loving pictures of peasants picking large bunches of grapes and other fruits. Old film footage that was like how it had been. Then the film told of the coming of the enemy and the peasants desire to stay and fight. They built tunnels and co-ordinated the resistance from there. The film then focused on the exploits of a seventeen year old girl who led a platoon to fight and kill American soldiers. Was she real too or just 'like' the truth must have been? But there was real footage here too. Footage of bombs falling. Footage of fighting. Footage of the tunnels themselves. When the video ended the officer led me to a map which showed the Cu Chi area in relation to Saigon. He pointed to the villages which skirted the area, and the army camps. There were, he informed me, 250 kilometers of tunnels in the whole area. 16,000 people had lived in them. 10,000 of them had died. He pointed to some jagged pieces of shrapnel.

'Bomb fragments,' he then rattled off some statistic that I tried to remember but it eluded me. Did he say 60 kilos of fragments for every square meter of land? I must have got this wrong. Or was it 6,000 fragments?

He pointed to an idealized cross-section indicating the three different layers of tunnels: the first at eight feet, the second at sixteen feet down and the third at twenty-one feet down. There were bunkers just under the surface protected by log roofs. There were wells. There were kitchens.

'Now, we will visit the tunnels.'

I was suddenly aware that this officer spoke an extraordinarily good, clipped English. He turned to me.

'Where are you from?'

I wanted to say Britain, Germany. I flirted with Canada. But the pause was too long.

'America,' I admitted.

He smiled a cool smile.

We walked along a path a short way. There was an open hole.

'Foxhole,' he said. 'From here our soldiers would shoot and then they would disappear underground. Your troops would come with dogs and tunnel rats and try to follow.' He smiled his cold smile again.

I thought about his phrasing – 'try to follow.'

'We will go down here. Mind your footing.' I followed him down into a subterranean chamber then stooped into a tunnel. It had been wired up so that there was lighting. The officer pointed at this.

'The lighting is for visitors. In the war there was no lighting. Also this tunnel has been widened just to make it easier for you to see.'

We scrambled along until we came to a bunker.

'This was the hospital.'

He pointed out the salient features of the operating theater How everyone had to crouch in the tunnels if the bombers came.

'How far did the bombs penetrate?' I asked. This was clearly a good question. The officer patted the tunnel wall.

'It was very difficult to build these tunnels because this earth is very thick clay. On the other hand, it is strong and it can resist the bombs very well. But the heaviest bombs with a direct hit will destroy even the deepest tunnel.'

The tour continued. The officer paused at a section that had been freshly plastered over.

'This was a toilet. We had to put a cover on to stop the smells. This was for emergency use only. Usually we waited until the enemy had gone then we went up above ground.' That smile again.

We visited the general's room.

'You see the hammock? If a bomb explodes the hammock just sways back and forth.'

We visited a conference room.

'This is the room where the Tet Offensive was planned.' Or maybe it was just 'like' the room where the Tet Offensive was planned. What did it matter? It was like any conference room. There was a long table and a podium at one end. That's where the similarities ended.

'Here is a bamboo trap,' pointing to a corner of the room, a pit in the earth with bamboo stakes protruding, covered with a thin camouflaged surface.

'If anyone went from one section to another they would need a guide. Only the General knew the whole system.' That slight hard humorous pursing of the lips.

'I don't know if you can do this section, it is the second layer down.'

'Carry on,' I said gamely, 'I'll follow.'

'This section goes round two corners and continues for sixty feet to the next hole. Do you suffer from claustrophobia?'

'Not particularly.'

The only way I could move was to sit on my haunches and bend forward thrusting my shoulders forward ahead of me. Still my shoulders brushed against the sides and I feared at times I would find myself wedged in. The air was hot and close and my knees ached with the unaccustomed pressure. The roof dipped and the tunnel seemed to narrow. I couldn't continue like this. I had to scrabble slowly forwards on all fours. I understood how easy it would have been to panic. Round another corner and there was light pouring into the chamber ahead of me from above. I looked at my mud smeared watch. It had only taken five minutes. I emerged to find him crouching at the hole mouth. He shook his head.

'You could never have been a Vietcong.' He grinned.

I grinned back. It was funny.

As we walked along the path he indicated with his feet a number of airholes. Then we descended into a kitchen bunker.

'We could only cook with very dry bamboo to reduce the smoke.' Then he showed how the smoke itself was filtered through chambers so that it emerged elsewhere.

We sat down at a table and a woman in black dress, the dress of the Vietcong, served tea.

'This is what we ate.' The officer picked up a yellow root and dipped it into a dry mixture.

'Manioc roots dipped in peanut and salt, or sesame and salt.'

'I guess you needed the salt,' I hazarded. It tasted fine. I thought about what he had just said: this is what we ate. We.

'Were you, yourself, here during the war?'

'Yes, and so was she,' he said indicating the woman. 'She was a cook.'

'She must have been a very young cook,' I said gallantly and was rewarded with a slight smile.

'What do you think of Americans now? You must hate us.'

'The war was a long time ago. Then you were our enemies. Now, it is peace. We welcome you as we welcome everyone.'

It was a good speech. I didn't believe a word of it. I remembered uncle Tom's vicious hatred of the Japanese that never abated with the years. There was a donation box in the corner. I wanted to purge my sense of guilt with a five dollar note. Then I thought of how they would laugh at the sweating fat American who tried to buy them off. I kept my money.

'That was a very interesting tour,' I said and shook his hand. His hand lay mute in mine. I took this as a comment but it may not have been. They are not great handshakers.

*

Why am I writing this story? (what a very singular word for these fragments that will or won't fit together into a seamless whole) For Benjy? But it may be best for him if he never reads it. Who needs this burden? Should we not all start fresh, new? That would be good, I think. What is the past to us? A burden. Yes. It's heavy. It weighs us down. We should be quit of it. But how can we be? That is the problem. We need it too, this memory that provides some explanation for the present. The past is a key to many conundrums. But though I have all the arguments – have long ago weighed up all the pros and cons – and know how much we need this memory, this understanding, I pause when I consider Benjy's position. No. It will be hard for Benjy – and it may be very much harder for him if (if? I am only fooling myself if I cling to this faintest of possibilities) – no, not if, when – when he comes to know his past. For Benjy, alone of his generation, alone of all the people now living in this world we call America, for Benjy alone, this history would best not be known. But there is no possibility of that. So I must start this story even though it has not yet come to an end.

Benjy is nigh on four years old. Maybe in twenty years time he will be ready to bear this burden. Maybe, hopefully, by then, the world will have moved on. Maybe he will read these chapters as if they are crumbling archives of another time and place. Maybe. But I hold out little hope of that. Benjy? If you ever read this, forgive me. I know the wrong I am doing you. But I am a stubborn man. You and I are victims of circumstance. And, I tell myself in mitigation, you need this record too to make sense of your past. But I need to do this. This is for me not you. I need it for my own sanity. Understand this: I'm angry. I can hardly contain this anger. I wish to smear profanities across this page. Planes crash into the World Trade Center and we're supposed to start everything afresh. New hates. New wars. We still haven't learnt from the past. We're fated to repeat the errors of Vietnam in Iraq. We start from a position of total ignorance of our enemy and then we dehumanize and abuse the enemy and then we shout out about how misunderstood we are. We! We cannot conceive the fact that God is not on our side. God is on the other man's side. We are the betrayers of the human spirit. You see, Benjy? I am angry and I let loose a torrent of words. But anger leads to mis-statements of the truth. It's not true that God is not on our side. But it is true that God is on the other man's side too. God? Why bring God into it to murk up the waters. What has God to do with it? Benjy, just know this: we've done much that was ugly, wrong, evil. We? Yes, we all bear responsibility. Or do we? I waver back and forth. The government, the state, the powers that be... are they acting on our behalf or are they too our enemies? Are the Timothy McVeighs right? If I fight evil does that make me good? Or is it the evil in the hearts of all men that goes to war – one combatant no better than the other? Or is the moral dimension a veil of illusion: is war the inevitable first dance between opposing nations, peoples – no whys or wherefores necessary; the rules of engagement hardwired in our souls, so that, no matter how hard we try, we cannot step aside and look? No. Yes. I waver from one answer to the next. And time rushes on, propelling us on, away from these questions to the next crisis and we stumble along trying to keep up and at the same time trying to hang on to something of that past that has been, that past that we need to sift through more carefully if we are to reach some level of understanding, some level of simple human understanding, some sense of completion.

*

Jack

    Let me tell you a story. Once Upon A Time, on a dark crisp night, just after midnight, a beautiful, blonde girl let herself out of her home and went down a small lane half a mile or so to the railway track. Living there she knew the times of every train. There were no lights on in any of the houses nearby. She knew she was alone. She felt a shiver of raw nervous excitement at the thought of what she was about to do. Did she dare? She lifted her skirt and took her pants off. Now she could feel the cold air against her sex. She looked around fearfully but there was no-one there. her breath was crystallizing in front of her. She quickly drew off her sweater and unzipped her skirt. She let it drop. She was naked. She was clothed in the deep cold of that dark night. Her flesh quivered with the pagan spirits whose commands she was obeying. There was a rumble in the distance and a hooting. It came closer and closer and then there was the engine and the glare of the headlight beam and she spread her legs and arms wide and shut her eyes and a shaft of cold air whipped through her legs and up the crack of her buttocks and there was a great whooooosh! And the train was upon her and devouring her. And she remained transfixed as the train carriages rattled by her not six feet away from where she stood. And then it was gone and she was suddenly alone and cold and feeling very vulnerable. She hurriedly dressed and ran back home. And when she got back to her room she climbed into her warm bed clothes and tucked herself warm in bed and tingled all over.

Chrissie excited something in Joe. And it was true, Chrissie exuded a lazy sensuality, a certain undefinable sluttishness that made the cock twitch – even, it had to be admitted, my own, much retracted, cock.

There were other stories that I invented about her but that was the best. I imagined her breaking into a supermarket late at night and running naked round the aisles, smearing herself with cheesecake and cream and spraying herself with champagne. I saw her everyday. I made sure of that. She was on the check-out desk at the library. She walked to and from work every day. It was only ten minutes door to door. I

*thought to myself: yes, girl. You're mine. I'm going to have you.
But for some reason I took my time about it. Perhaps there
was something about her that armored her. A look she had.
I wasn't sure I wanted to grab and take and throw away this
pleasure I had of seeing her and imagining stories about her.
Naturally one of them involved the library. I imagined she
had herself locked in with a gorilla. A gorilla, for Chrissakes!!!
Or a Chimpanzee, or some big monkey, does it matter? And
she sucked him off. Stupid stuff. Sometimes she was out late.
Some days the library closed at nine and she would go and
have a drink and then walk home. Drakesberg is a safe town.
Not much crime. Shoplifting is about as bad as it gets. One
night I felt the hunting and fishing urge and lay in wait for
her. About ten o'clock she starts to pat-pat-pat in her high-heel
shoes along the sidewalk. Drakesberg is more or less closed up
at this time. She click-clacks along. I have already planned
ahead. I have parked my car not far from her house so that
I can make a getaway. I walk behind her, padding softly,
but not so soft she doesn't hear me. I want her to know I'm
there. That I'm getting closer. I know she feels a sense of threat.
Not much. This is good old safe-as-houses Drakesberg where
nothing happens, ever. She wonders if she will get home first
or whether I will catch up and pass her. But she's near home
and doesn't feel too worried. I get closer and closer, timing the
distance, so that I will overtake her just before she gets home.
I feel the pleasure the hunter always feels when he's stalking
his prey knowing it's a sure thing. A certain kill. There's a path
goes off to the left, down to the railway track just before we*

reach the door of her house. I am now only ten feet behind her. There is a street lamp at this point. She has started to walk more quickly and I too have lengthened my stride. We are walking in sync. Oh joy! eight feet, I am floating in the ever-present tense of dreams, six feet. I am almost on her when suddenly she turned and stooped down on the ground.

'Huh!' I'm surprised. She looked up at me.

'Oh hi! It's you! I wondered who it was.'

She knew me! I always think I'm invisible. That's dangerous. She turned from me and looked once again into the darkness behind a shrub.

'Can you hear it?'

'What?'

'I think it's a kitten. I think it's stuck.'

I crouched down too and listened. There was certainly some animal whining pitifully in the dark.

'It's there!' she whispered. I saw it too. It was a kitten that had been tied to a stick at the side of the path just beyond the circle of light from the lamppost.

'Poor kitty!' she said and went to untie it. I gave her a hand by taking my knife out and cutting the string off from round its neck.

We were allies, it seemed. And then we were outside the door to her home.

'Would you care for a cup of coffee?' she asked and when I nodded she gave me the kitten to hold while she got her key out.

Now, the fact is, I still planned to abuse her but I had been put off my stride. I needed to get my head straight again – or crooked – or whichever way it was before.

We went in to her very messy home. Jesus. I started to clear up straight away, army style.

'Hey, I'm sorry about the mess. Just ignore it OK?'

She fixed up a nest for the kitten and the coffee was boiling. I didn't wait. I just took hold of her and turned her round. I expected a struggle. I was going to hit her and... well, she just sighed and put her arms round me and said: 'Anything you say buster!' and somehow we got to her bed and we didn't have any clothes on and we had a glorious fuck and I fell asleep in her arms.

*

Yes. It should all be over now. Two years and more now since Maddie went and left me. Left Benjy. Ran off. She left a message that she was too young to settle down. And maybe she never connected with Benjy – the son of a man who raped and abused her. Was that it? I should feel angry. Because of her, Norma left me – or I left her – whatever way it was. And she too is gone. Disappeared into the vastness that is America. And Maddie too. Just disappeared like she never was. And me? I remain. Beached.

Benjy lies curled up hogging the middle of our bed. I lie perched at the edge of the mattress feeling sorry for myself, and glad that I have him. At least I have him. I feel so pitifully sad for myself. This can't go on! Come on, man, get a grip on yourself! I yell at myself soundlessly, impotently. But I just feel devastated with sadness. Helpless and emptied. Three o'clock in the morning is not a good time for me.

Seven o'clock in the evening is different. I can't let Benjy see that I'm a hollow man. Got to make him believe this world is as solid as teak, strong as iron, firm and dependable as concrete. Hey man, I say to him, give me five – and he gives me five and we're buddies.

'Got to wash your teeth properly now,' I tell him as he stands on the stool in front of the mirror. I want him to believe the world is full of hard certainties.

'Time for bed. Say goodnight to grandma!'

'G'night gram-ma.'

'Goodnight honey, you sleep tight.'

'Yes, gram-ma.'

I pat his leg for half an hour wishing him to sleep. He is a restless, mobile being. It takes a while for the cylinders to switch off. But when they do, he is gone finally. I watch him closely. His whole face flutters from time to time as if he's trying to open his eyes but can't. I love him dearly, this son of mine who is not my son. What would I do without him? And his face is a liquidly mobile and plastic surface of his dreams.

By the time I come downstairs to the kitchen, Ma has set the dinner on the table.

'He's asleep at last,' I tell her.

'You spoil that boy. Sitting with him till he goes to sleep. He's going to have to learn to go to sleep by himself.'

Ma was never one for spoiling kids.

'It's good for both of us.'

She looks at me with that expression. The one she always had for those occasions when she wanted you to know she knew it wasn't going to turn out good if you persevered in whatever it was that she disapproved of.

'Hmm! Well, that may be, now let's eat. You go and help yourself.'

Stew and potatoes and a bowl of boiled carrots. We ate in silence.

After dinner we both cleared up and Ma settled herself down in front of the television. I could hear the canned laughter. I poured myself a large jug of water and filled a glass with ice. Then I pecked her cheek goodnight and took myself off and Benjy upstairs to the bedroom.

*

I always wake with the sun. She was fast asleep, snoring slightly, not a pretty sight. I got up. Wide awake. The neighborhood was still sleeping and I could still feel inside me the urge to assault and inflict hurt. The idea came to me to tie her to the bed. I found some strips of silk for tying robes and tied her arms against the bed head and her feet to the bed base. She was a heavy sleeper. I went to the kitchen and looked around for the right knife. I picked up a long knife with a serrated blade. I was going to cut her up real ugly. She was waking up when I got back. She was tugging on her arms and legs but still not really sure what was happening. She still didn't understand that she was all tied up and that I had a knife. She kind of focused on me with the knife as I came in the door. She gave me a nice long languid smile.

'Hey, buster. You're something. You fuck the bejazus out of me and then you get up and make breakfast.' She kind of pouted.

'Come here buster. I want to whisper something in your ear.'

I took the knife, got on top of her and stabbed down.

'Hmm!' she nibbled my earlobe. 'You really know how to rouse a girl. You got me all tied up and you got a knife. Guess you can just about have your way with me.' She wriggled her body under me. This time I fucked her with a kind of hard fury but she didn't notice that at all.

'Ride em cowboy!' she kept shouting till I was done and flopped on top of her.

'Wow!' was all she could say, and then, a few minutes later, she whispered in my ear: 'How about taking your knife out of my sheath and my knife out of my pillow and cutting me loose. I'm hungry.'

We disengaged. I untied her. She fixed breakfast while I stared out at the gray day that looked set to rain. The railway tracks were down there. And as I was watching a train came along and emitted a long, sad, piercing whistle and then clattered on out of sight. Going somewhere. And I was going nowhere. And she put her arms around me and hugged me.

'I hope you aren't having any ideas of getting on any trains and leaving town.'

'Not for a while,'

'Not never, buster. You're mine.'

Then, as we were sitting across the table from each other digging in to left over ham and scrambled eggs and toast and coffee, she stuck her hand out across the table.

'By the way, my name's Chrissie.'

We shook hands.

'Well Joe,' she said to me, 'let's just take it as it comes, OK? I've been hurt. Guess you've had your problems too like everyone else. Let's just take it easy and have a little fun. I'm in no goddam hurry to go anywhere. You want to leave, just pack up your bags and go. Don't make a big song and dance about it. '

Up till then I'd had this kind of tension in me. Like I was still planning to hurt and abuse. Or just quit and run. But suddenly a new kind of energy just rose up in me from the belly, a slow soft warm energy. I can't explain it. I guess I just kinda liked this piece of ass. Funny, isn't it? She just accepted me the way I was. That had never happened to me before.

*

The house is full of spaces. Each one has its own atmosphere. In the evenings, I have a choice of the sitting room with the television permanently on, or the dining room, cold and brittle with the family silver and Ma's wedding pictures on the sideboard, pictures of her and Pa – other pictures of Pa, formal pictures (this Pa who is long since dead and gone, gone before memory had a chance to thicken in the mind and stick, this Pa I never think about (did Joe remember him? I'll never know. Or rather I know what he told me which is that he remembered him clearly but I didn't believe him, thought he was just showing off, getting one up on me) – portraits of Joe and me, our formal wedding photographs – Norma looking so much more mature than me.

And then there's the kitchen with its shiny, washed up for the night feel. I prefer the bedroom with Benjy shifting and turning in his restless sleep. I was just three when Pa died (minor surgery that somehow went wrong). Joe would have been eight. Maybe that accounted for some of it, the things he did. Are we to be solely responsible also for all those accidents of fate that have impacted and changed us – and the way they have impacted and changed us? And yes, I suppose we must be. Cruel though that answer is.

Here, in the bedroom, I am alone, at last, with myself. There's no-one here to judge me. Except me. I pour my first stiff whiskey of the evening. I keep the bottle in the box along with Joe's papers. The box is labeled 'Joe's army stuff' in thick red felt pen. I know that keeps Ma from prying. She knows what she doesn't want to know.

But Ma, dear Ma, poor Ma, is like granite – I think of her as a kind of Mount Rushmore – a face made of rock, a soul of rock, the kind of rock you could build a house on. The solid rock of permanency. She has iron-gray hair done in a bun. She has hard stubborn eyes. And I am fifty-five years old and like a child again and she is taking care of me. And Benjy. And for how much longer? Snap out of it, Jack, I tell myself futilely. Snap out of it!

I'm a lot better than I was say this time a year ago. Then I felt I was swimming against the steady current of everyday life. Swimming and losing ground. In my head everything was cool and clear but dealing with the simple things in life – like going to work and doing the shopping – was an effort. I didn't know when I was suddenly going to find myself helplessly standing somewhere with tears streaming down my face unable even to get a shirt sleeve to my eyes. It didn't happen often but it did happen. A gaping chasm of pain opening up the ground at my very feet. Force six and seven Richter-scale events. But I'm better now. It hasn't happened for a while. I now feel up to most of the casual exchanges the day has in store for me. I may be slow but I get there. It's not that I don't want to respond, God knows I do. It's just that the words don't come to me as quickly as they should and by the time they do, the moment has passed and then I have the choice of saying the words or not – either way it's clearly weird.

But, as I say, it's getting better, I'm getting better. Dr Sondheim called it acute depression. Dr Bardbach hasn't named it yet. I don't know. I don't feel down. I just feel removed (except for anything to do with Benjy. I'm there for Benjy. One hundred percent. God bless him.) I feel my mental processes have slowed down. Thought proceeds at the pace of a wooden ox-cart loaded with rocks. It's a desperately slow business but I get there in the end, somewhere, maybe not where I should, I don't know.

'I can't get it straight in my head,' I said not so long ago in this spinning along present from which I persist in remaining abstracted. Dr Bardbach nodded his head slowly, his face pale and lined. I guess he isn't far from retirement age. I feel comfortable with him. He'll have seen most things, heard most things. His lower jaw is gently, softly flabby, the result, I guess, of too little exercise. All the listening he has had to do perhaps. Not speaking, Not exercising his jaw muscles.

'I don't think it is straight,' I added. This too, he seemed to say, he could accommodate, accepting the possibility with another nod. I was glad of the response. This was my second attempt at therapy. Dr Sondheim had not been a success. Perhaps because he was very much younger than me. Perhaps because he thought I was spinning him an elaborate fantasy – or was that just my flawed perception, my not so elaborate fantasy? Perhaps because he was blond and blue-eyed, firm-jawed, and crisply, briskly dressed. Tie and blazer. I had sensed in myself with him a conflict of energies, of understandings, of ultimate objectives even. I think he wanted to 'fix' me. I could feel it in my belly, a certain queasy buzzing. I had lasted five sessions. His blue eyes had stared coolly, impassively, unblinkingly, it seemed, for the length of each fifty-minute appointment. Such cold, pale blue eyes. And I had read into every slightest movement or tone of dress a judgment against me.

'Don't you have anything to tell me?' I had asked.

'Ultimately, only you can interpret your existence,' he had said in his bland, emotionless voice. 'You need to explore it. That's where the healing is,' depressing me even more than I already was. I listened to myself all day everyday as it was. I didn't need someone else to throw it back at me. I wanted someone to lighten the burden, to listen and comment and, ultimately, of course, to take the problem away from me so that it no longer weighed on me, so that I could forget it and move on to other things – my life, for example. Yes, I wanted to get on with my life. And if it was just me listening to myself then what did I need him for? I charged a hell of a lot less by the hour.

'It's all over the place.'

Dr Bardbach cleared his throat and I waited for him to speak.

'Perhaps,' he said, 'It doesn't matter where you start as long as it all comes out eventually.'

My turn to nod.

'You see,' I tried to explain further, 'I don't think it's me. The way I see it, it's everybody. Or maybe it's just America. Or it may be everyone who has ever lived.'

Dr Bardbach seemed to ease back into his chair. He made a vague movement of his head and hands as if to say, 'Good, go on, keep talking.' So I did. I started to tell him about Joe. Then (I'm conflating things here, merging the sessions I've had into one dialogue) somehow I was talking about Benjy – and so I had to explain about Maddie and how her arrival in my life had impacted on Norma and me. Then, somehow, I found we had run out of time. Dr Bardbach shifted forward in his seat and tapped a finger regretfully on his watch to indicate we had come to the end of the session. But he listened to me to the end and then, standing up, he came over and patted me sympathetically on my shoulder.

'Perhaps you need to start writing it down. Maybe that will help you get it straight.'

What intuition was this? Alice had said the same thing just last week.

'I've thought of that,' I said.

'And?'

'I've written some of it. But still, it's a bit here, a bit there. I want to make it all fit together.'

'Maybe it doesn't fit together, hmm?'

'Doesn't?'

'Maybe truth is a paradox?' His voice inclined up, teasing the suggestion into my thoughts. He opened the door and led me out to the staircase, speaking as we walked, holding my arm.

'You know, we generally see truth as if it were a kind of jigsaw puzzle with different pieces all fitting together to make a single static picture. But why should truth be static? Why can't it be dynamic? And if it's dynamic then an image, a frame if you like, at one point will show a different arrangement of events than a frame at another point. Do you understand? And then, if we try to freeze these two frames simultaneously, so that they seem to both exist, to be both true, at one and the same time, then we will have our paradox,' His head kept nodding. 'Hmm?' asking me to at least contemplate the possibility. He kept his hand on my arm as we paused at the top of the flight. He cleared his throat. 'Or maybe,' he continued, 'it's a question not of paradox but of parallax, keeping two images of different depth in a single focus.' He gestured his point firmly. His hand, I noticed, was strong, with short fingers, stubby, the hand of a craftsman.

I had a sudden image of a river flowing.

'You mean truth can have many tributaries?'

'Exactly, truth is a river with many tributaries. And what if the river itself divides into two, or three streams, each running separately down to the sea? Maybe one stream runs east while another runs west? Hmm? At one and the same time there can be three or four different, even incompatible, yet simultaneous truths. Is that not also possible?'

I laughed. (I marvel at this laugh. It is such a rare laugh.) 'You sound like the philosopher who said: come to me with your problems and I will make them more complicated.'

Dr Bardbach chuckled.

'Exactly.'

I shook Dr Bardbach's offered hand and started to descend the stairs. I hadn't laughed in a long time. But it wasn't a real laugh just the awkward whinny of nervous release.

'And now, here's another thought,' he raised his voice so that I could hear him clearly as I retreated from him down the stairwell. 'Think about this. If you're standing on the river bank,' his chest heaved with the joke of what he was saying. 'Ask yourself this: Is the river flowing towards you or is it flowing away?'

I smiled. It was something I'd have to think about. And as I continued to descend the stairs, I realized that if what he had said was true, then nothing was straight and Truth-with-a-capital-T was absolutely capable of being crooked and deceptive and perverse, quite capable of contradicting itself. Bastard, I thought to myself, though whether it was Dr Bardbach, myself or the whole damn world I was referring to I wasn't clear in my head – some combination, perhaps, and more besides. Bastard!

Chapter 6

'So, is this what you do all day?'

I had taken Alice to the ridge in the park that looked down on Oxford College. We were sitting, courtesy of Mrs Ethel Hawksworth, or the memory thereof, and her friends who had donated it, on my usual bench. Alice had folded her arms round my right arm and had dug her hands into my jacket pocket, her head resting on my shoulder.

'Not everyday.'

It was our third coffee date in a row. I was feeling a little more comfortable with the tactile element, with Alice's need to hug and hold arms – though we hadn't quite reached the intimacy of hands, the caress of fingers.

'What do you think about?'

I shrugged. 'Everything under the sun.'

'Do you think about me?' she teased.

I had to smile. She was grinning like a young girl.

'So! You *can* smile!'

And I had to admit it felt strange, like a cracking of lips glued taut by frost or ice. It was something I hadn't done in a long time.

'Well? You haven't said.' she persisted.

'These last few days, yes, of course.'

'Before that, when you didn't know me, before I talked to you, did you think about me then?'

'Not really.'

'You don't have to tell me the truth!'

'No? I can lie?'

'As long as they're good lies.'

'I fell in love with you the moment I first set eyes on you,' I said staring into her glistening laughing eyes.

'What a liar!' she pulled away putting on a huff.

'I was scared of you.'

'Were you?' all concern now, kindly.

'Terrified,' I admitted.

'Well, I'm going to eat you all up!' and she stood up and pretended she was a bear about to attack me. Then she did attack me, punching me in the chest, hard yet not hard yet not in any way pulling her punches.

'Hey!'

'That's for being a scaredy cat!'

I caught her hands as she made to launch another attack.

'You're good for me,' I said. 'You've made me lighten up.'

'Have I? Am I?'

'I'm not totally human yet, but I'm getting there.'

'Hah!' she said scowling with mockery but then her face softened into a warm contented smile.

'Good. I'm glad. I want to be good for you.'

And we sat in silence for a while and then she said 'You haven't answered my question.'

'What question?'

'What do you think about? If you don't tell me I'm going to get a can opener and open up your brain.'

'You don't really want to know.'

'Yes, I do. I do!'

'I don't think about fun things.'

'I know,' she smiled. 'You're a miserable thing. I know that. I just want to know about some of the things in your head. I want to understand. I want to get to know you.'

'All right. So be it. This is something I was thinking about yesterday afternoon.'

And I proceeded to tell her. The thought I'd had was this: We all carry a heavy burden of history. The past weighs down on us. And it's worse the more we know. The more we're aware of it the more it crushes us into the dirt. They say the sins of the father fall on the son. But what of the sins of the great great grandfathers? How far back do we have to go till the sense of shame no longer touches us, no longer raises a blush? Are we responsible in any way for the past? Or is it only the present that comes under our moral jurisdiction? And how much of that present? Am I responsible for your acts? You mine? The weight of history is the weight of impotent shame.

'You ever heard of the battle of Sand Creek?' I asked Alice.

'Should I have?'

'Yep. I guess so.'

She made a face at me, mocking her own ignorance. And so I told her the story and, as I tell her, I hear the bugle blowing in my mind early one morning, the cavalry charge, the long line of blue soldiers on their fine mounts, the Indians, Cheyenne, curious, emerging from their tipis. The concern. What should they do? It's nothing, says their chief, Black Kettle. They're just showing off. They're just going to ride through. Nothing to worry about. We're at peace with the paleface. We signed the Treaty. He stands there himself in the open, unarmed, calm, assured, holding a flagpole that's flying the American flag. But then the shooting starts. Just a peaceful native Indian village, early one morning. A minor massacre in the stream of history. Over a hundred people killed, three or four hundred by some accounts, people who weren't at war with anybody. Women. Old men. Children. Shot, trampled. Just a couple of hundred people killed because someone took it into his head that the Indians needed to be taught a lesson. What lesson? Never trust a white man? And the question I ask myself is this: am I responsible in any way for the events of that day?

'Well, how can you be?' Alice responded with even common sense, 'You weren't there, were you?'

'No, I wasn't there, way back in 1864. But trace back the ancestral tree, follow the collateral branches. You can pretty well guarantee that there is a link somehow between me or you and someone who took part. There's even a website dedicated to the proposition that between any person and any other person in the whole country there are only six intermediaries. I know someone who knows someone who knows someone... and so it goes. If it works in the present no doubt it will work in the past too. Do I share collateral guilt? Or should I not get too hung up about it? And, anyway, why should it matter to me? Why should I feel any sense of responsibility? As you say, it doesn't make sense. But then, almost exactly a hundred or so years later a platoon of soldiers go into a Vietnamese village and kill a couple of hundred or so innocent villagers, two, three, four, five hundred women, old folk, kids, babies. In a village called My Lai. Why? To teach them a lesson maybe. It couldn't have been more aptly named. My Lie. The big American lie that we're the Good Guys, capital letters, neon, with mustard and ketchup, the works. With God on Our Side.

Alice was looking at me big-eyed and nodding at my sudden passion.

'And even now, they are still digging out Nazis who killed Italian villagers, French Jewish children, had been death guards at Ravensbruck and Dachau. Nazis. They're fair game. But G.I. atrocities against the Vietnamese...?'

I let the thought hang there in the silence. Let it taunt me. Shame me. Lieutenant Calley, Captain Medina... those were the names that stuck in the mind. But the kids today, they didn't even know there'd been a war in Vietnam. That was old stuff anyway. Stuff their dads talked about sometimes. Dullsville. We expect the Germans to still feel shame about the Jews but we should feel sorry for what we did to the Vietnamese? Forget it. It's ancient history and we're the good guys right? God save America and all that. That was Maddie's world. It would be Little Benjy's world. The bad stuff of the past wrapped up in sanitary towels and disposed of. 'Cos we're the good guys bud and don't forget it. And will it happen again in Iraq? Has it already happened? And would we, should we, bear any of the responsibility? The question bugged me. Still does. It nags at me for an answer. In what way could I be responsible? But look at it another way. I am myself a product of the society that committed these acts. I share their culture. When it happens again – in Guatemala or Cuba or I don't know where – will I continue to be able to say: I wasn't there, I don't have any responsibility. Don't blame me!

Blame. That's the problem. People looking back, feeling guilty, more likely not, saying it's nothing to do with me, not wishing to shoulder the weight of guilt. But what of the future? When it happens again. Won't we then be a little to blame for not having done enough to make sure it doesn't. Isn't that what we demand of the Germans? That they make sure it doesn't happen again? Isn't that my job, as a history teacher, to make my young people aware, to make sure my students get the right message? And then again, I thought, but really, does it make any difference? Maybe we're just as much victims of the process of history. Maybe it just breathes through us, blowing us where it will, impartial to pain and suffering, to guilt and responsibility, like leaves on a fall day. I hope not. I prefer to pretend to the archetypical American virtue that we can all individually make a difference. That we are all witnesses. But, then, of course, I came to realize I have been framing the questions way too far into the heights of abstraction. Perhaps I have been trying to absolve myself of my own collateral guilt. For of course it wasn't the guilt of my great great grandfather that I am struggling to come to terms with. It is Joe's guilt. I know that even the Bible consoles me. I am not my brother's keeper. I know. But still... And once I reach that point my mind empties again and a silent wind blows through it and I sense a vast void inside me.

'Well,' Alice said in a muted voice, 'I guess the next time I ask you what you're thinking, I ought to think twice about it.'

*

C is for Common Coins.

> *All coins are the same, made with bellows, coal and fire.*
> *Some, from shape or size, have value, succeed, are proud.*
> *Others, lacking value, are common, stained and useless.*
> *But this common coin needs just one other common coin to*
> *be of use.*

*

C is for Caodaism and Coconut Monks.

Joe got it right: ice-cream churches and circus religions. The Caodaist churches were creamy yellow with paintings in blue and pink around the outside. Like a Walt Disney church with a single eye dominating the front. We passed a dozen on the way to the cathedral complex at Tay Ninh. The main cathedral was bizarre. On the outside it was a church. On the inside, how can I describe it? Pink pillars, writhing with blue dragons, stretched in two files from the altar in the front to the one at the back. The rest of the space was empty, spacious and cool like a mosque. The ceiling glittered with mirrored specks against a blue background: space and the universe. At one end the altar was emptiness and at the other it was clutter. Emblems of half a dozen religions perched below a circular globe of the universe. There was a hush of white robed clerics, male and female. They gave it the necessary solemnity and dignity. Without them it would have been Disneyland. According to the guidebook Caodaism was formed by a judicious selection of the main tenets and beliefs of Christianity, Buddhism, Islam and Chinese folk religion. The founder claimed that Sun Yat-sen and Victor Hugo were apostles of his creed. Did they know? Easy to laugh at it but it seems to me that a belief in the cosmic energy of a knowing universe is not so laughable.

But merely mixing Buddhism, Christianity and Islam was not sufficient for the Coconut Monk. He stirred the religious pot again and formed a belief compounded of Buddhism, Christianity and Caodaism. It was said that he had lived for three years eating nothing but coconuts on an island off My Tho town in the swirling waters of the Mekong river.

From the riverbank in My Tho the Mekong didn't look so grand. The island, I was assured, was just around the corner. I took a boat and away we went. There was a strength in the waters of the river that was all the more obvious from the precarious vantage of a fifteen foot motorized skip. We headed for a point in what I took to be the far shore but when we got there we rounded a point and an even wider stretch of water materialized I saw that the river had formed long boomerang-shaped islands – several kilometers long but narrow – a hundred yards at most. The waters concerned me.

They seemed to be flowing inland. Perhaps this section of the river was tidal. Ahead I could see a curious contraption sticking up from the point of the next island – I could see it was an island because a car ferry had rounded it ahead of us. The contraption was a flimsy edifice of poles and metal sculptured fittings: a pagoda, a rocket, a sickle moon. A ticket to look cost half a dollar. There was nothing to see apart from the edifice which from close up I could see had walkways and ladders. I declined the temptation to climb up. There was too an ancient gong, which, my guide informed me, the Coconut Monk rang at mid-day when he ate his coconuts. There was a jar there too, made of concrete and plastered with broken ceramic pieces. It was a four-sided jar. On each side was a photograph of the monk. In one he was a young earnest lawyer. In the next he wore the white gowns of a Caodaist priest, in the third he wore the saffron robes of the Buddhist and in the last he looked like Laurence Olivier playing Cardinal Richelieu: surplice tied up to the neck with a heavy cross dangling on his chest. His head was shaved except for a small circlet of hair. He was still alive, I was informed. He was over ninety years old. He lived in the village we could see on the far bank. Not a bad life. Found a religion and charge visitors. Commit some act of mild hardship for three years. This religion would no doubt last. There was a lot of money in it.

*

Wash looked towards Maddie who was sitting on the porch.

'Girl, go get some food on the table. We got a guest.'

I remembered the provisions in the car.

'I've got some steaks. They won't keep. I'll go get them.'

I got to my feet.

'Set yourself down. We got the girl to do all that kinda palava. You girl...' Maddie turned her head.

'Girl, go get the steak and stuff outa the car and cook us up something to eat. Isa gettin' hungry. And my brother's brother here getting hungry too, I reckon. Am I right?'

I nodded and sat down. Then got back to my feet.

'I need some water to wash this whiskey down.'

I went to the sink and while I filled the glass I looked out of the window. Maddie reached the car and opened the driver's door. I had a sudden thought I'd left the key in the ignition and that she would jump in and drive off. Which would be good for her but bad for me. If she made it. I checked my pocket. The key was there. Wash noted the movement.

'She tryin' to run out on us?'

'No, I was just checking.'

'She ain't got the balls for it. Don't you worry.'

A few minutes later Maddie came back carrying a couple of bags which she put down. Then she headed for the door again.

'Where you think you going?'

'There's more bags in the car.' These were the first words I heard her speak. They shivered, fearful but still truculent. 'You want me to get 'em or not?'

Wash yawned.

'Yeah. Go get 'em.'

I'd been up here a couple of hours now but Wash's eyes were still boring holes in me, sizing me up, testing me. Maddie came back carrying more bags.

'There's still some whiskey out there. You want me to bring that in?'

'More whiskey. You doing me proud brother Jack. Hope you don't plan to hold out on me, now.'

'Don't worry. There's four more bottles out there and they're all for you. I can't drink much these days. My kidneys...' I said vaguely, hoping he wouldn't pry too much, seeing as I didn't have any kind of kidney thing. Just can't hold my drink too well. Too many sober years with Norma to blame for that.

*

C is for concubine.

On Being A Concubine
Cursed is this fate of women who share a common husband.
While the first wife lies warm under a blanket
The concubine has to suffer the cold.
Occasionally he deigns to visit
No more than twice a month at most
I might just as well not be married
People vie for sticky balls of rice
Those who snatch one think they're lucky
But soon they find the rice is stale
It is like doing unpaid hired labor

If I had known this before I would have stayed single.

*

It doesn't show much right now but I know soon that Maddie's going to be swelling with the babe and I should be holding and cuddling her and all that shit. There she is swelling with the child. And I feel sicker and sicker. One day I got to talk to that child and it's going to say 'Dad'.

Fact is I know I can't be no 'Dad' for nobody. A dad's somebody you got to be proud of and look up to. Maddie's nothing to me but I always wanted a child. I always wanted to hold my own baby in my arms. I want to have my very own child. Who's going to look at me with love and open eyes. How can I look him – or her, maybe it's a her – in the eyes? I'm dead inside. One day they're going to look me in the eyes and they're going to see I'm dead. They're going to despise me. What am I going to say to them? One day I won't be able to keep the dam back. It'll all flow out. All the shit I've done. Oh Christ! I think one day I'll just put a gun barrel to your belly and pull the trigger. That's right. But you know what? I've tried to picture it to myself. I can't do it. Can't even picture it. Goddamn.

*

'So, you going to bang the bitch tonight? Remember, you're standing in for Joe. Joe always get real spoiled when he come up here. You say the word, she is yours, man.'

I knew he was just testing me.

I looked at Maddie and she looked back sullen, blank. We needed to talk. She needed to know how things were.

'Sure.'

'You sure you up for it?'

'Sure. Why wouldn't I be?'

'Joe didn't think you had the balls for it.'

'That right?'

'Damn right. That's what he told me. I swear on the good book itself. He was sitting right where you at right now and he said: My brother Jack is a heap of shit.'

'He said that?' I was shocked that Joe would say such a thing.

'Yeah. Ask the girl. She heard him. Hey girl. He say that or not?'

She twisted her mouth.

'Yeah,' she said finally, unwillingly.

'I'll have to talk to him about that when I see him next.' I said sourly.

'Yeah. You talk to him.'

'So, why are you telling me?'

''Cos I want to see you get mad. I want to see what you made of. Are you a chicken or are you a man?'

'Me?'

The mood needed lightening, fast.

'I guess I'm two thirds chicken.'

Wash stared at me hard for a long minute. Then slowly he let his face break open into a wide silent, rocking mirth.

'Yo! Ain't we all man! Join the club. Man who ain't mostly chicken most likely end up dead.' And he slapped his leg. Then he turned to Maddie.

'You heard the man. He going to give you a good time tonight. Fuck your sweet pussy rotten. So you best go make yourself pretty for the man.'

Our eyes met and this time she held the look.

'I got a shampoo in my bag if you want to wash your hair,' I said to her, conscious that these were the first words I had spoken to her.

Her eyes lit up at that. She gave a quick nod.

'OK.' I stood up. 'I'll just go get my bag.'

I went out to the car and got my bag. What about the gun? On impulse I decided to slip it into the bag. Best to have it close to hand. I opened the glove box. Time and space froze solid. The gun was gone. Shit! Had Wash got it? He hadn't been out of the cabin since I had arrived. It had to be Maddie. What had she done with it? I forced myself to calm down and compose myself. If I wasn't careful she might decide to shoot me too. I took in a deep breath and then carried the bag inside.

'Where do I sleep?'

Wash waved his hand in the direction of the back room.

'That's where Joe sleeps.'

'That'll do me fine.'

I got the shampoo out and went back into the main room. Maddie held her hand out to take it but I sat down with it still in my hand.

'You got a smoke for me?' I asked Wash.

'Sure man. Just roll ups.'

'That's fine. I don't smoke much. Thought I had a pack in the glove box of the car.'

I looked up at Maddie and locked my eyes on hers. I gave a little shake of my head. I hoped she got my meaning. I didn't want her coming back with the gun in her hand shooting us both up. I wanted her to know I was on her side. She was biting her lip.

'Turns out I didn't.'

When I was sure we understood each other I lobbed the bottle to her.

'Here!'

'Go use the outside tap,' Wash growled at her.

A few minutes later I was still struggling with the tobacco and paper trying to make a decent roll up. Seeing the mess I was making, he gave out a loud guffaw.

'Here! You making a real mess of that,'

He took the tobacco and paper from me and deftly rolled me one. It was a long time since I had last had a cigarette and the smoke caught in my throat. Wash shook his head as if to say there was no hope for me. Or maybe he decided I was such a putz he needed to do something about me. I heard the water from the tap splash on the ground. Wash gave me an exaggerated wink and beckoned me with his finger. I followed him out on to the porch. There, by the corner of the building, by the tap, Maddie stood naked, soaped up, her hair a mass of soap suds. Her golden brown skin shone in the late afternoon sun. It hit me in the stomach. It felt like I was winded. She was – quite simply – beautiful. She saw us looking and made a vestigial move to hide herself, then shrugged and carried on, ignoring us. I felt several electric shocks in the groin. Maybe it was the whiskey, or just being away from Norma, or the adrenalin. Whatever it was, I wanted her. And her frail, bruised, hurt vulnerability only made the wanting worse.

CHAPTER 7

Morning proper. Benjy is awake and once awake he is impatient. He wants to do things. He has plans. I am an obstacle in the way. He clambers over me. I used to be a heavy sleeper but since I started to share a bed with Benjy I am a hair-trigger sleeper, the slightest movement and I'm awake, whiskey notwithstanding.

'Ow!' I say as he trails a sharp finger-nail across my side.

'Sorry, Daddy.'

'What are you doing?'

'Watch TV.'

It's one skill he has picked up with ease: the ability to press the buttons on the remote. He knows what he's doing. Or so it seems. Maybe it's all random, trial and error. All he has to do is keep clicking and finally something will happen, some program that he wants to watch will come on. The television is downstairs and he doesn't like to go down alone. He starts to pull my t-shirt.

'Come on Daddy.'

'No way.'

'Yes way.'

I hear the door to the bathroom and I check the clock. Ma is up. The household has woken. In ten minutes it's my turn. Breakfast will be on the table at twenty past seven on the dot. Always has been and always will be. My head is heavy but I know I have no choice except to savor the ten minutes Ma takes in the bathroom.

'Hold your horses,' I say as Benjy is reaching up for the door handle.

'I don't have a horse, Daddy,' Such literal seriousness. He keeps me sane. What would I do without him?

After breakfast we walk to the kindergarten. On the way he surprises me with a question that had to come up sometime. I've been expecting it with dread, surprised it has taken so long.

'Am I black, Daddy?'

How do you explain to a little four-and-a-half year old the complexities of race, the stupidities of men, the words that are in us that we want to pluck out and hurl into oblivion, the words he must know, nevertheless, to survive?

'Yes, Benjy, you're a beautiful little black boy.'

'Are you black Daddy?'

'No, I'm white.'

'How come?'

'Well, my mummy is white and my daddy was white so I'm white.'

'But you're my daddy.'

'That's right. (I sure fell into that one!) I'm your daddy. But you've got another daddy, and he's...'

'But you're my real Daddy...?' There is worry and concern in his voice.

'Yes, I'm your real Daddy,' I try to reassure him. 'I'm the Daddy you're going to live with for ever and ever. You and me and grandma. We're one family.'

'But how come they make fun of me at school?'

'Do they?'

'Yeah.'

'What do they say?'

'They say I'm no good. They say I'm dirty. I'm black.' The cruelty of children.

'Well, they're wrong. You're good. You're as yummy as chocolate. You like chocolate, don't you?'

'I don't understand.'

'Well, OK, when I said you're black. Well, that's not true exactly.'

'I'm not black?' Was it hope or hopeless confusion that caused his voice to wobble?

'No.'

'But...?'

'It's like this: Your daddy, your other daddy, was a black man – actually he had a fair share of white blood in him too (blood? The primitive language of ancestral roots) – but your mom was like the rainbow, so you just go back and you tell them: 'I'm a rainbow. I am all the colors in the world.' Can you say that?'

'Rainbow?'

'That's right.'

'I don't understand Daddy.'

Oh God. How could I explain everything? But I had to do it and keep doing it, I told myself. Don't start out by lying. And how was I to explain Maddie's own rivers of genetic blood? She was a Lumbee Indian and who or what was that? *E pluribus unum* with a vengeance. And it was strange that we had that in common. She too had grown up not far from Lumberton, North Carolina, as we had, and so Lumbee was something I knew about. And I remembered that day... It was raining the day we went from the Outer Banks to Roanoke. A cold heavy drizzle that nevertheless was unable to dampen our interest in the curiously small circle that was the fort. The overgrown mound was barely approachable with the ground turning to mud. Here, among these trees, was the first settlement of English men, women and children. Here, right here, the very first European child was born on American soil – Virginia Dare. Virginia, daughter of Ananias Dare and his wife Eleanor, who was herself the daughter of the leader of the expedition, John White; Virginia Dare, who must, later, have had a brother for this was very likely, or so she believed, the line of Maddie's own descent. I felt enormously privileged to be a witness at this conjunction of past and present.

We spent some time trying to visualize the scene but it was not very satisfactory. Having seen the outer banks and the huge sheltered bay between these long sand banks and the mainland, it was obvious why Roanoke had been chosen as a place to build a settlement. If Walter Raleigh had wanted a base from which to launch harassing attacks on the Spanish further south then Roanoke was the obvious place. But why this point on the island? The shore hereabouts seemed inhospitable. Not that we were able to see it clearly and in the more than four centuries since that day they landed in 1587, it was probable there would have been a few changes. And, also, of course they hadn't stayed there long. They had arrived in 1587 and three years later were no longer there. Duh duh da duh. The theme music of suspense. The Lost Colony.

We watched the film that told their story. Maddie watched it with great concentration. Afterwards she was furious.

'Why are they always saying this word Lost, Lost, Lost. Don't they know we been found? Why is it so hard to admit?'

'Hey! Calm down!'

'No, I won't calm down. I'm serious. Why? Can you tell me? You're the big history man here. They love this Lost Colony stuff. Killed by the cruel Indian. Wooo! Makes shivers go down your back, don't it. Huh?'

'People are looking at us.'

'I don't care if people are looking at us. I want to shout in their damn faces. I want to say that man there in that film is my great great great, how many greats I don't know, grandfather. I want to say these damn Indians saved your people. See, even I'm confused 'cos I always think I'm a Native American person and that I am not a white person, that I am opposed by white people, but here in this film I am on the side of the native people and also I am on the white man's side 'cos that's my name. I'm a Dare.'

'It's good for the tourism business. There's no point in having a museum to the Lost Colony if a hundred and fifty miles away there's another museum that says: Hey Look here! We're the Found Colony. We're the descendants.'

'Yeah, you sure got a point there.'

'And anyway, we've got the Mayflower Society and the Pilgrims and Plymouth Rock. We've got another myth about who are the real descendants of the first colonists of this fair land. And the nice thing about them is they're rich and white.'

'Yeah. We're the wrong color. But how do you explain us, then? A lot of us have the same names as the people in the Lost Colony. And, when you white guys found us we were already speaking English, and farming and living in houses.'

There were other sides to the story but this was not the time to go into them. And anyway Maddie would not think better of me if I were to give them head space. I was on Maddie's side no matter what.

'There's none so deaf as those who will not hear.'

'That is the truth of it!'

And it did seem to me interesting how the history textbooks that we used at school made no mention of the Lumbee people of Robeson County in southern North Carolina and their very reasonable claim to be the true descendants of those brave Elizabethans who upped and left families and friends knowing their futures would be hazardous in the extreme, yet still taking wives and children. Who would set out to colonize the moon like this? Shouldn't we celebrate this wonder? These people who were prepared to build up lives on the edge of an unknown continent – which, unknown to them, was on the edge of another colonizing venture: Powhatan's growing tribal confederacy. And therein lay the problem for Powhatan was strong and certainly not going to let any settlement of unaffiliated white men and women grow that did not recognize his authority. And in any case the white men were a rough and ready lot who do not seem to have had a proper sense of what was needed to survive in this new land that they wished to make home. People who depended overly much on the scarce resources of friendly local people, a people who quickly tired of the novelty of these crude and belligerent men. All that is known is that in 1587 a small group of people landed and started the work of establishing a settlement: building some form of protective wall, building homes for shelter, clearing the ground for agriculture, finding and maintaining a good, unpolluted, water supply, establishing areas for elimination and so on (or so we imagine, we who are more organized in our thought than they ever could have been, more clean and obsessed with privacy – how did they organize the business of pissing and shitting, men and women? What tensions were felt, if any, about how this matter should best be accomplished? My guess is that people just went any old how into the bushes and trusted to luck that they didn't step on another's deposits). These adventurous fools or foolish adventurers were left there while the leader John Smith went to get more supplies. There were delays. Three years went by. Then in 1590 when John Smith returned, there was no sign of the settlers. However, looking at it in a positive light, there was no sign of violence. The departure had been orderly. Apart from that, the historical records provide only small whispers – a tale of English speaking people here, a massacre of white people there. The dream text of authorized history is that the cruel Indians killed them, massacred them, burnt them, scalped them: killed that first baby to be born on American soil – white baby – poor Virginia Dare, possibly before she could even totter on her two legs. Those bastard Indians would have shot that poor baby through the heart with their bows and arrows. Or was she snatched up by some demented bloodthirsty warrior, caught by the legs, her brains dashed out of her against a tree trunk? There's a dream text sufficient to justify the slaughter of Native Americans ever since: Take this for little Ginny Dare! Easy to stoke the coals of racial anger.

But then you have to explain Maddie's people. Who are they? Where did they come from? How is it they speak English, spoke Elizabethan English that was old-fashioned by the time the next wave of colonists made their way down through the swamps and along the coasts, Scots by and large seeking to settle on good fertile land and establish new lives? How is it that they share the names? Half the surnames of those men and women who were part of the Lost Colony will be found today in the telephone book of Robeson County. What is the statistical likelihood of that? All of them Lumbees. And there are only forty thousand Lumbees. But there are no answers. Only silence. There is no desire to explain. Muddy waters. The symbolic truths too potent. The Mayflower Myth too entrenched in our Oxfords and Harvards and Yales. And it will not be shaken while the text of our mythic history remains steeped in the hostility and opposition of the races: Black versus white versus red. What do you do with a group of people who are red and white and black – because escaped slaves, both white and black, and even some freed Negroes found community among the Lumbee people? It's a myth that goes against the grain and so we have suppressed it. That's the truth. That's the whole truth of it. And in this other dream text of history little Ginny Dare grew up and married an Indian man – an Indian who fished the swamps, hunted the woods, tilled the land, and she gave birth to a little child who was not half this and half that but wholly new and complete. And little Ginny Dare had a brother, maybe two, maybe more. And they married Indian girls who must have been comely because somewhere down the line they gave birth to Maddie. That's right. I'm a believer. There is no doubt in my mind whatsoever, that Maddie Dare is a direct descendent of Ananias Dare of the Lost Colony of Roanoke.

And that means Benjy too, wherever he comes to lay the anchor of his identity, is a descendent of those first colonizers.

And what is it we want of history – a narrative that we can be proud of? Or the truth no matter how awkward?

And I thought of the names of some of those Indian tribes who fed into her bloodline, that most likely flowed into the arterial river of the Lumbee, names almost forgotten now. I sounded them out silently in my head. Catawba, Keyauwee, Sugaree, Waxhaw, Eno, Shakori, Saura, Cheraw, Tuscarora, Pamunkey, Occanock, Metompkin. Mixed up and blurred into each other by the churning wheels of history. At one time separate, distinct and hostile. At another time blended into a new whole. And we are all mere insects inhabiting such a small, short moment of space and time – and yet we take ourselves so seriously as though our identities are and have been for all time and will be forever.

All of this I had visited and revisited many times, quietly, in my thoughts. Now I had to pass the burden of them on to Benjy.

'You're a rainbow of colors. You've got white blood and Indian blood and black blood, African blood. You're unique. Do you know what that means? It means you're very, very special. Do you understand that? You've got something that most other people don't have. You've got the blood of all America running through you.' I was getting carried away. Deliberately. I wanted to make it sound grand, something to be proud of, not some measly mealy-mouthed compromise, some failure of identity.

'Got that?'

'Yes, daddy.' He stared into my face with that direct stare of the wholly innocent, staring down with all seriousness into the dark depths of my own and it took all the effort I had to return the look, to stare back into his eyes. I could sense it coming, another question of great profundity.

'Can I have some ice cream?'

'Yeah sure.' Ice cream? He'd caught me in the guilt trap. 'Later. After school.' Ice cream? What can he be thinking of?

And then, at school, I hand him over, this precious being, into the hands of his enemies, his friends, his future. He's happy. He's already pulling himself out of his jacket in excited expectation of the fun of the day ahead.

'Bye bye Daddy.'

'Bye bye Benjy.'

'See you later alligator,' he says.

'In a while...' I pause deliberately to let him provide the ending.

'Cocadrile.'

'Yeah right. Give me five.'

We slap hands and then he runs off and I am left thinking I should have been talking about Native Americans not Indians. Maddie would have... would prefer that. But even they, I ruminate, are not true natives, true aboriginals. They just had a thirteen or maybe twenty thousand year start on the rest of us. We're all of us immigrants to this new land. Black and white and red and yellow: all these absolutes, separate and individuated. Not measures of the reality of the underlying truth – just concepts, just ideas. In the end, when we've traced the thread back to its origins, we're all Africans. 'Fraid so Kansas. No denying it Missouri. Now we're stuck with our parallel communities founded on falsehood.

I catch sight of Alice and we smile. We have definitely become a conspiracy.

'Look,' she says to me. 'Why don't I pick both kids up after school and take them to the house and then you can come out whenever you like. Have some time to yourself. And then, why don't you?' she paused to check if I was up to speed with what she was saying. 'You can stay over. Benjy can sleep in Kathy's room and there's a spare bedroom,' she smiles. 'You'll be safe.'

I offer to do some shopping but she waves me away.

'Just go and enjoy your day doing whatever it is you want to do and I'll see you later out at the house.'

*

It's just come back to me. The dream I had last night. I dreamt that Maddie came back and said she had forgiven Joe. I had hugged her gladly when she said that; as though a warm, and radiant, honey-glowing sun now flooded through me. I was so happy. Incredulous too.

'Do you mean that? Really?'

'I guess so.'

'You know he died thinking you were carrying his baby.'

'Yeah. I let him think that.'

And then, even in the dream, though this memory was true, I laughed as I remembered when Maddie gave birth, finally, after much heaving and screaming, to her little baby. And I was there mopping her brow with a cloth and holding one of her hands – saying 'Come on, baby! Come on! Push! Push!' – and the midwife and the doctor standing by. Then suddenly, a sudden whoosh of motion, this greased up, gray and slimy sack of being suddenly sloshed into the doctor's arms and I can still remember their utter consternation, their mouths dropped open as they saw something immediately that I didn't see, and they wondered how they were going to tell me this, tell me what I already knew, that I was not the father of this baby, for it was clear as day the father was black. And I laughed at their bewilderment and their wondering how they were going to break the news to me. And I suddenly took it all in, remembering suddenly there was a question to be answered and I looked at little Benjy and nodded and whispered to Maddie.

'It's Wash's baby,' I whispered but the midwife, suddenly tense and nervous, misheard me.

'We'll wash him later,' And she placed little Benjy on Maddie's belly. And Maddie took hold of the little fellow cautiously, tentatively, unsure.

But I fell in love with him. The sins of his father surely did not fall on this son. Surely to God not. Please God, not ever.

And the doctor, feeling he needed to draw my attention to something I appeared not to have noticed, said: 'He's a dark little fellow, isn't he?'

I just smiled at him. Some confusions are too vast to bridge with explanation.

'He takes after his father,' I said and returned my attentions to the tired mother.

And then I woke and the happiness dissolved in the gray light of dawn.

Maddie never did embrace her fate, her son. Not with her whole heart. It was an effort that, one day, became too much for her. I came back from Vietnam to find she had gone, leaving Benjy with Ma. That's when I began to fall apart. There was no note. She did ring once, twice, to appease her guilt. And then nothing. I kept waiting and hoping. There's nothing that guts a man quite so hard as hope turned bad.

*

And Joe too had his dreams.

I still have dreams – crazy messed up dreams – of rice paddies and dikes and tree lines and mat shed hooches and damn banana trees and coconuts with wide fronds waving in the sky, innocently. One time we got landed at a landing zone by chopper. Let me tell you about the choppers. The noise was something phenomenal. You couldn't hear yourself think and the whole machine is shuddering and clanking and there's a great hole where the door is. You know what they said when that press photographer took the shot of the man falling from the helicopter: 'He was not co-operating with his interrogators.' Not co-operating? That's a good one. Chopper's not the place to hold an interrogation. We got dropped at this LZ somewhere in deepest Vee-etnahm. Wall to wall rice paddies. We jump into the gunk and spread out. The tree line was 2,000 meters away. What are we doing this for? Who knows? It's just a sweep. It's hot and the mud sucks your feet. You're chewing gum and thinking it would be nice to see corn fields again. No-one in sight. No boy on a buffalo. No old man repairing a paddy wall. We should of noticed that. The tree line was a thousand meters away and it's a nice quiet day. There are troops up ahead on point. Could have been me. Could have been anyone. The sun is strong now and the sweat is pouring from your armpits and you're thinking of partying tonight at base camp and that pretty nurse you said hello to and having a beer. Five hundred meters Nothing moving. No sign of any enemy. Why are we doing a sweep? Because some AID worker thinks he's got information that there's a division or two of NVA in the area and the top brass are pissing themselves laughing. Two divisions? No fucking way. We'd have heard them coming. Tell you what. We'll do a sweep. See what we come up against. Fucking AID workers think they know everything. Three hundred yards and the men on point are ten feet from the tree line. Then all Hell breaks loose. The whole fucking world exploded. I was down in the gunk in no time flat. I hardly dared come up to breathe. I could hear myself screaming to myself: God, please, please, pleeeeze! Oh God! Save me. Don't let me die. I don't want to die! I backed up real slow. Everyone still alive got their asses out of there. I guess they had snipers up the trees. Did a lot of damage. Finally they called in support fire but they got the range wrong and it was exploding all around us. It lasted for hours. It was a real fucked up operation. In the end they napalmed the tree line. That was one up for the gooks.

'They'. Let me tell you about 'They'. They was everybody. They was the enemy. They was the Fleet Air Arm. They was everybody out there that was trying to kill you. They was the people who ordered up artillery support. They was everybody except you: you and your fire team especially. You were in this little bubble with your own people, your team. Your only task was to stay alive.

Who was in our fire team? In the beginning there was Wash and Me and Teddy O'Rourke and Flamingo Perez and Fredericks McMillan and Ken Kobel and Danny Smith and that kid who got shot on the first day in the field. Shot in the leg. Lucky bastard. Luckiest grunt there ever was. Then came Junior Jameson, which made it three blacks and four whites if you could call Perez white. But we had no trouble that way after O'Rourke spat in Wash's face and called him a nigguh and Wash kicked him in the balls and had his knife at his throat and O'Rourke spluttered in the dirt, going redder and redder in the face. Then the Sergeant came.

'What the fuck's going on?'

Wash calmly climbed to his feet.

'Just showing O'Rourke how to defend hisself case there's a bayonet charge.'

'That right O'Rourke?'

'Yes sir, that's how it was sir!'

'Good! Carry on!'

O'Rourke watched the Sergeant march off and then spat on the ground and held out his hand.

'Guess I was a fool.'

'Yessuh! Mr O'Rourke, you was a fool but I guess you ain't a fool now.'

After that there was no trouble.

Then O'Rourke had his head blown off right next to me and the gunk, like jell-o, splattered all over me. When? Where? It's all a mess in my head. It was in downtown Veee-etnahm. Who cares? God and America didn't care. Why were we there? To contain Communism. You can't argue with that. Might as well say Fighting Against The Devil. What did it matter? There was no point being for the war or against the war. The only point there was was survival. We didn't know if we were the good guys or the bad guys. Or to put it another way, we knew we were the bad guys but we didn't like to think about it too much. Thinking didn't help increase your chances of long term survival, the only thing that counted. We went in cherries, we came out hard cases or in body bags. It didn't take long to lose our virginity. Fred took shrapnel in the face. Flamingo just disappeared. We never found him. Not even bits of him. Maybe he took off. Maybe he's still alive. So Woody Walters and Lenny Davis and Ken Troot and Manny Levitz came in and out of our lives. Woody lost a leg to a mine and Ken shot himself in the foot and Lenny took a shot in the belly and leaked all over himself and died before he could be medevaced. And then there was...What the hell does anyone care? In the end it was just Wash and me who'd been there from the beginning. We weren't particularly close to start with but when the others got it... in the end there was just us. It seemed natural. We were the survivors. Within six months we were the old men. The cherries tried to stick with us, copy us, survive like us.

CHAPTER 8

That first morning, Waking in Alice's house. I listened out but no-one was stirring. I decided I'd had enough of lying in bed waiting for a noise. And what a great pleasure it was to be in a new house. I tiptoed to the bathroom and inhaled its feminine lavendery essences.

I was fiddling with the kettle when Alice came padding out of her room in her billowing white nightgown and slippers.

'I thought I heard you.'

'Did I wake you?'

'No. I'm an early riser. This is my favorite time of day.' She looked out the window.

'If the rain keeps off and it warms up a bit like the weather report said it would, we can go down to the pool and have a picnic.

'Pool?'

'There's a natural pool about a mile or so upstream.'

'Sounds good.'

'The kids can splash around.'

'It's not too cold?'

'They don't mind the cold. Only fuddy duddies like us...'

But before she could finish the sentence there was the sound of a crash from Kathy's bedroom.

'Oops. Let's see what they're up to.'

A bedside lamp was lying on the floor but the kids were having too much fun bouncing up and down on the bed to pay it any mind.

'UP!'

'I can jump higher than you!'

'No you can't. I can…'

'I can! I can!'

'You'll break the bed springs!' I shouted and moved to grab Benjy.

'Oh don't be silly!' Alice admonished. 'Let them have fun. Let's leave them to it while we get breakfast ready.'

'Are you sure…?'

'Come on.'

But almost immediately there was another bang as Kathy herself fell off the bed on to the floor. Benjy, glorying in his victory continued to bounce.

'I'm the highest. I'm the king. I win. I win.'

Katie screamed and wouldn't be mollified.

'Come now, little man,' I grabbed him by the arm and lifted him struggling to my shoulder.

'Let me go! Let me go!'

'We're going to have breakfast.'

And still Kathy would not be consoled.

'Come. We're going to have pancakes. Who doesn't like pancakes?'

'Pancakes! I want pancakes. I want…' Benjy screamed.

'I don't want pancakes,' Kathy shouted. 'I don't want anything.'

'Come on, now, Kathy,' Alice's husky voice hinted at naughty pleasures. 'You and I are going to make pancakes for these two men.'

'I don't want to…' Kathy struggled. But within a few minutes she was stirring eggs in a bowl while Benjy and I wobbled around the room like ungainly ballroom dancers, his feet on mine. Thank the Lord for making children so easily distracted.

*

The first bottle of whiskey was gone and Wash had started to make inroads into the second. I brought the other four in from the car. I guess I hoped that Wash would drink himself comatose. That would make things easy. But it was going to be a long night. It was just after five now. The shadow of the mountain had fallen across the cabin as the late afternoon sun sank behind us. Wash started up a small generator behind the cabin and lights came on. We moved out on to the porch and watched the world turn slowly gray Then the surrounding mountains settled behind the curtain of darkness and we were wrapped in the cloak of night. There was no moon to shed light. It was pitch dark. Maddie brought our food out and we ate in silence. When we'd finished she took the plates away. I sat and wondered about the gun. Almost certainly she had it in there hidden amongst the food. We were sitting ducks if she decided to just let loose. And why wouldn't she? And now that night had fallen Wash's manner changed. I felt we had made some headway now I wasn't so sure. I noticed he kept his gun close at hand.

'How long have you been up here?'

'How long?'

He lay back with his head propped against a cushion, giving the question more thought than it deserved.

'Forever, man. Seems like forever.'

'Why did you come up here in the first place?'

He gave me a hard look.

'You sure is full of questions.'

By now I was feeling more secure. Wash had a thick coat of aggression but there was something else there too, almost a vulnerability. It was hard to lay my finger on exactly what it was. All I knew was that Joe was part of this inner world and if I was to catch him off guard I had to pry him open.

'It's just that Joe didn't tell me much,' I explained. 'I mean he told me about you being his Vietnam buddy and he told me some of the things you did out there, but…'

'He told you?' Wash cut me off. 'What?'

'You saved his life. He saved yours. That kind of thing.'

'I sure done saved his ass,' Wash laughed. 'Oh yes. He was fucked if I hadn't of been around. Joe would be pushing up daisies I hadn't been around. That's the truth.'

He spat into the weeds beside the cabin.

*

We played it like the book for a month or two. We were on reaction patrol duties. Up in the hills. Out of touch for days and weeks. Feet rotting. No hot food. Moving. Always moving. Once we came to a village up in the hills. Truly beautiful. It was at the top of a kind of meadow. There was a stream flowing past. We sat and watched it all day and all night, tucked into the bushes, hidden from view. Eight days we were there watching. We watched life, normal life. Women fetched water from a well. Others washed clothes in the stream. Kids played in the dust, old men smoked pipes. Not many mature men. Some. A dozen or so. We watched it like it was a movie. It was so quiet we all fell into a dream-like trance. How could there be a war when a place like this existed? I guess we knew they knew we were there. But no-one messed with NVA uniforms or flags of the wrong sort. Nothing like that. It was as though they were completely isolated from the war.

'Man, this is paradise,' Wash whispered to me. 'War's over, Isa gonna find a nice sweet little meadow like this and Isa gonna dig myself in real deep. No shit!'

I wonder what happened to that village? Maybe it's still there. Maybe I'll go back there one day. Trouble is: I don't know where the fuck it is.

Another village. We knew the Cong was there. Another patrol had taken fire. As we approached it there was sniper fire. ping-ping. Just one gun. No-one was hurt. We took a sweep through the village, checked out all the hootches. Nothing. As we were leaving the sniper opened up again. Ping ping. Either he wasn't a good shot or he had a lousy gun. Only this time he got lucky. Wash took a bullet in the arm. Nothing serious. But he was out in the open. I yelled at the others to shoot at the tree tops as I raced over to Wash and dragged him to cover under a tree. Then I looked up and I could see a foot dangling among the coconuts. We were sitting right under the fucking sniper. I couldn't get a shot at him from where I was so I ran backwards and emptied a magazine into the fucking tree. Coconuts fell everywhere but there was no sign of the man. I swear to god he was up there. He'd hollowed out the top of the tree. Maybe the whole tree was hollow. Anything was possible. Funny thing. Wash was hit by a coconut and knocked flat out.

We called in support and they napalmed the whole fucking village.

How many died? Who the fuck cares? Wash was choppered back to base camp but he wasn't bad enough to buy a ticket home. A week later he was back with us.

*

Early afternoon. The air was surprisingly warm. The pool was brimming over. Cold frothing water gushed down the tumble of bare gray rock at the far end.

'Don't worry. It's not deep. They'll be fine. Can you swim Benjy?'

Benjy stood cautiously on the banks examining the pool. He'd never seen a pool like this before. We'd been to the local indoor pool a couple of times – but never in the open air under the umbrella of trees with the sound of birds in the distant canopy. The air was surprisingly warm, almost like early summer.

'Just take your clothes off.'

Benjy shook his head.

'Don't wanna.'

I sympathized The water must be cold.

Kathy saw this was a competition she could win. She peeled off her little knickers and stepped boldly into the pool.

'See, Benjy,' she called to him. 'It's easy.'

Benjy watched her wade to the middle where she was still only waist deep, her skinny white arms held high to avoid getting wet. Then bouncing up and down she plunged under the water and came up again laughing.

'Come on Benjy.' She called. 'It's fun. It's fun.'

Benjy stopped struggling and allowed me to take his clothes off and then he too was gingerly stepping into the water.

'Isn't he such a lovely color?' Alice commented. 'Such a handsome color.'

The dark coppery brown of his skin gleamed and shimmered in the reflected light of the pool's surface.

'Come on,' Kathy called. 'Don't be scared.'

'I'm not scared. Look at me daddy. Da-ad!'

'I'm looking. You're doing great!'

'Come in daddy.'

'No. I'm talking to Alice. You play with Kathy.'

And I lay back against the mossy embankment and looked through the tree branches at the sky.

'This is one of my favorite places.'

'I can see why.'

High above us was a clear blue sky and the sun, a sharp brightness, scattered light through the leaves of the trees falling to where we sat. Alice lay propped on one elbow keeping her eye on the kids.

'I often bring a book down here and imagine I'm Thoreau sitting by his pond.'

For a while nothing more was said. Apart from the children who were shrieking with laughter the woods around us were silent

'It's quiet.'

'No-one else seems to come here.'

There were many things to be said between us but the presence of the children constrained us. Then, after some minutes of silence, she started to talk. I felt she was talking more to herself than me. I was just being allowed to listen in.

'Sometimes I lie here and I imagine I'm wrapped up in a tangle of vines – I'm in a castle – I'm in a solitary space surrounded by magical barriers. I am beautiful and pale. I'm in a deep and bottomless sleep. I'm the sleeping beauty waiting for my prince to come slashing through all the obstructions to find me. And when he finds me he can't help himself. He leans over me and presses his lips gently against my lips and when I feel the touch of his lips I open my eyes and immediately I am awake. The spell has been broken. And I hug the handsome prince and we dance to the sound of birds and butterflies and ladybugs And I live happily ever after!'

She smiled and stretched her arms, exuding deep contentment.

'Oh, dear prince, when are you going to come and rescue me from my prison?'

Then looking at me with wicked humor she said: 'Are you my prince?'

I shook my head.

'I wish I could be.'

But the effort it took to say that caused me to feel drowsy. I wanted to sink into a deep sleep. I didn't want any demands to be made of me. If only there was a hole I could burrow into. Perhaps she understood something of the cold chaos of my feelings. She teased my eyes open by tickling me with a blade of grass.

'If you're not my prince, who are you?'

'You're the beauty,' I muttered. 'I guess that makes me the beast.'

'Oh no! You're too gentle to be the beast.' She smiled. 'I prefer it that way.' Then her expression clouded over and she looked away towards the kids.

'I had a beast in my life once.'

She shook her head at the thought.

'But he's gone. He'll never trouble me again. Never again. Never ever!'

Later, we trooped back along the forest trail, Benjy riding on my shoulders and Kathy running ahead of Alice who, from time to time stooped to pick a flower. About a hundred yards from the road we came to a clearing. The embankment sloped down to the stream. Half-way down there was an irregularity, a slight but distinct mound.

'Wait here,' Alice called and clambered down. She placed her little posy of flowers on the mound.

'What's that?' I asked.

'It's just a habit.'

'It looks like it could be a grave.'

'Maybe.'

Then she started to clamber back towards us. On the way she stooped to inspect something.

'Oh kids, come and look at this.'

'What is it?'

Kathy and Benjy scrambled down the slop towards her while I followed behind more clumsily.

'Do you see this?'

She was pointing at a small plant.

'Do you know what this is called?'

The children looked at her and shook their heads. Their eyes wide in expectation of some wonder.

'It's a Venus Flytrap.'

'What's that?'

'It's a very special plant. Do you know what it eats?'

They shook their heads.

'It eats insects. Look, they fall into this little pool here and the liquid at the bottom dissolves them. Isn't that interesting? We eat plants and some plants can eat us.'

'No, they can't. They can't,' Kathy shouted dancing up and down.

'Can they, daddy?'

I put an arm round him to reassure him.

'No, only little insects.'

'I'm scared of the forest, daddy.' Benjy started to pull on my arm. 'Let's go. I want to go.'

'Wait Benjy,' Alice said. 'It's all right. I was just teasing you.'

'I want to go home.' Benjy pleaded.

'Do you want to know a big secret. A very special secret?'

'No, I want to go home.' Benjy was quite beside himself now. Kathy was made of sterner stuff.

'What's the secret, Mummy? I want to know the secret.'

'The Venus Flytrap needs something very special to survive. Can you guess what that is?'

'Water?'

'Air?'

Alice shook her head.

'I give up. Tell me. Tell me.'

Alice paused to make sure she had their complete attention.

'They need fire. They need to be burnt up. Isn't that strange? If they don't get burnt up they just die off. But the fire spreads their seed and the new plants are strong and healthy. Isn't that interesting?'

But Benjy still urgently wanted to go. He tugged my arm furiously.

'Come on daddy. Come on!' So we left the Venus flytrap to its fate and let the kids run ahead of us back to the road and the house.

And later, reflecting on the day's events, I asked myself this question: is that true for us too? Do we need to be burnt, hurt bad in some way, in order to be healthy?

CHAPTER 9

Sitting with Wash took a lot of energy, a lot of concentration. Conversation stuttered along. Destinations were arrived at in a roundabout fashion.

'How'd I end up here?' Wash spat into the grass beside the cabin. 'Long story.'

Fireflies flickered, dancing here and there.

'Goddamn bugs!' Wash said flapping his hand at them. He looked at me and laughed.

'Hey. So you think I'm just a goddamn urban nigger?'

I shook my head.

His face grew solemn.

'Truth is I love it up here...' he grimaced and spat on the ground. 'And I hate it. Drives me crazy.'

He let the silence settle on us again a while. When he spoke again his voice had a new edge to it.

'How'd you like to live up here with no-one to talk to for weeks on end, always having to keep your eyes peeled, not knowing who might sneak up on you?'

'Who? Who'd be sneaking around?'

'You never know who might be sneaking around in the dead of night.'

'Do you ever see anybody?'

'Not much. Strangers ain't welcome round here.'

He poured himself another half tumbler of whiskey and offered me the bottle. I still had plenty. I shook my head.

'How bad is Joe?' he asked suddenly.

'Bad.'

'Will he lose his leg?'

I mulled over the options and decided not to go overboard.

'Oh I don't think so. He'll be up and around soon enough, I guess. Maybe in a few months.'

'Can't wait that long.'

'What?'

'I got to get outa here.'

'Yeah?'

'Yeah. Driving me crazy. Now you're up here, maybe…' He didn't finish. 'Got to do some thinking.' He knocked back some whiskey. 'Where's that girl?'

I looked around. Maddie was still somewhere inside the cabin. I was nervous.

'Girl? You get your ass out here.'

I heard her say something to herself.

'What's that girl? You say something?'

I was relieved when she appeared without anything in her hands. Wash was twitchy and once he started shooting I didn't reckon much on my chances of getting out of the situation alive.

'I didn't say nuthin'. You want somethin'?'

'Yeah baby. I want your sweet loving.'

He grinned at me.

'Get your dress off baby.'

I started to get to my feet.

'I'll leave you two to get on with it.'

'Stay where you are brother Jack.'

He patted his gun to show he meant business.

'I don't trust no-one and I sure don't trust you. Reason I'm still alive is cos I don't go round trusting people just cos they brothers of my good friends. You understan' me?'

'Sure, man.' I said and sat back again resting against the wall of the cabin.

'Hurry up baby,' he croaked.

Maddie unbuttoned her shift and let it fall off her shoulders. She wasn't wearing anything underneath.

'Let me smell you baby. Let me smell your nice clean body.'

She crouched beside him and he buried his nostrils between her breasts.

'Oh. That's good baby. That's good.'

He unbuttoned his pants.

'Put your lips round my friend here. He needs the warmth of your sweet lips.'

She bent over him and her head bobbed up and down.

'That's right, baby. That's right. That sure feels good.'

After a while he took a knife out of his back pocket and cut the string that hobbled her. Then he sat her on his lap and held the point of the knife against her chest as she rose and fell on him.

'Don't you stop now baby.'

Then, just as suddenly, it was over.

'Oh yeah!' he sighed and she stopped moving. They rested like that for a few moments then he pushed her roughly aside.

'Get off of me, bitch.'

She scrambled away and picked up her shift.

'What you doing?'

'Just gettin' dressed, that's all.'

'You ain't finished, girl. You got to take care of my friend Jack here too.'

I coughed. I wanted to say no, no, go away, no, I'm not going to do that. But somehow the words didn't get said. She just shrugged and dropped the shift again. Her breasts swayed and the shadow in her loins caused in me a great ache of wanting. She crouched down beside me and took hold of my zipper. I helped her with one hand and touched her tentatively at first with the other. Slowly I caressed her, savoring the warmth of the contact. Then I was stroking her buttock. How long had I been faithful? Faithful every single day of my marriage to Norma. Now, here I was with a strange girl's lips around my prick while I had a finger in her cunt and I was loving every tingling second of it. Then, after a long while, she sat on top of me and I entered her. Or did she swallow me? Her hips rose and fell and I closed my eyes. Was it shame? Or to better feel the soft friction. Then I felt her finger tickle the base of my testicles. Just a light brush of the skin, a kind of calling card. Surprised, I opened my eyes and looked in her face. There was just the subtlest warmth. I blushed with the shame of it and leant forward and buried my face in the warmth of her breasts. Oh sweet soft apples. And then a force rose up in me, dark, electric. I turned and had her on her back, thrusting hard, even though it must have hurt her, until I too came in a mighty culmination.

'Oh Jesus!' I moaned as I rolled off her.

'Oh yeah,' Wash chuckled. 'Ride 'em cowboy!'

Only then did I remember she was pregnant, possibly with Joe's baby, and I felt a deep but distant shame.

*

The kids had thrown themselves on the cushions to watch cartoons on TV. I drifted out on to the porch overlooking the valley but the sun was behind the house now and the porch was cold in the shade.

Alice called out to me from the kitchen: 'Want a beer?'

'Sounds good. Are you going to join me?'

'Sure. I'll just put something in the oven first.'

I went and got a jacket from my room and by the time I got back Alice was sitting in the rocker with two cans open on the floor beside her.

'Here's yours,' she passed one over and I sat myself down on the other chair.

'How are you doing?' she asked. 'Are you stir crazy yet?'

Smiling, I shook my head.

'I can't tell you how much I'm enjoying it here.'

'I'm really glad.'

We didn't speak for a while, both relishing the peace of this late afternoon but also, I guessed, not knowing quite what to say. Knowing perhaps where we were headed but not precisely sure how we were going to manage it from here. I didn't mind. The longer it took the better. And I was happy to leave the running to her. It seemed to me that she had a better idea of what the possibilities were. I didn't want to break any spells, and anyway I was scared. Scared but also pleased I was handling things OK as they were. Please let nothing ruin the next few days, I prayed.

We looked down at the tangle of trees and bushes as they followed the fold of the hill and the deep cut of the stream below.

'How long have you been out here?' I asked eventually. A safe question. A small turn of the key to unlock some of that past that was still unknown to me. Who was she? Where had she come from? And why was she here? Wasn't that Bogart's approach to Ingrid Bergman in Casablanca? If it worked for Humph it might work for me too.

'I bought the place two years ago when I moved here.'

I nodded.

'When it was time to run from Dick, I wanted to go somewhere he would never think of looking. I just got on a plane and flew down to Richmond – why Richmond? I have no idea. Maybe it was just the next plane out – and then I bought a car and just drove around until I landed up here. As soon as I got here I felt at home. It really felt like I was escaping to some paradise. I didn't want to be in town so the realtor showed us some properties out in the boondocks and I fell in love with this place. So that's the story of how we came out here.'

'And Kathy likes it?'

'She loves it. For now anyway.'

'Does she talk about her father? Does she miss him?'

'I don't know. We never talk about him. I told her I never want to talk about him. One day we'll talk. When she's older. All I know is Big Dick Baker is out of my life forever.'

Her eyes were fierce with her resolve.

'Maybe Kathy will want to get back in touch with him.'

'Over his dead body!'

'What?'

'Over my dead body.'

'You said 'his' body.'

'A slip of the tongue.' She pursed her lips. 'But it's the truth. If he, or any man, ever tried to abuse me again and I had a gun in my hand I'd kill him right there. That's something I know as a matter of fact.'

'Was it so bad?'

'He smacked his hand right across Kathy's face. He left the whole of one side of her face bruised. She was not much more than a year old. You think that's acceptable?'

'No,' I hurried to assure her. 'Of course not.'

'But he was here, you said. He gave you the Cadillac.'

'Oh yeah. The Cadillac.' But she didn't say anything more on the subject. 'I guess I'm just allergic to men who abuse their women. Did you ever lay your hands on your wife, on Norma? Or Maddie?'

I shook my head.

'Sorry. Silly question. You're not the woman abusing type. But tell me about Norma. I don't know anything about her?'

'Norma?'

I shrugged. What was there to say? We were college sweethearts who, fearful of the life that was opening up in front of us, tied the knot in the last week of my MA program. When I got a job in Oxford she felt it was natural to quit her course and come and join me. We settled into a domestic life of sedate habits. We joined the local Baptist congregation. We grew old before our time. I told Alice all this.

'No kids?'

'No. No kids.'

'You didn't want them?'

'They just didn't happen. It didn't bother me but I know it did Norma. She wanted kids.'

'And were you a good and faithful husband?'

I nodded.

'Of course you were. You're the good and faithful type.'

Was she mocking me? I gave her a quizzical look. She seemed to understand what I was thinking.

'Because you're good and honest and a wonderful person.' There was no mockery in her face. 'And that's why I want to know you better, be your friend.'

She stood up then and bending over me planted a kiss, light as a feather, on my lips.

'And now I'd better check on our dinner.'

And she left me there feeling again and again in the replay of memory the soft pressure of her lips.

*

Was I so pure and innocent? Ever? Is this not the sterilized, vacuum packed, chemically-bleached propaganda put out by the Saturday Evening Post? I remember putting a frog in Angie Kupinski's underpants. First attempt on a girl's asshole. I was eight. I remember I put a rubber band on Jack's pecker and told him it would drop off. I was ten. Put wasps on light bulbs and watched them melt and stick to the glass and writhe in fiery agony. Age twelve. I remember Danny Fernandez and I Jacked off together and grabbed at each other's balls at age thirteen. Pure and innocent? We shot the bird out of the tree and when we saw it was only wounded in the wing we shoved a twig up its ass and cut its throat with a rusty razor blade that Danny always carried with him. Age fourteen. We got Isabel Nash to strip and show us what she had and grabbed a feel. Age sixteen. Rape and murder, are they so very different? It seems to me there is a natural progression. In my case there was a progression, natural or not.

When I came back I couldn't settle. I was all over the country. I was doing fine. I was getting good experience. I liked sales. I liked getting out and meeting people and sweet-talking them into some deal or other. I used to tell my nigger jokes. They got me a lot of customers. Heh heh!!

One night, late, I went for a drive. I couldn't sleep. I just drove round town. It wasn't all that late maybe. There were whores on the street. I stopped by one. Yellow-skin, Hispanic girl. Don't remember anything else about her except she was a sweet brown skin girl who looked to melt all over you. I told her to get in. I tell you straight I didn't know what was in my

*mind when I did that. I guess I was thinking... I don't think I
want to go into this right now. I'll talk about it later. She was
my first peacetime kill. Tell you the truth I don't remember
the act so much as the feelings I had. A great anger tore right
through me when I came, like a streak of lightning I took out
my knife and ...You don't want to know and I sure don't want
to remember.*

*

D is for Dalat. A town in the hills. Joe was here once. I have
the postcard. Built by the French in 1912. A pink Cathedral on
one commanding site is looked down upon by an equally pink
Protestant chapel on a higher hill. There is a lake. The market is
brimming with massive mangoes, bulbous blackberries, succulent
strawberries, ample avocados, crisp cabbages, opulent onions,
bulging beans. I discover some round white shiny vegetables I have
never seen before. I think of onions, eggs, peeled potatoes, turnips.
Nothing fits. The stall keeper much amused waves a long purplish
aubergine in my face. I look from one to the other. Light dawns:
eggplant, of course. I looked for Joe. He wasn't here.

The town is not as pretty as it ought to be. It is an oddity.
pony-traps bring farmers to market and home again. Ancient
Peugeots wheeze up the hills. Peugeots. Not just the cars here but
diminutive buses everywhere. They appear to date from the thirties.
yet they are still going strong. They are a good advertisement for
the company. There are rusty, banged about DeSotos too that give
new definitions to the bottom end of road-worthiness.

The motorcycle riders who take you up into the surrounding hills are mostly, it seems, ex-ARVN men. They are all of a certain age. Forty-ish. Their motorbikes are East German Simsons, 70ccs which cost, my rider says, US$700. Where did he get the money? He talks vaguely of working in coal mines. I interpret this as 're-education'. He's not married. 'I can't afford it.' Vietnam is opening up. How does he think of that? 'On one side it's good. More tourists. More work. On the other side there's inflation. Everything will cost more. It will be more expensive to buy a house. I can see it coming. I worry about it. I see opportunities. But I can't do anything about it. I've got no money. What can I do?'

His friend reminisces of the days he was an ARVN helicopter pilot. 'I remember those days. I lost a lot of good friends. American friends. Man I remember those fire-fights,' he nodded sadly. It was a long time ago. Later, we were talking about families 'I was in Colorado one time. I wanted to marry a Chinese girl. I wrote to my mother. She wrote back and said I should come home and marry a Vietnamese girl. So I did. That's my bad luck.' he shook his head, then it was back to business. He turned to his ride: 'OK where are we going tomorrow?'

I think of going to the Montagnard village but the authorities want to charge ten dollars for a visa, five dollars for a car, seven dollars for a guide.

'They hate the Montagnards, man,' a young German traveler informs me. 'They fought with the Americans. This is their revenge. The Vietnamese authorities keep them isolated in their village and don't let anyone in to see them. I know one guy went in without a permit. He was picked up immediately by the police post there. He had to pay a fine. But none of the police could speak English. He couldn't speak any Vietnamese. So they pulled in this tribesman, this Montagnard. He was about fifty years old and he could speak fluent French and English. It turned out he was a lawyer. But he was interned in this village. He had to work in the fields. He came in and spoke to my friend: 'Listen. I am not one of these bastards. They say you have to pay 30 dollars for a fine. This is too much. I suggest you offer them five dollars, all right? So say that to me. Wave your hands a bit. But smile. Don't look angry. Always smile.' Then he turned and talked to the Vietnamese and then he turned back and said: 'They have come down to twenty. Still this is too much. Maybe you will have to pay fifteen but I suggest you offer them ten dollars now and apologize for the error.' It was a good story but I never did get to see the village.

*

Later still. The stars were pinpricks of light in the blackness of deep space. And it was strange to think these stars that we could see no longer existed as we saw them. Time had become timeless. My mind was wondering and that was dangerous. I forced myself to focus again on what Wash was saying.

'I grew up in South Philly.' He chuckled mirthlessly. 'The love of brotherhood has sure passed that place by. Oh yes.'

The second bottle was empty. I drained my glass.

'Any more whiskey?' I asked.

Wash looked at the empty bottle sourly.

'Girl. We need another bottle of that whiskey. And I mean now.'

Maddie shuffled out of the cabin with the bottle and handed it to Wash.

'You can be our geisha girl, our good old Saigon bar girl.' He yawned. 'Keep our glasses filled.'

She nodded her head wearily.

'Sure.'

She opened the bottle and filled our glasses.

'Brother Jack,' he raised his glass in benediction. 'We have fucked together. We have bonded man to man.'

I raised my glass and drank. I avoided looking at Maddie.

'A man has to have his sweet pussy else he ain't a man.'

He was grinning amiably now, a mean amiable leer that I didn't trust for one second. But he seemed to have loosened up. We were not yet equal in the eye of the Lord. Not in his eyes. But we had shared pussy and I guess where he came from that counted for a lot.

'Tell me Jack,' I waited for him to finish but he seemed to chew on his words.

'Tell me about the first time.'

'First time?'

'Yeah. The first time you ever get yourself laid.'

I flashed an image of Norma. A shameful fact. A virgin husband. Well, not virgin by the time the wedding ceremony came along. But up till now Norma was my one and only sexual partner. I was going to have to improvise.

'I was eighteen. On a date with a girl, it was maybe our third date and well, it just happened.'

'Nothing just happens, Brother Jack, lest we make it happen. Am I right?'

'Sure. That's the way it was.'

'And what was her pretty name?'

'Name? Um, Betty, I think.' Betty? The woman who runs the bookshop? Did I…? No, surely not.

'Betty? That's a clean white name. Betty. I like that. I ain't never fucked no Betty. Guess that's something I'm going to have to rectify.'

'What about you?'

He chuckled.

'My mama made her living on her back if you get my meaning. She had herself a habit, a white powder habit. That's how I got to be running deliveries of the white powder round the neighborhood. I was fourteen then. The hookers thought I was cute. They'd give me a little on the side. I was bunny hopping since I can remember. Oh yeah.'

'Drugs?' I prompted.

'Yeah,' sounding bored. 'That was one of my hustles. Man grows up quick in my neighborhood. Time I was seventeen I had my own stable of bunnies. I was the fifth biggest pimp in the street. Oh yeah! So proud of myself. I had the best suits made for me. Real flash I was then. Didn't last long. Got greedy. Stepped on the wrong toes. Got muscled out by the competition. Had to make myself scarce. Fast. I was down at the enlistment office before you could say boo.'

'Yeah?'

'You bet your sweet ass. I hadn't of, I was dead. Some people you don't mess with.' He shook his head. 'Jack, there is some evil dudes out there.'

His voice had dropped and way off, a long way off, I heard a kind of coughing noise, short and sharp. Wash cocked his head.

'You hear that?'

He paused and we heard the sound again.

'You know what that is? Wolves. It was Joe told me. He got talking to one of the dudes in the program. They is re-what? What is the word? Setting them wolves free in the wild to live likes they used to. Wolves! Fancy that! One day I'm going to come face to face with a wild snarling wolf. That will be one poor sucker of a wolf. One poor dead sucker. I'll skin it and hang the pelt on the cabin wall. Here lives Wash the wolf killer. Oh yeah. That's the way it will be.'

I was glad the words seemed to be pouring out of him now; some dam had broken in him and he needed to speak. The more he talked the less I had to. That suited me just fine. All the time I had one eye half angled at the door. Any moment I thought, she's going to come running out shooting that damn gun. I cursed myself for being such a fool as to have it in such an obvious place as the glove box.

'…black pussy?' he was asking me something but my thoughts were scrambled.

'What's that?'

'Black pussy. You ever had some of that?'

'No, I never had a black girlfriend.'

'Who said girlfriend? What's this girlfriend shit?' He was laughing at me hard. 'I'm talking deep pussy, man. You never had no black pussy? You never cheated on your mamma?'

I shook my head.

'The black man likes white pussy so I guess it makes sense that the white man has a hankering for black pussy. If he hadn't of there wouldn't be so many yellow skin niggers. What they call it? Miscegenation? I'm all for a little miscegenating.'

He cackled softly at his joke.

*

Fragging holes. Oh Boy! This was about two thirds of the way into our term. We got a cherry lieutenant, Harvey Hammond, Lieut. Hammond sir! He was full of shit and polished brass. He was always on our tails. One day, we find a shaft. The fire team is spread out. I'm with the lieutenant and he says to me: 'You're slim and wiry, Gauss. Go in there and smoke 'em out.' I look at him and I look at the hole and all I know is that there's no fucking way I'm going in there. I shook my head. 'No way, sir! Absolutely not!' The lieutenant pulled out his sidearm and pointed it at me.

'Gauss,' he says, 'I'm ordering you to go down that hole.'

I looked at him and then I looked over his shoulder. Wash had crawled up to a rock about ten yards away.

'No fucking way I'm going in that hole!' I said. 'You want to shoot me, that's your business.' I said it loud enough so as Wash could hear.

'*This is your last chance!*' *Hammond said,* '*I said go down that hole.*'

Wash coughed and Hammond spun round.

'*Lieutenant,*' *he said,* '*I happen to know that Joe here suffers from claustrophobia.*' *Hammond could see Wash's gun was casually pointed at him. He was a fool. Full of his own sense of dignity and authority and red-blooded American gung-hoism.*

'*I'll do it then,*' *he said and crawled into the hole. We waited a few minutes hoping the enemy would do our work for us. No such luck. Five minutes later, he called up.*

'*I'm coming out.*'

*Wash and I looked at each other. We knew what we had to do. I took out a grenade, pulled the pin and rolled it down the hole. He saw it coming. He just had time to say: '*Oh fuck!*' before it took his head off.*

CHAPTER 10

Later, after dinner, Alice and I took our glasses out on the deck. We were both feeling pretty mellow.

'That poet, poetess, can you still say poetess these days?' she asked.

'Waitress?... actress?'

'Seamstress, manageress? Perhaps not. A disappearing species.'

'Mistress?'

'Oh yes! Some words will never blend into the impersonal unisexual.'

'What about her?'

'I just love her to bits. Tell me about her.'

'Well, I really don't know very much. She lived about 200 years ago. That's all I know. Except of course that she is enormously popular in Vietnam today and, or so I was told, still considered somewhat shocking. Isn't that something? To remain popular and shocking for two centuries?'

'Why don't we know about her?'

'Maybe we have to kill each other before we can get to know each other.'

'Is that a world truth?'

'Maybe.'

'For countries or for individual people?'

There was a challenge in her expression. I nodded, then shrugged.

'Maybe both.'

'Look. You've never published these translations before?'

I shook my head.

'We're going to publish them. That's going to be our project.'

She stood up abruptly and turned away to look out of the window.

'I wonder who the shocking popular poets of Iraq are.'

I had nothing to say to that.

She turned back to face me. 'I've got something to show you.' And she went off to her bedroom, returning with a newspaper cutting. She thrust it at me.

'Read this.'

The article told the sad story of a young Afghani woman, Nadia Amjuman, a woman who was killed by her husband because she wrote poetry. She'd had the temerity to learn how to write. She'd had to do this in secret while the fundamentalist Taliban ruled the country. If they'd been caught they'd have been killed. In the end she was caught and was killed. 'What should I say about sweet things when I have bitterness in my mouth?' she had written. Her husband had beaten her until she was dead.

I shook my head at the horror of it.

'What would they have done to Ho Xuan Huong?'

She reached out her hand towards me and I, surprised by the gesture, jerked back. She smiled.

'It's all right. I won't hurt you.'

And her fingers lightly brushed my cheek. Her touch burned. I was still not ready for this new level of intimacy. I felt as if I had hit a wall. It had been a good day but now it was time to retreat into myself. But before I could signal this she had moved herself to my lap, wrapped her arms around my head and fixed her mouth to mine. Oh yes! Oh gosh yes! I had forgotten so much. I had forgotten the warm, tingling sweetness of a soft, lingering, hesitant kiss. Our lips read each other's like the blind read Braille. What new knowledge were we uncovering? Tongues tentatively touched dark nameless depths. And I was afraid of what would inevitably come after.

I tried to say something but it came out as a croak. Eventually I managed to say it. 'You don't know what you're taking on.'

'You underestimate me.'

And we stayed entangled like that for an hour or so.

'I haven't necked so much since I was a teenager,' she laughed.

'Nor me.' I too had to smile.

'Do you want to...?' indicating her bedroom.

I shook my head, my eyes pleading with her not to take it as a rejection.

'That's fine.' She smiled and patted my cheek. 'It really is. And tomorrow's another day.' She kissed me again before allowing me to get to my feet.

'By the way,' she paused. 'I hope it's OK with you but I've arranged for Kathy and Benjy to have a sleep over tomorrow night at Wendy Shoemaker's, you know her? Her son Jared is in the same class. They're good friends. Do you think that'll be a problem?'

Not for Benjy, I thought. I was pretty sure he'd go for it like a shot.

*

Here's another time how Wash saved my life. We were on patrol. There was a swampy place we all knew was crawling with VC. They would engage us, shoot us up and then disappear into the swamp. We were proceeding very cautiously down a trail. I was on point that time. The way Wash tells it, I've walked past this bomb crater and everything seems hunky dory when all of a sudden Wash sees a movement. Just a head popping out of a foxhole. This guy takes aim at me and suddenly there's a burst of fire. I hit the deck. Wash crows.

'Got the fucker!' and then to me: 'You were a dead man my friend.' There wasn't anything left of the man's head. We fragged the hole he came out of.

So we owed each other. It's not a debt that gets repaid. It's a debt that goes on for life. I was born charmed I guess. I never got a scratch.

*

'You ever kill a man, Brother Jack?'

I shook my head.

'Ever fired a gun in anger?'

Again I shook my head.

'Boy what kinda life you been leading?' Wash laughed.

'Oh Jack, don't get me wrong now. That kinda shit is no good.'

He took another swig of his whiskey. He had slowed down some but I noticed he never let his fingers stray too far from his gun.

'First person I killed was a accident. Didn't mean it. Just happened. If he hadn't of woked up while I was burglarizing his apartment, he'd still be alive.' He shook his head. 'I was jus' fifteen.'

He started to chuckle.

'But, you know something, Jack. I am glad I killed that mother.'

'Why's that?'

'Why's that?' Repeating my question. Enjoying the rhetorical stance.

'Cos I got myself a reputation. I got respect. From that day on, people saw me they said to themselves: There goes Washington Thomas. Know what? He killed a man when he was only fifteen. Yessir.' He laughed to himself.

'Could be I woulda been killed myself if I hadn't a reputation.'

'Why's that?'

'Why's that? Cos they wouldn't been scared of me. Would they? But now they knew I was the kind of cool dude that didn't mind if I killed myself a man now and again. That's their mentality. Mine too. You know a guy's a killer, you be careful of him. He could just kill another person any time, no skin off his nose. Know what I mean? But a guy like you, Jack, you done never killed no-one. Don't need to show you so much respect.'

I tried to read a message in this rambling. Was he trying to tell me something? I couldn't tell. I let it slide over me.

'You're just a soft white guy, Jack. Know something? You don't never want to go to no prison. Soft white guy like you end up sucking big niggers' dicks. And that's the good bit. You paying good money for anything to grease yo' ass cos, when evening come, they going to stick you. And you going to make like you having fun. You don't, you going to get messed up real bad.'

'You were in prison?'

'What's it to you?'

'Nothing. Just talking, listening. Just want to hear your story, that's all. You've led a very colorful life.'

'A colorful life? Listen to the man,' He chuckled. 'I've had a nigger full life. Don't give me that color word.'

He grinned mirthlessly at his joke.

'Yeah. I done a stretch. Three years, seven months and a few days on top of that.'

'What for?'

'For not killing a no good pimp I shoulda. He only got a scratch and I got busted.'

He spat into the dark.

'But, you know. It's a strange world, ain't it? I mean, if I hadn't of gone down, I'd be dead and buried by now I swear on my mother's grave.'

'How's that?'

'How's that?' The dark shadows on his face exaggerated his mocking expression.

'Cos Jack. It done got me out of a very sticky situation. Very sticky.'

'One day you should write your life story.'

He spat again into the dark.

'Maybe you write it for me. We hole up here all one summer and I'll tell you my whole story and you write it down. How about that?'

I nodded and smiled. I wanted him to think it might happen. That it was possible.

CHAPTER 11

Waking this second morning I felt the ominous presence of the specter. As always I held my breath for what seemed an immeasurable length of time. It was the same dream I always had. But this time, thanks to Bardbach, I was looking harder, looking for a detail I may have missed. Trying to read it fresh as if for the first time.

I'd told Bardbach about the dream, this waking dream. As I struggled out of sleep, a dark presence seemed to hover over the bed. Substantial and shadowy. Both a threat and a comfort. I didn't know what to do with it but when it was gone I felt an obscure sense of a muted but immense loss. I wanted it to come back.

'How long have you been having this dream?' Bardbach asked.

'It seems to have been with me forever.'

'Maybe it's not a dream?'

'What else…?'

'A memory, perhaps.'

'Memory?'

'Could it be your father?'

'Oh Gosh!'

I felt suddenly awash with feelings I hardly recognized: a hot and eager hope, a powerful aching desire, a need to be comforted. I sensed a distant, heavy, familiar odor on the nostrils.

'Perhaps he came to say goodbye before he went to hospital. He died in hospital you said?'

'Yes, that's what I've been told.'

'He stood over your bed and kissed you and said goodbye.'

'Thank you,' I said. 'Thank you.'

'Hello,' I hesitated. 'Father? Pa? Dad? What do I call you?' The shadow lifted, retreated, dissolved, disappeared. I was sad. I hoped it would come back. I had a lot to say to it. I wanted it to come closer and hug me. I wanted to be embraced by that heavy odor of something I seemed to know but recognition of which lay just out of reach. How important a father is. I can only hope that I can be a worthy father to Benjy. I was overcome by a sense of bleak inadequacy. Then I fell back into a fitful sleep.

*

'So how'd it happen, man?' Wash was chewing on a toothpick.

'What?'

'The Goose.'

'Goose?'

'Your brother. Joe. His accident. What happened?'

'Oh. He got drunk,' I lied. 'Had an argument with the wife. Went for a drive. Drove into a tree. Got smashed up pretty bad.'

Joe rolled himself a smoke and lit it.

'Something 'bout all this here don't make no sense.'

I waited for him to get to the point.

'Why'd Joe tell you 'bout the cabin?'

'He was in a lot of pain. He told me to come and help you out with, you know, food and so on.' Lying was coming easy to me.

Suddenly Wash lifted his gun and pointed it at my head, flicking the safety off with his thumb.

'You better be telling me the truth my friend or you be a dead man. You understan' me?'

I nodded.

'You packing?'

'What?'

'Carrying, man. You carrying?'

'I don't understand.'

'You got a gun on you?'

'Oh a gun?' I tried to look him straight in the eye but didn't quite manage it. 'No.'

'You're lying man. I knows a liar when I sees one.'

'No gun. Really.' I patted my pants.

'In your car man. You got a gun in the car?'

I shook my head.

'I never carry a gun,' I said. This time it was the truth and I could look him straight in the eyes. I felt sick in my stomach. I'd never had a gun pointed at me before. Never. Wash studied me for a long moment then just nodded and clicked the safety catch back on. Streams of sweat poured off me.

'They'd better not be.'

And I wondered again what Maddie was doing. When was she going to come out gun blazing?

*

C is for chewing betel.

Offering Betel
I offer you a folded leaf of betel
I have just added the juice of a lime
If our feelings for each other are true
Chew it thoroughly. Turn it richly red.
Don't let the parts stay separate.
The green of the leaf, the white of the lime.

*

I woke before dawn. Moonlight brightened the trees outside (I had left the curtains open and was glad I had done so). There was the soft moan of a stiff wind. The branches of a tall pine swayed. My hand sought the comfort of an early morning erection but no comfort was to be had. I watched the branches as they swayed. The air in the room was cool but I was nicely warm under the covers. The emptiness in my groin was as vast and cold as the distant galaxies.

*

The village was hidden among the trees. There was a full moon.
We made our way from hooch to hooch. We were looking for

cadres. They must have been warned. There were no men at all in the village. That in itself was an admission of guilt.

'Where the fuck are they?' I yelled at a woman who had a baby at her breast. 'Where's your husband?' She shook her head. I knew she knew. I grabbed the baby from her and dangled it by its ankles. 'I said where the fuck are the men?' She shook her head. I pointed the gun at the baby: 'One more time. Where the fuck is your husband?' I was in a rage. All I could see were the blank impassive stares of the women and children and the old men. 'If you don't tell me I'm going to blow this baby's brains out. Got it?' She just shook her head and stared at the ground and I couldn't stop it. I couldn't stop myself. The rage. This awful anger in me. I threw the baby on the ground and put two rounds in it and its guts plopped red and I thought to myself: 'Well, you've gone over the edge kid. You've done it now.' But the rage wouldn't let up. The rage and disgust at what I'd done so I grabbed the woman and flung her outside and emptied the magazine into her. I cut her body in two with bullets. I couldn't have her live and tell the story of how the grunts had killed her baby. I couldn't have any of them left alive to tell that tale. I fragged the hootch which wasn't clever. Bamboo splinters flew everywhere. This was not a nightmare. This was real.

That wasn't the only baby I killed, Jacky boy. One day I saw a woman cycling down a road with a child in front of her on the bar and another behind her. It was a peaceful day. Nothing had happened except we hadn't slept for three weeks. Four hours on two off. For three weeks. I blanked out. Must have fallen asleep saw them coming at me. Waves of NVA pouring down the hillside towards me. Nothing I could do. In my mind I kept shooting at them and they kept coming and finally I cracked. I couldn't take it any longer.

'Fuck you fucking bastards!' I yelled and jumped up and sprayed the road with bullets, emptied the whole magazine. When I calmed down and saw what had happened, there was a bicycle and three dead bodies in the middle of the road. A young woman and two children.

*

My thoughts such as they were had made me restless. Neither awake or asleep, I had turned from side to side. My throat was dry and I needed a drink of water.

There was a light knock on the door but before I could respond, the door opened and Alice eased herself into the room.

'You awake?'

I grunted. The warm fresh odor of her skin as she bent low over me shaking me gently made me heady with ease. I wanted to be enfolded by it.

'I want to show you something.'

'What is it?'

'Come.'

'What is it?' I repeated. 'What's the time?'

'Come on. Get up or you'll miss it.'

I got out of bed and followed her, tiptoeing, into the children's room. They had both been tucked up in the one bed but now they were spread right across it, bedclothes askew, eyes flickering with dreamscapes. We stood over the bed marveling at them, Kathy on one side of the mattress, Benjy on the other..

'They look so innocent. Little angels.'

'You'd never think they were little devils.'

Alice took my arm in hers and I stood still, not wanting the warmth to go. Eventually she felt we had marveled enough and tugged me and we retreated as silently as we could to the kitchen where Alice busied herself making coffee.

Children: angelic or devilish. Discuss.

'I've never understood the idea of original sin,' I said later over toast and coffee. 'How can sin be a state that we are born to without having done anything bad?'

Alice shook her head sharply.

'We're all of us dirty creatures. Animals. We shouldn't idealize ourselves too much.'

Alice punctuated this with a hard look.

'Unless you believe in God. Do you? Are we here on a mission to prove ourselves?'

'I've lost the habit of faith,' I smiled apologetically at the words. Norma and I had been regular church goers. But when she'd left me and Maddie had taken her place I had not felt welcomed by the congregation. I had gone once by myself, still feeling the attachment of the sense of community. I had found myself feeling invisible, blotted out. Smiles had missed their mark, had certainly not been returned. It had been habit not active and fiercely held belief that had led us to join this church those, what? Twenty? coming on thirty years ago when we had first arrived in Oxford and we thought church membership would lead to social communion – and it had. We had made friends. But they, I discovered on her departure, had been more Norma's friends than mine. Something that hadn't occurred to me until then. So be it. I didn't return.

'Animals? Yes, perhaps that's all we are. But then there would be no original sin. It's only if God – a specifically Christian God – exists that...'

'Those kids,' Alice interrupted, pointed at the bedroom where they were still fast asleep. 'We think they're innocent but they aren't. It's just that their tiny minds can only conceive of tiny evils. Their tiny bodies are less capable of carrying out truly evil acts. They want what they want and they'll do anything to get it.'

'Is that a definition of evil?'

Alice shrugged.

'It's too early in the morning for philosophy.'

But the thought stuck in me. If sin is a stain on our souls and we are born with it, then it can only be because we share the guilt of all our past humanity. We are all responsible for every massacre there has ever been. But only if God exists and our lives have a moral purpose. And that's a big if, as I liked to say in my schoolmaster's pose. Otherwise it's just my urge versus yours. And evil, I told myself, is more than just an obsession with satisfying urges: it is the infliction of pain on others, and the desire to do so for the pleasure that it will give, the satisfaction of it, the sweetness, even. Or are there categories of evil? Is the truth of evil a slippery beast that slides past any easy definition?

We took our drinks outside to the porch where we sat and watched the layered sheets of mist lift off the valley floor. Somewhere a strident bird whistled. We leaned in silence on the wooden fence. It was a cool and damp beginning to what promised to be a good day ahead.

*

We hadn't been laid for two months. Wash and I talked about it. It was getting serious.

'Let's get ourselves some pussy,' I said.

Wash just licked his lips I guess. It was his way of saying yes. Just the two of us. We sneaked off from the perimeter of the fire support camp. We knew where we were going, a village two miles off. We moved along the trails with all the acquired professionalism that ten months of fear and rage had seared into the mind. We didn't expect trouble and there wasn't any. When we got to the village we selected a hootch and went in very quickly and quietly. There were three women, a teenage girl, four kids, two teenage boys and two men. One of the women was OK to look at and the girl too. We weren't fussy. Wash gestured for them to come out. But I stopped him.

'Ao dai!' I said, 'Put on your ao dai.' The flowing skirts of the national costume.

It took five minutes for the women to get ready. They knew what was going to happen. I expect they had resigned themselves to it. We lead them away from the village. They looked so pure and immaculate in their white cotton skirts.

'Take them off.'

Slowly they peeled their clothes off. I was hard and stiff and ready to cream myself.

'Lie down.'

They lay down and we took them. God it was good to feel warm pussy circling the dick. We both came quick. Too quick. We felt cheated. It wasn't enough reward for the effort we had put in. They wanted to go. Wash took out his knife and shook his head. The girl complained a bit and so Wash caressed her with his knife a little more insistently. He let the blade run from her throat to her nipple to her belly to her cunt. The girl shivered with fear. Wash had brought KY jelly. He turned the girl over and smeared her ass and his dick and plunged it in. My fuck simply sat and shivered. I told her to play with my balls but her heart wasn't in it. I took out my gun and pressed it to her head. This seemed to do the trick. I could feel the urge return and she too seemed more motivated. I plunged inside again. It took a long time and when I felt it coming I clicked off the safety switch and blew her brains out. There was a sudden delicious contraction of her pussy and I came. Wash saw what I had done and smiled and slit the other girl's throat. Her blood spurted everywhere. Daddy, what did you do in the war daddy? That's what I did. I get a hard on every time I think of it.

Why is it you remember all the worst things? We were only there thirteen months – thirteen goddamn months that stretched into a lifetime – no, an eternity. Seems you could put that behind you. Pretend it didn't happen. Hell. Four fucking seasons in hell. Heaven and Hell that was the name of a bar in Saigon. Pink and dark interior. Thinking back, as the war deteriorated, we all deteriorated, the whole fucking scene. Girls, Jack naked on a platform shaking their sweet little buns. Press of men drinking their beers and the girls came up to you and said: Hey Joe, you want fuck-fuck, you want suck-suck and they'd grab your crotch and do it right there. Common. Often saw a grunt fucking a girl on the platform and she's sucking someone on the fringe of the action. Now that was fun. Heaven and Hell. That was the name of the bar. Good name too. I was there once. Seven days. I lived there. And then I had to go back to the war. Those were the good times. The times of euphoria. The times you wanted to blow the whole trip. You knew death was round the corner. Your death. Someone else's death. What did it matter? Oblivion, joy, sleep, forgetfulness, absolution. Ah! The absolute purity of the sudden fuck. The deep-throated chuckle of laughter and orgasm. The shimmying, shimmering duplicity of life. What does that mean? Just an orgasm of words.

One day, I got in conversation with a war groupie, a journalist, he called himself a stringer. We were looking at the tits and asses.

'Imagine these girls were ugly as sin. How long do you think the war would last?'

Yeah it was as obvious as that. These girls were ugly, no way the war would last another day. Everyone was having so much fun. That's why we had a war. Jesus. I knew I wasn't going to have so much available ass when I got back home.

'You want suck suck?' a girl asked.

'You bet!'

She unzipped my pants and sucked away while I guzzled my beer. She sucked me dry and all the time I was talking to this stringer. I saw the cum slip down her chin as the sweet line of honey ejaculated in my brain. Yeah! That's what the war was all about, Jack. Believe me.

*

This thing with the eyes. Sometimes Benjy and I play this game. We press our faces close to each other eyeball to eyeball. Noses get squashed. I'm not sure what the rules are. Does he want to see who can stare longest without blinking? I think that's the game. But we play it very seriously. No-one ever seems to win. Maybe it's just a sense of connection we're seeking. I think that's closer to the truth of it. We're looking for the contact, recharging ourselves. Or are we trying to see into the depths beyond the visible.

*

Does God exist? What an old fashioned question – almost juvenile. You believe or you don't believe. No-one argues about it any more. God is just one option among many in the cultural supermarket. That was Jack's phrase `the cultural supermarket'. Jack's not dumb. He knows a thing or two. He's gone shopping in the responsible liberal episcopalian section. I'm pretending to be in the hard-ass blue-suit section but I'm really in the in-deep-shit mother-fucker section.

God? It's somewhere to start.

Jack says he sort of half believes, What kind of wishy-washy side-stepping is that. Norma believes. Jack just goes along with it. Doesn't make sense to me. I can't believe in a little old white-bearded man who lives on a cloud. Pa didn't go to Heaven. He went to the worms. His spirit was loosed unto the universe. Some crap like that. Crap is a very good theological word.

I am sitting here with my neon lamp and my Jack Daniels and my stupid little exercise books. But I got to do something while Wash humps the gal. I almost feel sorry for her. She hasn't had much of an existence and soon she won't have any. Wonder what meaning her life has had for her.

The meaning of life? It's almost a joke. Hey Guys! Here's a guy who's searching for the meaning of life! Har har har! Yuk yuk yuk!

But where else can you start? Are we just jumped up monkeys? If one monkey kills another we don't get all up-tight and morally offended about it. But one man kills another then there's evil loose on the land. If one cluster of monkeys gets into a fight with another cluster we just say it's territorial. If we're fighting then God's on our side and the other side is the devil incarnate. Fucking Commies!

Is man special or is he just like all the rest of creation? Is killing a man the same as killing a pig or a rat? If he's different what makes him different?

Pigs don't drink whiskey! Quod erat demonstrandum. QED. Oh fuck I'm drunk. But it's the only fucking way I can get the fucking thoughts out.

Let's say God exists. Then why does he cause so much fucking pain? Why does he allow O'Rourke's head to be blown away? Why does he allow me to cut up cunts? Isn't the argument that we're put on earth to prove ourselves: see whether we're good enough for Heaven? If not, then we go to Hell or purgatory or limbo or whatever. But really, what's God trying to prove? That he can make something good? Something bad? Are we to blame for our own fundamental nature? If I'm born bad is that my fault? If I'm made bad is that my fault? Who should the man blame for his evil thoughts? Who should I blame for the urge that is in me to hurt and go on hurting? To do things that disgust even myself? Am I responsible for the urges that howl through me like squalling hurricanes? Who is to blame if I have evil thoughts and do evil things? Me? Or is God – if He, She or It exists – to blame? Me? I blame the government. Joke.

If I choose to do evil, both the part of me that delights in evil and the part that chooses to do evil are given to me by God. How can he object? Goddam it I want to know! How can he judge me? He ordered David to castrate ten thousand Philistines. That's the God I'm talking about! God made us in his own image! God is both good and evil. Christ! This is beginning to make sense.

If I am one of God's experiments then whatever I do is right. All experiments are successful. They show that something works or doesn't work. They show that something is, or isn't, true. That is the purpose of an experiment.

OK, let's look at it from another point of view. If I am somehow responsible for my own fate then I must be somehow in control of my fate. What happens to me must reflect what I am, what I am thinking, the things I do. O'Rourke had his head blown off. Surely he did not reap what he sowed. His head was blasted into crimson pulp. What evil deed did he do to deserve that fate? His head disintegrated into a bloody mass because it was in the way of the fucking bullets – not because he had evil thoughts or did evil things. He was too young to have done anything truly evil. What about Wash and me? We did some evil, vicious things. Look at us. Not a scratch. I kill a baby. What does that mean for the baby? It hasn't had time to work out its fate. How can God know if the nature in it is good or bad? Doesn't make sense. Maybe it goes to Heaven anyhow. In that case I've done the baby a favor. It goes to eternal paradise. If it had lived it would have risked going to eternal Hell. Pass the bullets and let's kill more babies.

Who the hell wants to spend eternity praising the Lord? That's what they preach. That's what they say people do in Heaven. Doesn't sound like much fun. But if God is cruel, like he must be, then maybe he enjoys the sight of all those fuckers on their knees praising him morning to night. God as a concept doesn't have much going for it. If I were God I sure as hell wouldn't want people praising me the whole fucking time. I guess it would get fucking tedious.

Let's take a look at the other side of the coin. Let's say God doesn't exist. Let's say God is just another word for Nature. Nature is everywhere. Nature is the energy pulse of the universe. Then every living being has nature flooding through it. Life is the flood of nature's energy. There's no morality, no ethics, no God, no religion. Just Nature, just cosmic living energy. What then? Then it doesn't matter if it's an ant or a tree or a sheep or a whale or a man. It's all equal. A living unit of being. So to kill an ant, or to kill a germ or a virus is the same as killing a man. As far as Nature cares it's all one and the same. Hands up anyone who's concerned about killing germs or ants? No-one gives two hoots. So as far as Nature is concerned there is nothing to worry about when it comes to killing human beings.

OK let's backtrack again. If all there is is Nature, then we are all expressions of nature. Our fate is Nature's fate. What nature has given us is what nature wants us to feel and think and do. If we feel hungry it is nature telling us we need to recharge, so we go and fill our stomachs and then we feel good. If we feel lust then we go out and fuck a cunt and then we feel good. If we feel lust and we don't go and fuck a cunt we are going against nature's will. We are acting contrary to our destiny. If we feel the urge to fight and kill then we must go and fight and kill. Then we are fulfilling Nature's plan. No use asking: why are we fighting this war? We aren't doing it for any goddamn intellectual reason. We're doing it because our gonads are saying let's kill the fuckers. Not my gonads or yours maybe but the President's and the Senate's and

Congress's combined load of male hormones are saying let's go fuck somebody. Who can we go fuck? Who can we go kill? Let's shoot off some jism. Let's shove it up somebody's ass.

The only questions a man needs to ask himself is this: What does my body want? What do I need to do to satisfy its most fundamental needs? Then, for answer, all I have to do is go do it. That's the only right there is. So don't ask: Is America right to do this or that? That's not the question. The question is this: What does America want in order to satisfy its own needs? Other people's needs can go fuck. This is a trial of strength. You got needs that are contrary to my needs then I got to fight you. I got to kill you. Got to get you to conform to my needs. If you don't like it then I got to kill you. Otherwise you're going to force me to bend over and offer you my asshole. That's the way it is. Either I got to be subservient to your needs, or you got to do what I want you to do. It's a fight to the death. Might is right. The Good is always with the victor. Man is by birth a killer. Cain killed Abel. Homo sapiens came upon Homo Neanderthalis and slaughtered his distant cousin. This was no territorial war. Man was sparse on the ground. There was land and water for everyone. No. It was a fight for genetic survival. Nature's cruelty coursed through our veins. We needed to fuck the Neanderthals for we knew this: if we didn't do it to them they sure as hell were going to do it to us!

*

'When you just a dumbass, street punk who don't know any better you just jail meat. Vietnam was the best thing that ever happened to me. That's the truth. Yessir.'

He licked the paper of another cigarette and rolled it tight. His actions were slow and deliberate.

'Know what we called Joe?' Wash laughed. 'We called him Goose. Yo Goose! Follow the Goose. Do what the Goose man says.'

Joe 'The Goose' Gauss? Why not?

'He had this way of walking when he was on point duty. We'd follow that sucker and we'd be cracking up something crazy. He shook his ass. Oh yeah. The Goose.'

Another slug of whiskey went down his throat. How much could he drink?

'You know, Jack. I love your brother. We are more than mere friends. We are blood brothers.' He started to roll a cigarette. 'But this world ain't good to a black man and a white man being that close. Vietnam was different. We forgot all that crap. It was just Wash and Joe, Joe and Wash. We was pals, buddies. Then we come back Stateside and…' He shook his head at the futility of explaining it.

'Joe came up to see me one or two times. People in my neighborhood look at me strangely. What's with the white dude? They'd ask me. It wasn't comfortable. We got to meeting up elsewhere. Find a city somewhere where neither of us knew anyone. Only way. We had some black pussy and we had some white pussy and we had some Chink pussy too, and Latina. Oh yes. Good times. And when Carmen threw me out for putting it to her thirteen year old sister – and I tell you that little girl was not complaining, no sir – well Joe sorted me out. And then. Then… Oh Yeah!'

He lapsed into silence. His head bobbed forward, then, jerked back.

'What was that?'

'You were saying Joe sorted you out and then… something. I didn't catch what you were saying.'

Wash nodded slowly, trying to pull his thoughts together. Maybe soon, I thought.

'Then he had this brainwave.'

'Brainwave?'

'Oh yeah. For sure. I got to tell you 'bout this brainwave. But first I have to piss.'

He struggled to his feet. I expected him to go to a bathroom inside but he just stood on the edge of the porch and a long silvery stream of urine flowed out to the dark. I could feel the need myself. I stood up and unzipped my fly and pissed out into the dark. There's nothing unites men so much as the brotherhood of the open air urination.

'Whoa. Feels better, now, don't it?' He laughed. Then he broke out into song.

'Come on baby light my fire, oh yeah baby. God, those were good times. Good music. What's happened to music. It's just…' he struggled to find the words but ended up just shaking his head in disgust.

'You were telling me about the brainwave.'

'Brainwave? Oh yeah. That's right. Well, Joe said to me one day. Wash, what you doing with your life? What you doing? You pissing your life away on this and that and the other thing. One day you gonna end up dead. Real dead. Why don't you get smart? Make one big hit. One big motherfucking killing. Then just disappear. Never go back. Lie low. We'll get ourselves a cabin in the mountains and we'll just chill out. Never worry about anything ever again. Oh yeah Man. That was a brainwave. You see, everything's tied up in the suburbs. If I was to hit some racket, they'd all know it was me and my life expectancy would drop from very low to zero. I'd have no time to spend it. They'd give me a one way ticket to damnation soon as look at me. But lots of hustlers keep stacks of the green stuff in their own homes. They don't trust no banks. And they sure don't want Uncle Sam knowing they is behind on their taxes. Know what I mean? I knew that for a fact. So it seemed to me that Eddie 'Moose' Perkins was my man, my target. He had a lock on my local area. He kept a tight ship and he had a cute as hell daughter who was going on seventeen. I decided that he was going to be my hit.' He started laughing. 'Yo! I tell you, before you make a hit like that your adrenalin is just whooshing around your belly like nobody's business. I waited till three in the morning. I waited for him to come home. He had two bodyguards but I took them out before they even know'd I was there. You see I had myself a silencer. Pfft! One down. What the hell? Pfft. The second goes down. What the hell's going on here? He shouts and then runs to his door. He's dropped his night's takings on the lawn but I'm not after that. I'm after all he's got stashed away back there in his house. So when he's at the door pfft! I shoot him in the legs. He keeps going though cos he's a big strong man so…' He mimed the shot. 'Pfft! Another shot in his back this time. He goes down. I open the door for him and pull him in. His wife is coming down the stairs so I say. 'Help me. Someone's shooting. He's been hit. Like I'm one of his friends. Well, she came running down, forgetting that she don't know me from Adam. We pull him in and he's gasping and crying and I am high as a kite cos it's all going down just like I planned it. And his wife is a big fat woman. Ugly. So I says to the man. You got to tell me 'bout where you hides your money. I ain't going to tell you, he says. You can shoot me, I don't care but I'm not telling. Hell, I said to him. I ain't going to kill you. I'm going to kill your wife here. Well, then she sees what's going on and she opens her mouth to start screaming, so I just fast as I can I just let her have it and I shoot her face off. Ouch. Never think I would do a thing like that. But the funny thing is she's not dead like I thought she must be. She's quivering on the floor in her blood and so I says to him, you want to tell me where the money is? And so he tells me it's in a trunk in his bedroom. I go to his room and find the trunk and, sure enough, I see straight away it's full of cash so I start to pull the trunk along the corridor and down the stairs. I'm half way down and the daughter comes out. I thinks to myself. You been looking at this piece of ass a long time. This is your last chance to do something about it. So she starts to shout out: 'What's going on?' So I grab her and put my gun in her face and that shuts her up real fast. I shove her on the bed and tell her to strip off her clothes. Man the adrenalin was pumping and she saw I was not someone to mess around with so she took off her clothes and waited for me to do what I was planning to do but you know. First time in my life. I couldn't do a thing. And there she was looking so damn cute. What could I do? You'd of did the same. I shot her between the eyeballs man. Didn't want any witnesses. So I hauled that trunk down the path to my car. There were some lights going on in the neighboring houses so it was time to exit the scene. That I did. Had over $700,000 in the trunk. I just drove off. No goodbyes to nobody. Oh boy! I felt so hot and wired I could not sleep for two whole days after that. I drove south and west and then found myself a Cherokee reservation and booked myself into a motel and called Joe and well, long story, but we ended up here.'

*

One time I was in the library. I guess I was waiting for Chrissie. I was browsing along the shelves. So many fucking books. Can't read them all. Why start? But sometimes I like to open a book and get some ideas. I like encyclopedias. They're full of facts. I just flip the pages and dip in when I see anything interesting. That's how I came upon Clausewitz. I was just browsing.

The entry started something like this: 'Karl von Clausewitz (1780-1831) Prussian general and military theorist. In his work, On War, *he....' I tell you I was stunned. There was a book on war? It had never occurred to me before. Then I thought about it there must be books on everything. I went to the catalog files and found they had a copy of the book right here in the library. I just read the first couple of pages. I'm not much good with words. I get tired real easy trying to*

squeeze the juice out of them. You'd think words would give
up their meanings straight away. Maybe it's just me. I'm not
as educated as I should be. I read the words again and again.
Then I asked to photocopy a page but the photocopier was out
of action but they gave me some paper so that I could copy it
out. This is what Clausewitz said about war:

War... is an act of violence intended to compel our
opponent to fulfill our will. Violence arms itself
with the inventions of Art and Science to contend
against violence. Self-imposed restrictions, almost
imperceptible and hardly worth mentioning,
termed usages of International Law, accompany it
without essentially impairing its power. Violence,
that is to say, physical force, (for there is no moral
force without the conception of State and Law) is
therefore the means, the compulsory submission
of the enemy to our will is the ultimate object.

'Violence arms itself...' Wow! The words kind of exploded
in my brain. I knew this was important. I have read this
paragraph over and over again. I have thought long and hard
about these words. 'Violence arms itself!' There it is. Violence
is the doer. Not me or you but the violence in us. Violence is
raw nature. Morality depends on countries and legal systems
and conventions that are educated into us. There is no God!
There are no absolute values. There is only the inevitability
of violence. For Clausewitz, war is inevitable. It is nature

expressing itself. Morality has no place. If you kill, so what?
Rape? Maim the enemy? Do it. The only object is to get the
enemy to submit. That is the only right. In a word: Fuck the
enemy any way you can before he fucks you. So everything I'd
done was OK? And since this violence was natural violence
anything I did to express this violence was OK. When I raped
and killed the cute librarian it was going to be OK. Amazing
what you can find in books.

*

F is for Fan.

'This is one of her most famous poems,' Anh explains. 'She uses the metaphor of a fan, a hand-held paper fan made of paper with a wooden frame consisting of – in the poem she says seventeen or eighteen slats attached to a wooden handle. So the fan can be folded up or spread out wide. But actually the poem is not about fans but about something else.'

'Is this a man-to-man type poem?' I smile.

'Yes, I think so,' she smiles back. I have rather fallen for Anh, but she, I suspect, is involved with Le. They both talk with a European freedom. There is certainly something beneath the surface – an ease between them. Not just the ease of intellectual parity. Le blusters fluently. 'I'm a scientist. I like connections to be clear, logical. Sometimes you can read too much into a poem.' He is putting some pinkish jelly from a jam jar to a larger jar and sends one of the students out with it. The student returns. He appears to have filled it with water but when the liquid is poured out in little cups I find it is hard liquor. Eleven o'clock in the morning!

'What do you call this?' I ask.

'It doesn't have a name.'

It was like a strong *sake*.

'It's good. Is this for special occasions?'

'I drink it everyday.' Le says unabashedly. So this is how he keeps his easy-going manner. This is how he maintains his sanity.

It is Ho Nguyen who helps me with the poem. Ho Nguyen, his name (to my ears at least) sounds like Hor-wheen, intercepts me one morning as I am cycling round the town of Nha Trang on a rather shaky bicycle. To stop or slow down I have to keep reminding myself not to squeeze the single handbrake. This has little effect. Instead the pedals must be pedaled backwards. I am sightseeing. I am looking for Joe. He isn't here. Was he ever here? I have postcards from him in Nha Trang. But it was then a different town. Suddenly Ho Nguyen cuts in alongside me and starts up conversation.

'Are you here on business?'

'Where are you going?'

'Can I talk to you?'

We cycle together to a monastery. There we walk around. Ho Nguyen is very careful of his bicycle.

'Might it get stolen?' I ask.

'Oh yes!'

There is a plaque with the exhortation: 'If your fate is bad, don't blame anyone else. You are the origin of yourself.' At least this is what I surmise from Ho Nguyen's translation.

'Can I come and talk to you later?' he asks, 'I would like to practice my English.'

'You can help me translate some poems by Ho Xuan Huong. How about that?'

'Oh yes!' His face lit up. 'We all love her poems.'

So Ho Nguyen came and we translated *The Fan* together. This is what we produced.

> *Seventeen or Eighteen sections wide.*
> *I never go anywhere without it*
> *Spread out wide or only slightly parted it still has three angles*
> *But either way, the paper folds can take a handle*
>
> *The hotter it is the more you have to cool yourself*
> *You fan yourself all night but that's not enough.*
> *You have to fan yourself all day as well.*
> *This fan is beautiful. Look at its rosy-pink complexion.*
> *Even the king loves rose-colored fans.*
>
> *The paper hole can take all handles, short and long*
> *Invaluable I've been since time began*
> *When spread out wide the skin need not be taut.*
> *When closed up tight something may still protrude.*
> *Heroes use it to cool themselves when there's no other breeze*
> *Virile men use it to cover their heads when it starts to rain.*
>
> *When he is enclosed in her embrace*
> *When he is fanning himself strongly*

Panting with heat he wants to know:
Am I getting cooler?
When will the cool come?

*

'Joe tell you I re-enlisted?'

I shook my head.

'When we rotated back to the States, we said Jesus, Thank God we survived that shit. But you know what? The weeks went by and I just could not get a handle on shit and all. I just didn't have any get up and go. I was lost. It wasn't real. And the thing was I had got used to being, you know, a white man. In Nam I was somebody, but back home in Philly I was just another goddamn nigger looking for a hustle. In Nam, I said do this, do that. Man, they jumped to it.'

Wash grinned.

'You know what? I was treating those Gooks like they was niggers and it felt good. I could see where the white man was coming from. So, I re-enlisted. Went back. Man, that was good. This time round I knew stuff. Knew my way around. This time I found I was enjoying myself. Girls, the bars, hell I had fun. And those gooks, they could see I didn't take any crap. This time round I was there for one reason. To have a ball. Oh those girls, man. I miss those girls. The cowboys would come round on their bikes, their Honda bikes, with their girlfriends on the back and you'd just take your pick. When you finished with them you just gave them a little gift. Ten dollars was the going rate if I remember right. Five for the guy and five for the girl. I could live like that forever man.'

He pointed to his scalp where there was a three inch scar.

'See this?'

He spat into the dark.

'This is what comes of being obnoxious. Yeah. Thinking back, I can't say I've been a totally righteous brother. One of them zips ripped me with a stiletto. Can't say as I blame him. Lucky it was just a slight stab wound. Could been a whole lot worse. This was close to my final rotation and I was completely gone. I had lost it. If the first time home from Nam was bad, the second time round was... was...' he struggled for words. 'I got so used to swaggering round saying I'm an American. I'm here to help you zipper heads sort your shit out. You gotta give me respect. You're just a slope. I don't have to respect you. That sorta shit. That's the way it was then. That was the mentality. We was all fucked up. And then I got rotated back that second time and I was still all psyched up to kill someone, to disrespect anyone who crossed my path. Joe, that's when I realized what a good friend Joe was to me. Joe took me hunting round these parts one time. We just camped out in the mountains. Oh man. That helped to sort me out. Oh I love Joe. He is my one and only true compadre. When he gets on his feet again we'll go camping. I got to get outta here. Tomorrow... you and me... we'll... Jesus, where's that whiskey?'

*

Alice was reading a book and I was swinging the kids on the makeshift swing Alice had fixed up in the garden, hanging from a tree branch. It was hot work and after a while I left them to chase each other and went over to the porch to sit down. Alice set her book aside with a sour expression.

'Betty recommended it to me but I can't get into it at all.'

'No?'

'No, it's one of those very sensitive, intellectual, smart novels, very acutely observed in a feminine, deeply civilized, thoughtful womanly sort of way.'

'And?'

'And it's a fucking pain in the ass.' She laughed.

She placed her hand on mine and gripped it.

'It's so good to have you here.'

I nodded.

'I like talking to you.'

'Yeah?' I pulled a face, mocking.

'Yeah. Intelligent conversation is so hard to find.'

'Intelligent?'

'Yeah. Don't put yourself down. Just having you here, someone I can speak my innermost thoughts to. That's really special. I appreciate it. I can't tell you how much.'

'I'm happy to be here too.' But as I uttered this smooth politeness I was thinking I can never ever speak about my inner truth. It is a pit of blackness, a sink of desperate fear. And when I think of the things that I hold most dear I find myself thinking of Benjy and knowing, more deeply than I have ever known anything, that I fear losing him. I would be utterly destroyed.

'Now, I was thinking,' Alice continued. 'Something you said to me the other day. Something about feeling a sense of responsibility for what our soldiers did in Vietnam and what they're doing now in Iraq.'

'Responsible? Maybe that's not the right word, but shame? Yes, I do.'

'And you feel responsible for what your brother did?'

'I guess that's closer. I feel it belongs to me in a way. Does that make sense? I have to account for it in some fundamental way.'

I paused. How could I express it? I felt an obscure but intense frustration in my chest.

'I don't know what the right word is for it but yes I feel a share of the guilt. I feel I should put some energy into righting it or making sure it doesn't happen again.'

'And what about my husband, say, who used to beat the shit out of me? Do you feel responsible for that? For him? Do you share his guilt?'

'Oh God! Am I to be responsible for every evil ever committed by man?'

'Isn't that what you're saying?'

'I guess it is. And maybe if everybody felt the same way...'

Alice laughed.

'I think you're taking on too much! I'm not one of these women that blames all men for the sins of some.'

'Don't you worry about the world?'

'Please! There's too much going on in the world that's bad and evil.' she shrugged. 'I guess I just don't think I can do very much by myself to rectify the situation. I think we just need to accept it and get on with our lives.'

'You're saying we shouldn't examine history and so learn from it? So we can avoid making the same mistakes?'

'Maybe, we should say the past is past. Let's forget about it. Let's focus on now. Let's change the future.'

'So history is useless – and a history teacher is worse than useless?'

Alice chewed on her lower lip as she contemplated me.

'Maybe, you should just live your own life and leave the big questions alone. That's what I'm saying. I'm saying, you can't rid the world of pain no matter how hard you try. But you can live your own life in a way that makes you happy and contented and a good friend, a good neighbor, a good member of the community, focus on bringing up your own kids to be nice people. I think that's all any man or woman can do – and I think it's enough. So what if the goddamn cavalry killed off a couple of hundred Indians a hundred and fifty years ago? Were the Indians saints? I mean, they never killed anyone in a mean and vicious and contemptible way? Didn't they invent scalping?'

'Well,' I paused. 'There's some disagreement about the origins. Some say...'

'I don't want to know!'

I had to admit there was something – a great deal – to be said for what Alice had been saying. I didn't need to take on the sins of the world. I was no Christ or Gandhi prepared to sit between the railway tracks to stop or derail the train of inevitable history. I was not going to change the world with my suffering. Christ no!

That wasn't me at all. I tried again to express something of my thoughts.

'It seems to me I have a choice. A very simple choice at that. I can either choose to think only of immediate and personal concerns – what I want today, what I want tomorrow, and the next day for me, for Benjy, for you and so on – in that case I am no better than a worker ant. I have no wider consciousness of the world and our place in it.'

Alice interrupted me.

'I am certainly not suggesting that you don't concern yourself with community issues and so on.'

'I'm talking about something far bigger and more important and more abstract than community issues.'

'What?'

'I know it sounds preposterous, but my thoughts – the things I want to – goddamn it I don't want to, I have to – the things I have to think about are what it means to be a man, a human being. It's an absolute thing. It's about right and wrong. It's about being a witness to the truth and acknowledging it and judging it. Absolute truths. The truth of what it is to be a man breathing and living at the start of a new millennium.'

Alice reached out her hand and gripped mine.

'Jack, you're just working yourself up into a terrible, frustrating mind game. You're never going to come to the end of it. You ask yourself crazy questions. Are you responsible for some horrible killings done a hundred years ago? How can you be? People kill people. That's a horrible, horrible truth – but what can you do about it? It's not your fault. You can't do anything to correct it.'

I pulled my hand out of my pocket and waved it in the cold air.

'Look, it's like this,' I said. 'I can keep my hand all wrapped up and cozy, in a glove say, and pretend it's not cold or I can take the glove off and feel the harshness of reality.'

'OK,' Alice waved her hand in the air. 'I'm not afraid to feel the truth too.' She shook her head. 'But if you were to take off all your clothes to feel the truth of the world you'd die of frostbite or hypothermia or whatever it is people die of in the cold.'

'You'd certainly be arrested,' I said with a laugh.

Alice's jaw dropped open in mock shock and horror.

'Did you just make a joke?'

'I guess.'

'Well, hell, give me five!'

And we slapped each other

'There's just so much harsh reality we can take,' Alice said and gripped my hand hard.

'Maybe,' I conceded. And I heard Joe's voice mocking me. *See Jack? No-one wants to know. They just fucking don't want to hear.*

*

F is for fish in a temple pond. The water is like thick green pea soup. From time to time a fish breaks surface and takes a gulp of air. It seems as good a metaphor as anything. Fish gasping for air. But a metaphor for what?

*

G is for girl.

A Girl Dozes Off
On a summer's day a warm breeze came from the East
A girl combing her hair on a porch dozed off
Leaving the comb in her hair
As she slept her top slipped down
Her firm full breasts, like two soft hills, lay open
The sheen on her skin flowed like a stream between them
All this was virgin, new, untouched.
Seeing this the passing gentleman found it hard
to continue on his way.
But, for shame, to stay was not possible.

*

H is for Ho Xuan Huong. Very little is known about her. A summary of the known facts goes something like this: It is believed that she lived in the late eighteenth and early nineteenth centuries. She was married twice, but each time as a concubine, that is not as a first wife. One of her husbands, on the evidence of one of her poems, was the magistrate in the district of Vinh Tuong, near Hanoi. It is thought that she was not a beautiful woman. She likened herself to the rough skin of the breadfruit. Her poems were the secret pleasure of a select group of men and women of literary tastes before gradually becoming known to the general populace. She wrote in colloquial Vietnamese, disdaining to write in the exalted poetic style of literary Chinese. She preferred earthier, often very crude, themes. She is now a popular favorite though much frowned upon by the authorities. Her poems, I was informed, are not studied at school but volumes of her poems can be easily bought at any bookshop.

*

H is for Hudson Report. I found this volume in Mr Hung's shop. The title stared mockingly: *Can We Win In Vietnam?* Completed at about the time of the Tet offensive in 1968, five authors, including the famous 'futurologist' Herman Kahn discussed whether victory was possible. The majority view – by a narrow majority (Herman, as Chairman, made use of his casting vote) – was that it was. Kahn who believed that the war was justified and victory possible nevertheless considered ten possible options. The first was 'Shameful and Undisguised abandonment: the United States withdraws from Vietnam almost unconditionally, with no serious concessions by the other side. This occurs less because of objective military weakness than out of 'war-weariness'.'

Well done Herman. Spot on. His own view at the time was that some of the views may 'seem to be relatively farfetched (the first and the tenth particularly strike me as being unlikely, though not completely impossible).' Poor Herman.

Another contributor to the report, Edmund Stillman, made the following assessment: 'According to proponents of the war, four major issues would seem to be at stake... we have been told that the American intervention is necessary, first of all, to contain

Communist China; secondly to contain Communism, thirdly to contain the tactic of... 'wars of national liberation' and finally to contain the very practice of aggression – to discourage assaults on 'world law'.'

So, if I've got this right, he was saying we fought the North Vietnamese but in our mind we imagined we were fighting China. Or we fought the North Vietnamese but in our mind we were fighting China and Russia, the Eastern Bloc and Cuba. Or we fought North Vietnam to stop a people from governing themselves independently. Or we blasted the hell out of them to stop them fighting?

Jesus Joe, did you know what you were fighting for? Let's say it was hormones. But how can I justify my actions intellectually if they are fundamentally biological? I grab something out of the bag. I say I did it because I'm against Communism. That smacks more of the reality of what happened. We respect authority too much.

In a round up discussion at the end of the book, William Pfaff made the following comment: 'We seem to believe that the only way to fight this war is to go out and get ambushed and then to kill a lot of people in the ensuing battle.' Joe would have liked that. He would have nodded his head sagely, wryly. 'Fucking right!' And it sounds an awful lot like what's happening in Iraq.

The question of use of arms was discussed. Their comments are unanswerable. Remember this was before My Lai: '...the United States has not shown too much compunction about indiscriminate killing. I think it is another one of the ways in which we have indulged ourselves with respect to this war in Vietnam... The weapons are bigger than the targets... Americans seem to prefer to do their killing from 30,000 feet. Apparently, we see an operative distinction between putting a bayonet in someone's belly and dropping a bomb on him from up high, We like the 'antiseptic' way... it is morally outrageous to take out a village to kill a guerrilla... It seems no more immoral to kill someone with napalm than with a bullet. But in the situation we find ourselves in Vietnam, or in any guerrilla war, you are fighting an enemy who is not clearly identifiable, who frequently is not fighting as an organized body on the battlefield, who comes from the population and retreats into the population. In this situation, then, it seems to me that the resort to use of indiscriminate weapons (eg napalm) is ethically wrong and politically catastrophic.' Somebody saw sense. That was in 1968. That was before My Lai. This was right at the beginning. Already it was believed that villages, whole villages, had been 'taken out'. How could America win? If you kill the people who are supposed to be your people and if you defoliate what is supposed to be your country (and which after your victory will have to be refoliated) how can you realistically expect victory? Two of the five authors of the Hudson Report can look back with some pride. They saw what was wrong. They drew the inevitable conclusion. And no-one cared to see the truth of what they said. Oh Joe! They were right. But they weren't right in time to save you. How can ideas save you from hormones?

*

F is for Fuck. It is late afternoon. Le is slightly disheveled by the day. Perhaps he is nervous, ill-at-ease. All the waiters at the hotel know him. He was their teacher. He was everyone's teacher. They clasp his hand. It is clear my own estimation has risen. I am no longer just the Fat American. I am the Fat American who knows Mr Le. Mr Le reveals that he is a man of many involvements. So many he seems to hold back from time to time for fear of claiming too much. But he makes it clear he has to run to stay still.

'I write books for a fee. They're published under someone else's name. I am involved in negotiations for inter-provincial trade. Everything has to be done in US dollars. In some parts of the country the government is no longer in control. Smuggling is open. Haiphong is the worst place. It is controlled by gangs. What do they smuggle? Gold. Look at the consumer goods in the shops. How do they come in? Who can afford to buy them?' It is true. Shops are full of tinned goods and a wide range of brandies and whiskies. I ply him with rice wine and we turn to poetry.

'One should always have drink by one's side when one discusses literature,' Le says. 'It loosens the tongue and it lets the mind soar.' I like this rather old-fashioned approach. It is no longer fashionable to 'discuss literature' in America.

We turn to a poem that Ho Nguyen has already said is too difficult for him to attempt. Mr Le seizes on it.

'This poem shows how clever she is. She uses the device you call spoonerism. In English, you do not have many options to spoonerize. Can we say that? Spoonerize?'

'Why not?'

The only spoonerism I could remember was changing dear old queen to queer old dean.

'In Vietnamese we can spoonerize in six different ways. We have a very rich language. It gives us many possibilities.' He nodded his head thoughtfully. 'Now this poem seems to a fairly simple poem about human destiny but there are two spoonerisms at the end of the first and last lines. These add an interesting meaning to the poems. Le stirred his glass and swallowed a large mouthful of diluted spirits. Then he started.

'The title is 'The Burdens of a Monk's Life'. So the poem should read like this:

> *Monks are burdened by a heavy weight of duty (too much*
> *fucking)*
> *You should not care about the little tasks in life*
> *The Buddhist boat is headed for Nirvana*
> *Unfavorable winds (twisted cunts) will only bring you back.'*

Le hardly paused as he uttered the words. His translation came out pat. So much for the idea that Ho Xuan Huong's poems were not translatable. But we were prevented from continuing our translating. A band was tuning up.

'You'll stay for dinner?'

'I have to work.' Le had turned his attention to the band. 'These are also teachers. They are my friends. I used to play with them. I play the guitar.'

So rich in skills and ability. His students were luckier than they knew. But he looked so emptied out.

*

It was sometime after four when Alice got back. I'd had a long bath and was lying on the couch listening to Mahalia Jackson, lost in my own thoughts, wallowing in the luxury of being alone in someone else's home.

'You look nicely chilled.'

'I am.'

She came over and sat down next to me, grinning.

'Now, I've got you where I want you.'

'Flat on my back?'

'That's right.'

She bent over me. 'Hmm. You smell good.'

She patted me on my cheek.

'You look ready for some serious cuddling.'

'I guess I'm as ready as I'll ever be.'

She smiled.

'Give me a minute. And when I call, I want you to come running.'

The call came about ten minutes later. I found her in bed, her bare shoulders a promise, a wide wicked smile on her lips.

'Don't look,' I said and she covered her eyes playfully. I undressed and crawled under the covers and felt the sudden blessed newness of her skin against mine.

'At last,' she breathed as our lips came together liquidly. This time my hands did not feel constrained.

'It's been a long time,'

'For me too. I thought we'd never get there.'

'I'm out of practice.'

'Don't worry. It's as easy as falling off a bike.'

'Oh yes?'

'And there's no hurry. No hurry at all.'

But it wasn't so simple. After a while it became obvious I wasn't responding as I should.

'I've got some weed. Maybe that'll help.' Alice got out of bed and rummaged through a drawer. Eventually, she found a joint and lit it.

'Take a few puffs. That might do the trick. And we need some Latin music to dance to.'

I took a long suck and held my breath while Alice busied herself with the music. The truth was I wasn't surprised. Another suck and then I handed it over as Alice crawled back under the covers.

I closed my eyes and followed the heightened dictates of lips and fingers. Her skin was smooth and supple to my touch. It tasted good. I worked my way down her belly.

'Oh. That's good,' Alice whispered encouragingly. It took a while but I brought her to her climax. I could tell she enjoyed it. She tried to reciprocate but I stopped her. It wasn't going to happen and that was OK with me. Hopefully it was just first time nerves and the next time would be better. Her fingers tickled me lightly until I clenched my legs and forced her to stop.

'It's OK. Really.'

'Are you sure?'

'Yeah.'

'Can you bring yourself off?'

I spent a few minutes trying but it wasn't going to happen. We kissed and cuddled some more and that was good. I was happy. Then Alice got up and came back with some wine and olives.

'Very civilized.'

'You bet your ass.'

We laughed and toasted each other.

'Was it me?' Alice asked eventually. 'I don't turn you on?'

'No. I really want to fuck you.'

'Fuck me?' Her voice had a hard edge. 'Screw me? Bang me? Ball me?'

'Make love to you. Is that better?'

'Yeah. A whole lot better.'

'OK. I really want to make love to you. I want to be your lover.'

'I like the sound of that.'

'But something's gone wrong with the mechanics. Maybe I'm just too old.'

'You're not too old. But you've been through a very traumatic time. It's not surprising really.'

She fed me two olives thoughtfully.

'You know, I haven't told you about my dad.'

'What about him?'

'I told you I married Dick Baker for his name. Actually, there was another reason.'

'Uhuh?'

'Yeah. My mum died when I was fifteen. Cancer. It was really a very bad time. Dad went kind of crazy. It was like he had a sexual frenzy. It was so inappropriate. He was propositioning all mum's old friends. I was so embarrassed. And then he turned on me. He was always touching me and patting me and I just didn't know what to do. Suddenly there were girly magazines in the bathroom and porn videos that a sixteen year old girl shouldn't be finding around the house. It was just awful. I had to get out. I really did.'

'Why are you telling me this?'

'Well, you know, you've let your sexual feelings dry up inside you. You've done the decent thing. My dad went the other way. But, you know, maybe my dad's way is the right way. You're too young to shrivel up and die. You need to get out there and shake your butt.'

'I know.' I said. I knew she was right.

Then, suddenly, apropos nothing that I could see, Alice rolled over to the side of bed, stood up and began to pull on her clothes.

'What's up?'

'Just had a thought. I'll be back in an hour or so. Don't run away.'

*

H is for history. I have two books on Vietnam's history. One is Stanley Karnow's Pulitzer Prize winning volume, *Vietnam – A History*. This is 686 pages long excluding notes and index. Only 38 pages deal with Vietnam before the French made contact. 406 pages detail America's involvement. The other history is one of Mr Hung's volumes which says on the cover: *An Illustrated Outline History of Vietnam, Saigon 1991*. There are no details of who the author is but I suspect the hand of Mr Hung. There is a note at the front that says: 'This was a textbook for foreign students in South Vietnam for 20 years 1955-1975. The original was not illustrated.' This book is 197 pages long. 148 deal with the country's history before the arrival of the French. The history book does not include any information on the American war except to include a nine-page chronology of colonial intervention of which the American involvement merits seven. There is a picture of a helicopter on the pad on the roof of the American embassy and a long line of people waiting to be evacuated. A man reaches out his hand to help a man? A woman? A child? It's not clear.

One history. Two different perspectives.

*

Alice had been gone fifteen minutes or so when I decided to give in to my curiosity. I pulled open all the drawers of her side table to see what she had there. In the first drawer I opened I found myself looking at a gun. It was a big solid gun, not the kind I would ever have described as a lady's gun. I lifted it out and saw a plastic folder beneath it. I knew I shouldn't but I lifted that out too. I pulled the papers out and spread them across the bed. One was a driving license made out to Richard Charles Baker. Amongst the other miscellaneous documents were the ownership papers for her car. They were in her ex-husband's name. After thinking about all this, I put them back in the drawer. There was probably a simple explanation. In any case, it was none of my business.

*

Wash stood up again to piss. I wondered if I'd have time to snatch his gun. Then what? It was past midnight. When was Maddie going to come out with the gun in her hand? And how was she going to handle it?

'You know what Joe and I do up here?'

He let the possibilities hang in the air while I shook my head. When was she going to come out with the gun?

'We go out into the woods round here and practice all our jungle fighting skills. We done bivouacked outside all our neighbors and watched them. Twenty four hours round the clock. Four hours on four hours off. Just like old times. We know all their habits. They have no idea. They don't know there's a black man up here in the hills. I reckon if they knowed I was here they'd come calling. We set out booby traps case any of them have the same idea about us. And if the Feds ever come to get us, well, know what? They in for a big surprise.'

'How's that?'

'We going to do the big disappearing act. They not gonna find nobody.'

'Yeah? How are you going to do that?'

'You an educated man, brother Jack. You heard about that cave place where the bull man lived.'

'The Labyrinth? In Crete? The Minotaur?'

'Yeah. I guess that's it. Well, we got our own labyrinth place here and I guess you can call me the bull man. Washington 'Bull Man' Thomas. Got a kinda ring to it, wouldn't you say?'

'Bull?'

'I'm not giving you any bull man. This ain't any bullshit I'm giving you. This is the truth.'

'A cave?'

'They lots of caves round here. But we found the king of caves – and we done kitted it out. Man could live a long time underground and no-one would ever find him. Not ever.'

'Where is this cave?'

His grin mocked me.

'That would be telling, now, wouldn't it?'

He pulled on his cigarette and blew the smoke out in a long exhalation.

'All sorts of caves round here. And you got to watch yo' ass when it comes to caves. Yessir. Can't just live in any old cave. You got to get yourself a nice dry comfortable cave. Then winter or summer it will stay the same nice temperature. Again, you need a cave that's got a stream running through it so you got your water source nice and handy.'

'I imagine almost any cave round here would be fine, no? I mean, it's all limestone.'

'I tell you, brother Jack, you is dead wrong. Some of the caves round here are damp, or they too narrow – you get yourself stuck, no-one gonna find you. One day in a thousand years maybe someone gonna stumble on your sad bones. Also, you got to be real careful when you find yourself a new cave. First thing you got to do is check it out. You see any bats or insects? If you see bats then it's OK but the word is some of these caves got poison gas.

You step in a puddle of water and the gas rises and kills you dead. You dead before you even hit the ground. You believe that?'

I shrugged. It sounded like the kind of story country people tell you just to scare you.

'We got a lot of dried food, army surplus stuff, stacked away there. Joe did a sweet deal with a National Guard officer. We got all kinds of weapons. We even got bunk beds. And we know these woods better than almost anyone else. I tell you man, if we have to, we can live up here a mighty long time.'

He yawned a long slow yawn. He was getting tired.

'It's been good talking to you brother Jack. I like you. A man needs someone to talk to. Chicks ain't the same. They don't see things the same way. Can't talk to a woman same way you can talk to a man. That's the truth.'

I got to my feet. For some reason I was getting nervous.

'What's the matter? You got itchy feet?'

'I got myself a numb butt.'

I stamped up and down to get the circulation going. What was Maddie up to? I glanced at the door. Wash noted the look.

'Yeah. I'm hungry. Where's the bitch?... HEY BITCH!' he called out.

'Yeah?' Suddenly she was there standing in the doorway, as if she'd been hovering just inside.

'Make me up something to eat.'

That's when I saw the gun in her hand behind her back. I saw she was shaking. Wash saw it too.

'What's up bitch?'

(Later she explained it to me. 'When I went out to the car to get the food like Wash told me to, I just had to check out the glove compartment. Couldn't believe my eyes when I saw the gun there. Before I even had time to think about it I had stuck it in with the food. But you and Wash was sitting yakking 'bout this and that, I had to hide it away till I had a chance to check it out. Then you go and you see I took the gun. I was sweatin'. I near had a heart attack. But when you say nothing I know you're there to help me. But even when you go and sit on the porch I'm just shaking with fear. I can't control it. I know if I don't get it right I'm going to die. I don't want to die. I hold that gun in my hand a long time and I think how am I going to do this? And can I really be sure you're on my team? I got to make choices. I got to make the right choices or I'm dead. Then I think I can't wait till Wash falls asleep 'cos he'll handcuff me to the bedstead like he always does. So, I force myself. Got to steady my nerves. And then he calls me out and I'm just about to come out anyway so I say to myself. OK, girl, here goes. And I come out with the gun behind my back 'cos I still haven't got it fixed in my head how I'm going to do this thing.')

She pulled the gun out and pointed at Wash, who couldn't have been more surprised. His mouth hung wide open.

'You fuck...' was all she could say. 'I'm gonna...'

I saw her try to squeeze the trigger but the safety catch was still on. Wash saw this the same time I did. I saw the relief and the snarl in his face as he recovered himself.

'You got a problem there bitch?'

'Shit! Shit!'

Maddie was screaming in fury and panic. I stepped forward just as Wash moved to pick up his automatic pistol.

'Give me the gun.' I pulled it out of her hand and clicked off the safety. Wash wasn't in any hurry. I could see he was going to kill Maddie now. I had to stop that.

'Hold it Wash,' I screamed. 'Hold it right there.'

He looked at me in surprise.

'I'm going to kill that bitch!'

'No, you ain't. I don't want to kill you.'

Wash froze then.

'Drop the gun.'

'And if I don't?' the query was soft with his anger.

'I'll shoot.'

'Why don't you shoot anyways?'

'Joe asked me not to shoot you, not unless I had to.'

'What's this to Joe?'

'That's why I'm here. Joe asked me to get the girl.'

'Joe? Asked you?' He seemed to find this very funny.

'Why he don't come and take her hisself?'

'Cos' he's dead.'

'Dead you say?' His face jerked at the words.

'That's right. He killed himself.'

'Killed hisself?'

The shock was clear. He rocked back on his heels.

'He asked me not to shoot you if I could help it.'

His face darkened in a snarl of pure anger.

'Well, maybe you's going to have to.' And he made to bring the gun up.

'Don't.'

But he was straightening up now and I had no choice. I had to show I meant business. I pulled the trigger and was surprised by the recoil.

'Shit!'

Wash dropped his gun and was hopping round.

'Shit! Shit!'

He clutched his leg.

'You done shot me!'

'I told you.'

'Jesus Shit! Didn't think you had it in you, brother Jack. My mistake.'

'Are you hurt bad?'

'What's it to you?'

'I don't want to hurt you.'

'Seems like you just grazed my leg.'

Now what? I had the gun pointing at him but he might try to rush me or go for his gun. I had to take charge.

'Take your pants off!'

'What? You gonna fuck my ass or something?'

'You heard. Get your pants off or I'll shoot. Next time it's for real.' As if I'd deliberately grazed him the first time, I thought sardonically.

'Get off the porch,' I told him. It occurred to me he might be able to whip his belt out and use it as a weapon. Or anything. I was quivering with the adrenalin rush.

'Now!' I shouted and pointed the gun at his head.

'Wait up, brother Jack!'

'I said *now!*'

I felt my finger tighten on the trigger. He saw it too.

'OK! OK!'

He hopped off and I pushed Maddie forward.

'Get his gun.'

She bent down and picked it up.

'I'm going to kill that son of a bitch.'

She pointed it down towards Wash, and he saw she meant business. He hiked his pants up and took off down the track. The safety was off and the minute she pulled the trigger bullets came spraying out. She couldn't control the gun and sprayed the distant trees. By the time she'd finished Wash had disappeared into the dark.

'He's gone,' I said.

'We got to get outta here.'

'He's gone.'

'You don't understand. He's got his cave. He's got guns and grenades and all sorts. We gotta go.'

She was right.

'Get in the car.'

I didn't have to tell her twice.

I spun the car round and took off back down the track. Soon I realized that Wash was a long way behind us and I didn't have to take the corners like a rally driver. I slowed down. Twice we nearly hit an animal. Their eyes lit up in the glare of the headlights. And then she started screaming. A mad wailing. It was the sound of an absolute unbelieving joy that didn't know how to express itself. I let her scream her head off and after a while she subsided into sobbing wretchedness. I concentrated on the road and after a while the tears stopped and she was silent. She started to shiver and I stopped long enough to give her a jacket to wrap around her shoulders.

'You OK?' I asked.

She nodded shakily, biting her lip.

'What now?'

'We go to the cops.'

She nodded.

A weighty exhaustion settled on me then and I could hardly stop yawning. I had to keep moving. After that we didn't talk much. It had all happened so quick and simple. Then I remembered I'd left my suitcase behind. Not that it mattered, just some clothes. Jesus, I'd done it. Joe, I said to myself, I have done it.

*

Then there is Sheena. Sheena? How can I explain her? I picked her up late one night. She was lying on the ground. A real whore! Haha! I loved her bald head and thick, sensuous lips. No tits of course. No cunt. What? A girl with no tits or cunt lying in the street? What the hell's going on? Just teasing you. Who? Who am I writing this for? Jack? Jack, you will never read this, thank the Lord. But this is for you, I guess. Not Chrissie. She could never in a million years understand what I'm saying. She'd react to it like it was a pair of dirty underpants. She'd pick it up between two fingers and make a face and put it in the washing machine and try to wash it clean, pound it clean, scrub it clean. Sorry Chrissie, it just won't come clean. It's pretty foul in here. You don't want to know. This is for me. I got to write myself into some kind of comprehension of what's going on. One minute I revel in thoughts of violent fucking. Then I'm overwhelmed with disgust. I want to plunge a knife into my own eyeball, stop myself seeing. Plunge it into my brain. Stop myself thinking these thoughts. There are times I think of curling up with a little old fragger. Just obliterate myself into nothing. But that's not the way I'd choose to go it if ever came to that. For some reason I hear a highpitched WHEEEEEEE! as a train rockets into the black tunnels of night. Chikety-chak chikety-chak chikety-chak chikety-chak. Like the screams of orgasm. Like the terror screams of death.

Sheena. Imagine a doll, you know a fashion shop window-dressing mannequin. Well that's Sheena. Actually she's just the head. Guess she was used to model wigs. I took a fancy to her, despite the fact that half the face was crushed in like someone took a blunt instrument to her. I love that about Sheena. She's been bruised by life and still she's there beautiful for me. I tell Sheena everything. She understands me. She forgives. She forgives all my trespasses against her and her kind. Her kind? Girls, Jack! Skirt! Cunt. Is that ugly enough for you? God it's ugly enough. I caress her face with an open razor as I whisper to her stories. She listens to me and she forgives. Stupid cunt. Her forgiveness is meaningless. I plead with her not to forgive. But she forgives me. In the end she had to go. In the end they

*all have to go. In the end you can't stand the judgment in
their eyes.*

*

'You sure are a sucker for happy endings!'

Alice is waving a pack of four white capsules in my face, a big
wide grin on her face.

'My friend calls this the love herb. It's herbal.'

'That so?'

'We're going to turn you into a Casanova.'

'You hope.'

'My friend says it really works.'

'So, now your friend knows I can't perform.'

'And you know her husband needs a little help too, so what?'

She popped one of the pills out and handed it to me.

'Go to the kitchen, get yourself a glass of water and swallow
this down.'

'It doesn't work straight away, I've heard.' My knowledge was
all hearsay.

'That's OK. We'll watch a nice smoochie movie and when it's
finished you should be ready to go.'

'Go?'

'Ready to roll.'

Hell, why not? I followed instructions and waited to see what
would happen. We sat down on the sofa and put on a completely
forgettable movie – man meets girl, chases girl, gets girl. But Alice
seemed to enjoy it so I went along with it. After a while I became

aware I was feeling a little light headed. Good. Something was happening. I don't think we made it to the ending – no doubt it was happy. That's the way we like them. Unfortunately there was no happy ending for us. We cuddled and kissed and caressed and eventually we both managed self-induced climaxes, in my case, one that had to be milked from my half limp member – somehow not worthy of the effort that we had put into the task.

'Oh dear,' Alice was sympathetic. 'Never mind. Tomorrow you can take a double dose, see if that's better.'

CHAPTER 12

I found myself wrapped round a pillow, curled fetally, stiffly, at the edge of the mattress. Alice lay sprawled over the rest of the bed. I turned to her and she groaned. I didn't want to wake her. Light was just managing to seep through a chink in the curtains. Alice, like Norma, like Maddie, liked a dark bedroom. I turned and snuggled up to her warmth, placing my face next to her breast. I sucked in the warm heady odors of her armpit.

'Hmmph,' she croaked and moved away. I followed and lay my face against her back with her breast in my hand. Then I let it slip down her flank to her buttock. I couldn't sleep and after a while it felt uncomfortably hot to be this close to her. I eased away and lay on my back staring at the ceiling. What ease! I thought. To lie in a woman's bed. To wake next to her. And to have nothing pressing to do except exchange caresses. Was that not something precious? What delicious dreams was she having? To have the time and space to dream, was that not the epitome of a civilized existence? Something wonderful to set against the sweat and anxieties of everyday. And already I was mentally preparing to get up to do something. But what was there that needed doing?

Nothing. Perhaps it was fear of this intimate softness, this exquisite closeness. Alice now shifted. I sensed she was waking. Then what? Would I have to go through the charade again? That pretense that I was a man who could offer her a stiff erection for the voluptuous stimulation of her morning cunny. And was cunny not a warm and friendly word, more affectionate and tongue tingling than any other?

Alice threw an arm across me and then pulled herself up to offer me a kiss. We kissed a morning kiss of friendly welcome. Her hand slid down my belly to my all too flaccid penis. A bitter thought came to me: I was the small dick to set beside her husband. I turned away.

'No, don't go,' she moaned.

Her hand continued to caress. It was not unpleasant in itself and I turned back and let my hand return the strokes. We kissed again. I buried my head in the nape of her neck, licking up and around her ears.

'Ooh! That's nice,' she encouraged.

*

H is for hustling. In Saigon everyone hustles. Business is business. But the way they hustle is so gently persistent and civilized. One evening, as dusk was falling – a short, sharp, tropical dusk that takes maybe fifteen minutes to complete itself – I was walking to the Rex Hotel for a much needed beer. The area surrounding the Rex is tout Mecca. A motorcycle owner lying back on his parked bike saw me coming and I saw him waiting. Our eyes locked.

He knew he should make the effort to try to persuade me to go for a ride round the city for a dollar or so an hour. He also knew the chances of success were low to zero. He quizzed me with a jerk of his head. I replied with a slight crinkling of the eyes and a minimalist smile. He was tired of hustling and I was tired of being hustled. He could see I was tired of being hustled and I could see he was tired of hustling. He could see that I could see that he was tired of hustling and I could see that he could see that I was tired of being hustled. For both of us, there was, in that brief moment, a complete comprehension of the situation. In a second. Between two people of very different cultures. I liked him. I liked what this expressed about everyone around me. There was the possibility of complete comprehension, real understanding. He let his head drop on the motorcycle seat and I went and had my much needed beer.

*

I forget her name. She was blonde, frizzy haired, freckled. Pink nipples, greeny-blue eyes. I picked her up at the 7-11. She wanted to live. She wanted out on the blue highway to excitement and fun and adventure. She found Mr Death. I took her out on the highway and squeezed her cunt and laughed and promised good times and fun times. We fucked her hard for three, four months until we couldn't stand the sight of her sniveling any more. It was winter then. We tied her naked to a tree and let her freeze to death. The gag kept back the screams. She lived through the night and into the

second day. I tried to fuck her against the tree but her cunt
was iced up and she was sagging against the ropes. Wash
wanted to slice open her throat. In the end he did. I plunged
my knife into her socket and cut out her left eye. We kept it
on the mantelpiece a while until we thought it was mocking
us. Wash got superstitious. We dug a hole and buried it under
leaves and twigs.

*

Maddie never could let the memories go. She'd wake up in the dark hours of the morning and shake and tears would stream from her eyes.

'What's up?' I would ask, trying to comfort her.

'I heard Tina screaming and there was nothin' I could do for her.'

We'd been here before. There was nothing I could do except try to give her some physical sign of comfort. I stroked her belly.

'I was so scared and Joe was using me and I had a good long talk to myself. I knew this was a bad story and there most likely wasn't going to be any happy ending. I knew what I had to do to survive. I whispered to Joe. I whispered to him. 'Joe, I'll be good to you. You let me get through this and I'll be good to you.'

I stroked her belly tenderly.

'Next morning Tina was a wreck. I saw Wash look at Joe and just kinda shake his head as if to say this chick is no good. Not worth spending time on. Tina was sniveling and all curled up. She was badly hurt.

'You want her?' he asked Joe. Joe grinned.

'Guess I do. This one here,' he pointed at me, 'is a pure pedigree fuckeroo.'

I guess I should have been pleased at the compliment but I knew what it meant.

'That so?' Wash said and unbuttoned his pants.

'Come here, baby, and give ole Wash a bit of your sweet tongue.'

I didn't even hesitate. Tina didn't last a day.'

Maddie was sniveling at the memory.

'They just stripped off her clothes and told her to run.'

'Go?' Tina asked. She just didn't understand.

Maddie quietly screeched out Tina's words for her.

'She jes' did not know. She stood there and shivered. She started to piss from fear. It leaked down her leg.

'Bitch. Get out. Go.' Wash screamed at her. She turned then and started to hobble down the path. They just sat and watched her as she kept on limping, not quite running, crying, looking back at us wondering how long she had. And then Wash picked up his gun. He was so calm and assured. He set out after her. I couldn't look then. I jes' listened to this awful silence of the forest. I jes' waited and waited. It seemed like an eternity but then, maybe five minutes later I heard the shots. Two, fired quickly. Then another. And another. What was he doing? I knew she was dead then. It jes' happened so quick. And you know what I think? Each person is a universe, a universe of dreams and hopes and possibilities. And the universe that was Tina had just been crushed out of existence.'

I sat there as the tears fell, stroking her foot, trying to tell her I was there, I understood her suffering. She could depend on me.

*

L is for Lotus pond. There was only the one. I saw it from the train window. It stood about fifty yards from a grove of trees and a house. It was a rectangular pond with lotus leaves draped on the surface and flower heads drooping, like a wilted, washed out tulip field. Two large white birds waded on its fringes. Cranes? It passed out of sight and I felt honored to have seen it. A lotus field in the middle of nowhere. Imagine that!

*

Ask the Moon
A thousand thousand years have passed
But the moon remains unchanged
Sometimes you're round, sometimes crescent, why's that?
How old is the white rabbit who lives up there?
And how many kids has the Moon fairy got?
So many things I want to know,
At night you shine white twinkling light
like the gleaming light of snow
Dear Moon, why do your red hot fires not glow so bright at noon?
Do you have to wait up there all night?
Are you in love with some darkly hidden secret sight?

'What darkly hidden secret sight might that be?' I asked. Ho Nguyen just smiled. "I think you know."

*

An afternoon of lovers' talk. Fingers circling flesh as we talked.

'I was thinking about you going up to rescue Maddie. That took some doing.'

'Yeah. I guess.'

'It was brave. Very brave.'

I said nothing.

'And you managed to get away. What happened then?'

I laughed.

'I got arrested.'

'Arrested?'

'Yeah. For rape.'

'Rape?'

'Sure. I'd fucked her. She was compelled to do it. So, it was rape. No two ways about it.'

'But you were also…! If you hadn't…'

'Sure, I'd have been killed.'

'So?'

'After she had me real scared, Maddie agreed to drop the charges on condition I looked after her until the baby was born. Until she could get back on her own two feet. I didn't have much choice.'

'But you loved her?'

'Infatuated. Head over heels.'

'And what did Norma say about all this?'

'She wouldn't let us in the house. That was it. Over. But you know what? I was glad.'

'Sure. You had a pretty young thing to wreak your lust on.'

'Yeah. Something like that.'

'So Maddie never considered abortion?'

'Refused even to consider it… even now I don't really know why.'

'Maybe she'd had enough violence imposed on her body. Didn't want any more.'

'Could be. I think also she was hoping for a girl. She was going to call it Tina after her friend. She was very disappointed she had a boy. I think part of her believed she'd given birth to another would be rapist.'

'Do you think she'll ever come back?'

'It scares me sometimes. I have a nightmare. She'll come back one day and insist she's the mother and she'll take Benjy away. It gives me the sweats just to think of it.'

'She wouldn't do that, would she? She'd be crazy to do that.'

'Crazy? When did that stop anyone from doing anything?'

I shivered at the thought and Alice put her arms round me to comfort me. I needed her comfort. We rocked like that for a while. It was good to be mothered.

'Benjy's such a nice boy,' she whispered. 'He's going to be just fine. A fine young man that you're going to be proud of.'

*

M is for My Lai. Stanley Karnow, in his Pulitzer Prize winning book, makes four references to My Lai. On page 31 of my edition, he writes: 'Morale further deteriorated following revelations of a massacre in which a US Infantry company slaughtered some three hundred Vietnamese civilians in the village of My Lai – an episode that led GIs to presume that their commanders were covering up other atrocities.'

On page 482, he writes a description of routine 'cordon and search' missions and adds the comment: 'These were routine missions, not outrageous atrocities like the My Lai massacre that occurred in March 1968.' On page 543, he writes a description of Vietcong atrocities in Hue and then adds the comment: 'Paradoxically, the American public barely noticed these atrocities, pre-occupied as it was with the incident at My Lai – in which American soldiers had massacred a hundred Vietnamese peasants, women and children among them.'

My Lai is one of those key words that reverberate down the years. It sums up everything. Yet Karnow does not describe what happened. He doesn't consider how it came to happen. He fudges. Sometimes it is an 'atrocity' or a 'massacre' and sometimes an 'incident'. Did three hundred people die or only a hundred? Were they mainly men with some women and children among them or were they mainly women and children with some men amongst them, or what? Karnow doesn't tell us. When future generations come to read about the war they will not find much on My Lai in the standard reference book on the subject.

The description in the Museum of American War Crimes in Ho Chi Minh City is rather different. 'On March 16, 1968, US troops committed a massacre of 504 inhabitants of the village of Tinh Khe – also called My Lai, Son Tinh district in the province of Quang Ngai. The raid, baptized 'Muscatine in Pinkville', was carefully planned. Several companies belonging to Barker's task forces engaged in the raid. Col Barker was in command of task forces of 1st Battalion 11th Light Infantry Regiment. The Division, commanded by General Samuel Koster, was mobilized for search and destroy missions. The Son My road was assigned to Col. Henderson. 'C' Company was under the command of Capt. Ernest Medina. Platoon Commander William Calley was responsible for the massacre. During one morning 504 civilians were killed: 182 women (17 pregnant) 173 children (56 aged 1-5 months), 60 elderly (over 60). 'Burn all. Destroy all. Kill all.' This was a standard order for mopping up operations.'

I stood for a minute's silence before this description. One should honor the dead. William Calley was lucky he wasn't a German SS officer. Then he might have been hunted down the decades to answer for his crimes. I believe he now runs a jewelry store in Atlanta City. And what about the others? I can hear a voice, a voice without a face, intoning: 'Yes, it was wrong. But remember it was done by our guys. Good boys who couldn't bear the strain of war. The real culprit is war itself. These guys should be left alone. Theirs is the guilt. They have to live with it.' But do they feel guilt? Or have they forgiven themselves? Was it an act of madness or was it planned? It wasn't done in the white heat of anger. Joe, you were there. How do you kill a baby in cold blood, Joe? Answer me, Joe. Tell me about the babies Joe. The fifty-six babies.

*

Late morning. We lay in bed naked, pleasured and sated, kissing and stroking and talking of this and that and smiling fondly at each other – as new lovers do. Lovers! Yes, the double dose worked. I rose to the occasion. And this time, as I slipped into her it was as if I was entering her with my whole being. I had forgotten this sensation. Now it came back to me full force. I was scared I would lose it, so pushed and jerked clumsily, intent only on my own pleasure and when it came I closed my eyes and when it was over I collapsed in a heap beside her, taking care not to squash her as I fell.

I think I fell asleep. Then I was awake. She forgave me for thinking only of myself. We cuddled some more. Suddenly Alice laughed.

'What is it?' I asked. 'Me?'

She gave me a light slap.

'Don't be silly.'

'What then?'

'Just a memory.'

'Tell me.'

'I don't know why I thought of it just now.'

'What?'

'A girl I knew when I was at college. Jenny something. We weren't close friends but she lived not far from us so I would see her quite often. She had these enormous tits. I mean, she wasn't a big girl. She was really quite slight and she wasn't tall at all. If she had been in proportion she would have been very attractive but she had these enormous tits – completely out of proportion to the rest of her. They were so big it was a joke.'

I smoothed my hand over her belly to her own firm breast and took her nipple between my fingers and rubbed gently.

'Umm, that's nice,' she said and kissed me.

'Of course everyone knew her as 'Big Tits'. They must have been fake. Must have been. Couldn't have been natural. But why did she do such a thing? She was, what? Five foot four at most and quite slim and she had to carry around these two enormous melons. It can't have been comfortable.'

I lowered my head to take her other nipple with my lips, nipping it lightly with my teeth. I remembered Jacob Mandel's little joke, slightly risqué within the confines of the staffroom but allowable on the grounds he was a biologist. 'A breast without nipples? Seems rather pointless.'

'What are you giggling about?'

'Nothing. Tell me about your friend.'

'The way she walked. It's a wonder she didn't topple over. And then there was this way she behaved. She was very hard and abrupt with other girls except when she was telling them about what happened on her dates. Oh God yes. She was always talking about what animals men were and how they were always groping her. Every week it was the same. She was always fighting them off. So she said. But God did she flirt. She would hum with sexual signals as soon as a man came within shooting range. It was fascinating to watch. I saw grown men crumble. She got at least one professor the sack for making a pass at her. Poor man. She was a double-edged weapon. No-one would be seen going out with her. They'd have been the joke of the whole campus. But, my God, they buzzed like bees around her room. I wonder what became of her. Now, she was weird.'

I tried to imagine her.

'Interesting paradox,' I commented.

'What is?'

'She wants to make herself more attractive. She gets all these signals from around her that big breasts are good. So she gets really big breasts and scares everyone off. She wants men to lust after her but when they do she despises them.'

'That's right.'

'So, here's the question: Is she a victim?'

'Maybe. Yes, I think she is.'

'But who or what is she a victim of? No-one made her do these things. You didn't do them. None of your friends got themselves enormous tits. You're all receiving these same signals but you didn't all draw the same conclusions. No-one pointed a gun at her and said 'Enlarge your tits, girl.' If she's a victim, she's a victim of her own brain.'

'Yeah, maybe.' She looked doubtful. Not convinced but not wanting to argue about it.

'We think the brain is in charge and out to benefit us in every way.'

'Isn't that the truth?'

'But what if our brains have a different agenda?'

'Oh God!' Alice crawled over me until she was nuzzling my neck. 'I don't want to go there.'

Then, a little later, after we had been kissing a while.

'Maybe our brains are just dumb. They don't know what's good for us.'

'In either case,' I stretched and yawned. 'We know we can't trust our own thoughts and feelings.'

'It's tough when you can't even trust your own brain.'

'Yeah. If you can't trust that, what can you trust?'

'Do you like this?' She bent down between my legs.

'I know I like it but can I trust it? Is it good for me?'

'I hope so.'

'Me too. I hope so too.'

Then she tickled the bottom of my feet.

'Come on, time to get up. Can't stay in bed all day.'

'No?'

'Definitely not.'

'More's the pity.'

But I let her get dressed first while I watched. Something in me was thawing out very nicely. And the thought stuck: if we have evolved then we have simply overlaid our ancient brains with new brains – but the old brains are still in place feeding their signals through to the whole system. The crocodile and the ape are still alive in me in my unconscious. I am my own enemy. Know your enemy? No way in hell I can ever know what's going on down there. How can I resist what I cannot know?

*

She was on a bicycle. I passed her and drove on a while and then parked by the roadside. I watched her in the rear-view mirror. A sturdy girl. Not the feminine type. But it seemed to me she would do. She was doing some cross-country touring. She had full pannier bags on the back. No-one would miss her for a while I reasoned. This section of road was not busy. She came abreast of the car and overtook me. I pretended to be consulting a map. I let her go on a while and then I started after her. I overtook her, pulled in sharply and screeched to a halt. It worked like a dream. She slapped into the rear end and went sprawling. I rushed over and pretending to be apologetic, picked up her bike and with a pin in the ball of my hand stabbed the tires. She was struggling to her feet. I apologized and she swore and I agreed it was my fault and I could see she was bleeding so I suggested she should come to my place to clean up and I would give her a good lunch and send her on the way with some money in her pocket. She was reluctant until she saw her tires were flat. I put the bike into the back and we drove up to the cabin. We played the part of kind hosts right through lunch. Her name was Linda, she said, and she was from Canada and she was cycling to Mexico. Wash rolled some grass and we had a smoke. Linda started to giggle and agreed that she couldn't go on in her state then Wash got out some cards and taught us some sort of game that required all sorts of forfeits. It wasn't long before she was blowing me at one end and Wash was hammering her at the other. Boy was she having fun. She stayed a week as our guest but then she said she had to get going. It was just her and Wash. I was at work. So Wash tied her up when he didn't need her. And when he did need her he kept her in his sights.

We'd got some guns by then. I had a contact in Blackrock who sold off army surplus. I got a few grenades for old times sake. What did I need a grenade for, for chrissakes? Bit by bit we built up a little arsenal. We made Linda walk around naked all the time. We felt this was a disincentive to escape. But after a few weeks she took off down the hillside screaming and yelling for help. Wash ran for his rifle and scope and went after her. She never had a chance. I sometimes imagine her running down the hillside, past thin silvery pines and her white body blossoming with red flowers as the bullets hit her white skin.

And sometimes, reading these descriptions, I put myself in Joe's place, wondering how it felt to be so much master of another person. Just knowing that you could do anything you wanted with them. Not just could. That you were actually going to do what you wanted no matter what. You simply did not care how they felt about it. They didn't like it, too bad. And I had to recognize the fact: it felt good to have that power over someone else, to know you really didn't care what they thought about it. My cock twitched.

CHAPTER 13

'What will you do when you leave college?' I asked Ho Nguyen.

'I would like to be a tourist guide, or to work in a hotel. I want a job where I can learn English.'

'Well, your English is good so that should be no problem.'

'You're wrong. It's not easy.'

'What's the problem?'

'I have no powerful connections to introduce me. I can apply for the job but the manager won't employ me.'

'Everything depends on who you know?'

'That's right.'

'I thought Communism was supposed to be fairer.'

'They are very primitive and also corrupt. They follow the old system. Before Communism my family was well-off. You know, I am a cousin of the king Bao Dai. He is still alive in France I think.'

'Bao Dai's cousin?'

'Not close. There are many cousins. I am separated by 14 generations.'

'Is that why things are difficult for you?'

'No. My problem is that my father was an interpreter for your army at Cam Ranh Bay. When Nha Trang was liberated he was exiled to a place where the soil is very bad. Since then he has struggled to live by growing rice and doing odd jobs. He is just scraping a living.'

'With his English can't he do some tourist-related work here in Nha Trang ?'

'You don't understand. I live here with my grandparents. Our family used to have some money before the war but now we are poor. We have nothing. There is no room for him in the house. When I graduate, I will be sent to a remote area too. I will have to live there for a few years before I can get a job in the town again.'

I didn't think living in a small village would be so bad. He could learn something. I said as much.

'You don't understand. Until two years ago I lived in the country. I understand the countryside. I know that life. It is not a life for a young man!' he was angry at my romantic notions. Here the countryside wasn't ease after the bustle of the city. Here the countryside was hard and mean and very very boring. I cursed myself for being such a fool.

'Your father didn't have to go to re-education camp?'

'No. But some friends of his did. One was there for thirteen years.'

'What happens there?'

'It is like prison. You have to work hard for long hours. The guards beat you up. There is not enough food. If they want to punish you they put you in small metal boxes and leave you for days in the heat of the sun. If they want to kill you they kill you. They just shoot you. Or they arrange accidents. My father's friend told us of some details. It is hard to believe. The guards are very cruel.'

I shook my head in bemusement. What leads people to such cold-blooded brutality? The impulse is there. Americans, Vietnamese, Cambodians, Chinese, Koreans, Japanese, Russians, British, French, Germans. No nation is exempt. Ho Nguyen smiled.

'These people are really primitive. One day the political official at the college asked to see me. He said: 'Young man, it seems you receive a lot of correspondence from foreigners.'

'That's right!' I said.

'You talk to a lot of foreigners.'

'Yes, I like to talk to foreigners,' I told him straight.

'Be careful,' he advised me, 'Not all foreigners are friends of Vietnam. Some wish to harm us.'

I laughed to myself. Harm Vietnam? How? How can I harm Vietnam by talking to foreigners? But such things will go on my record. Such things are noted. These people have very primitive ideas. I hope Vietnam will open up soon. Then the situation will change. I pray for change.'

*

M is for Mountain Pass.

> *A pass, a pass and still another pass.*
> *Praise indeed is due to him who carved this place*

The path uphill leads through a deep red gate
Rocks, deep blue with mottled moss, lead up through it
Pine tree branches shudder in the wind
Willow leaves dissolve in clouds of fog
No-one with any soul would not enjoy this climb
Your knees get tired but still you must go on.

*

P is for Pui. My last morning. I had nothing very much I wished to do. I would have a last browse around the bookshop. I would have a last conversation with Mr Hung. Before that I walked down to the riverside and walked along the side of the road a while. I saw a ferry crossing to the other side, to the matsheds. I hadn't been across to the other side. Why not? Just for an hour. I strolled along looking for the pier.

'Where you go?' a cyclo driver asked. I smiled and waved my hand vaguely in front of me.

'Where you go? Maybe I can help you,' a motorbike rider. I nodded and smiled vaguely and waved my hand in front.

'Where you go?' a hustler.

I waved my hand towards the ferry.

'I'm going to get a ferry.'

Where you going?' A woman, a boat woman from her clothes.

'Across the other side. Over there,' I pointed.

'I take you! Two dollars.'

I shook my head.

'I'll take the ferry.'

'How much you pay me?'

'One dollar.'

'Two dollars OK?'

'One dollar.'

'One dollar? Go across. Looksee. Come back?'

'That's right.'

'OK.'

There was something about her. She smiled a quiet, honest smile. There was no slyness or deceit in her face.

'OK!' I agreed. Why not? Spread my tourist dollars around a bit. I had been very aware how most of my money went to large companies, how little to the people on the street. She led me back the way we had been walking and then we marched on to a wooden pier where ten or so motorized skiffs were tied up. Immediately there was an argument. Two men lying in different boats invited me to enter their boats. The woman I was with started to scream and shout at them. She shook her hand in their faces. She charged back and forwards. I stood by and waited. I was with the woman. I made that clear. Finally, she pushed me into an empty skiff, which took some heaving and pushing to get free of the other boats. The men watched her with hostile eyes. Finally she managed it. The motor was on a long rod which was hooked alongside the boat. She unhooked it, poured some kerosene into the small tank from a bottle, placed a prehensile foot to hold the handle while she wrapped a string round the starter and pulled. The motor started up and we were away. She pulled a face.

'Bad men. They don't like me. I'm Chinese. They're Vietnamese. They want three thousand dong. I say crazy! I only get ten. Why I pay him three thousand?'

I liked this woman. She was a fighter.

'Where do you want to go? Cholon?'

'How long does that take?'

'Five, ten minutes. Very near.'

But I wanted to go the other way. I remembered a rickety little bridge a little way upstream. We were already half-way across the muddy waters of the river. She turned the boat.

'What's your name?' I asked.

'Pui.' She tapped her chest. 'My name Pui.'

'You married?' Children?'

'My husband...' she drew a line across her throat. 'Dead. Seven years ago. One child. One son. Fifteen years old.'

'You live over there?' I pointed back to the pier from where we had come.'

She looked at me.

'You want to see my house?' I looked at her and smiled and shook my head. She was not being disingenuous. It was a straight question. The implications were clear. They didn't have to be spelt out. We glided upstream. Here there were boys washing themselves. Deep brown bodies in the deep brown waters. We reached the bridge. It flowed over a small inlet. It was thirty yards wide. The bridge itself was a make-shift affair. I managed to demonstrate to Pui that I wanted to walk a while.

'Five minutes,' I said to reassure her.

The bridge had been put together by the local inhabitants. It started off three narrow planks wide. In places it shrank to two. At one point it was only one shaky plank wide. I could see the flow of the stream below. The flow of the water threatened to unnerve me. I looked instead at the far bank and walked on. I managed to reach the far side but half-way back I was faced with a cyclist wheeling his cycle towards me. I stood aside on a firm post and let him brush past. I made it back. Pui was nowhere to be seen but the boat was still there. There were children playing in the dirt. I looked at the houses that had been laid out around the side of a what looked to be a volleyball court. Beyond the houses were open fields. In Graham Greene's book this is where the Vietminh were. It was fatal to be caught here after dark. Fatal for a white skin. I imagined them then, on the roof of the Majestic Hotel, holding their pink gins, looking out across the river to where I stood. Maybe in the moonlight they see the shapes of the trees and houses. Here was the enemy. Here was fear. Here was the heart of the unknown, the heart of darkness. I passed the houses and looked in. Here there was a man slumped in front of a television. There a woman doing some sewing. A man came to the door to watch us. He smiled in response to my smile. Children caught sight of me and pointed and giggled. I was a funny sight. This fat American. Times change.

Pui took me back. We sat in silence as the river flowed past us. I felt very contented here in my silence. Pui was at peace with herself. She was earning enough for the day. I too was at peace. Vietnam had opened itself up to me. Only a little bit perhaps but you can't learn everything in two weeks. I felt at ease with this strange Chinese woman. I felt, if life were simpler, we might be friends. We are banks on the same river. But the river flows wide and strong between us. I handed her 12,000 dong before we reached the other side. I didn't want other people to see money change hands. She had unfinished business to deal with. Sure enough the shouting and raging started immediately we got back. Pui whirled round from one to the other and screamed and waved her arms forcefully, shaking her finger to mark her points. She turned to me:

'Tell them you only give me ten thousand.'

'That's right,' I shouted, 'I gave her ten thousand.' I walked off leaving them to it.

This was part of the compromise she had to make with life. I guessed she would hand over two thousand. I liked Pui. She was a survivor. Ho Xuan Huong would have liked her too.

*

P is for pierced drum.

> To Pierce a Drum
> *I am most sorry, yes indeed.*
> *My drum's been pierced, so hard were the beats*
> *Ah lazy days, five or seven drumsticks are broken*
> *Quiet nights, drumming once or twice or more.*
> *When you are young and healthy you can drum hard*
> *When you get old it's not so easy.*
> *The young can wrestle standing up or seated*

Oh please will someone come to love me
Make our flesh and skin come one.

*

'Want to play a game?' Alice's smile hinted at something naughty.

'What kind of game?'

'Close your eyes.'

I closed them and felt the pressure of the cloth as she tied the blindfold tight.

'Can you see anything?'

I shook my head.

I felt uneasy when the first handcuff went on and struggled.

'Come on. It's just a game. Don't you trust me?'

I went limp then and allowed her to handcuff both hands to the bedpost. I lay with my arms spread out, helpless. I didn't like the feeling at all.

'Hey!'

'Shh!'

Then I felt her fingers unbuttoning the shirt and pulling it open. Her hands massaged my chest then she went to work on my pants. When I was naked she started to rub me with different textures.

'Do you like this?'

It felt like sandpaper.

'Ouch. What is that?'

'Sandpaper.'

My heart started to race. I was feeling very nervous now. I was totally vulnerable. She could do anything she wanted.

'Ouch!'

Something was pinching into my belly. It seemed to burn.

'What are you doing?'

'Clothes pegs.'

'Jesus, Alice!'

'Is this ticklish?'

'No. Ow! Yes. Stop it. Stop it.'

'I'm going to hurt you.'

'Jesus, Alice. Why are you doing this?'

'What's this?'

I heard her open the side table drawer and a moment later felt cold metal against my cock. She pressed it under my testicles.

'What's this?'

'It's a gun.'

'That's right. It's a gun.'

'What are you going to do?'

'What do you think I'm going to do with it?'

'I don't know.'

'Guess.'

'Blow off my balls?'

'Does that scare you?'

'You bet it does.'

'This was Rich's favorite game.'

'That right?'

'He would cuff me to the bed and torture me. Not badly. Not so that there were ever any marks. But it was painful. Like this.'

She clipped a clothes peg to my nipple.

'Shit! Shit!' I tried to struggle but it was no use. I felt humiliated. I could feel a tear streaking down my cheek. I didn't want to cry but I had no control over it. And it hurt.

'Why are you doing this to me Alice?'

'You want to feel responsible for the violence of men? Well, then. Take your punishment.'

'That's not what I meant.'

'Yeah. You meant it the weak pinko-liberal way. Lots of angst. Lots of hand wringing but no balls. No action.'

'Shit Alice. Let me up.'

I felt the barrel of the gun trace a line up my belly and chest until it was pressed against the underside of my head.

'It's not your balls I'm going to blow away. It's your brains.'

'Why?' It came out like a wail. I was thinking of Benjy. Who would bring him up now? For myself, I just hoped it wouldn't hurt too bad. And then it came to me. This was how she'd killed her husband. He'd tracked her down. Somehow she'd tricked him into playing the game. She'd blown his brains out with his own gun. It explained everything. Now she was going to do the same to me. Somehow she'd discovered I knew about the gun. She knew I knew. It was all so pointless. I was a witness. She had to get rid of me. What was she up to now? She'd taken her weight off me. I could hear the rustle of clothes. Then her sex smell, pungent and earthy was in my face.

'Lick my cunt, buster.'

And she pressed herself down on my head. I licked. Laughter bubbled to the surface. Tears of release flowed down my face. It was just a game. It was just a game!

'Didn't you trust me?' she asked later.

'I didn't know...' I shook my head. I didn't have the words to express what I'd felt. The wretched funk. The fear sweat that had poured out of me.

'Rich turned me on to it. We both played the victim but mainly it was me. He liked to inflict pain.'

'So he was a sadist and you...'

'Don't wrap it up too neatly. It's true I like to feel abused but I like to inflict as well. It's good to be the evil mistress. When you're powerless, blindfolded, gagged and chained up and then to be fucked. Yes, fucked. Taken. Hard. It's a raw feeling.' She made a face. 'Trouble is I don't think this is your type of game.'

I shook my head.

'Pity. I'll have to put the whips away.'

'You've got whips?'

'Just joking.' She lit a cigarette, the first I'd seen her smoke. 'Yeah. When I'm a naughty girl I like to smoke.'

'So, you and Rich were heavily into S.M.?'

'The Marquis de Sade was Rich's guru. He had all his books. For myself, I could never stand all the shit stuff. He was a real sicko.'

'I don't know. I've never read him.'

'Oh yeah. It's autistic. But the sex stuff is different. It's totally amoral. It really turns me on. Here...'

She got up and went over to a cupboard.

'This is where I keep all the stuff I don't want visitors to see.'

She pulled a book out and threw it at me. It was a selection of his writings.

'Read through this while I make us some dinner. Want some wine?'

'I'll stick with beer.'

'One beer coming up.'

By the time she came back with it I had my nose deep in the book. I skimmed through a couple of rapes and an orgy or two until I came to a text that was discursive in style. He was arguing the case for his philosophy. I started to read with hard concentration. Resisting what he called 'Nature's voice' was criminal. We should not fight against our natural instincts. And among the most powerful of desires is lust. Instead of trying to shut ourselves off from lust, we should instead work out ways in which lust can be satisfied. To try to resist is pointless. To fight against our desires is to fight against nature. Instead, we should do what nature urges us to do. And if that requires us to be cruel, then we should not refrain from cruelty.

> Cruelty is simply the energy in a man [that] civilization has not yet altogether corrupted.

Women, he goes on to argue, are simply female animals and as is well known, female animals are there for the use of any passing male.

> If then it becomes incontestable that we have received from Nature the right indiscriminately to express our wishes to all women, it likewise becomes incontestable that we have the right to compel their submission, not

exclusively... but temporarily. It cannot be denied that we have the right to decree laws that compel women to yield to the flames of him who would have her; violence itself being one of that right's effects, we can employ it lawfully. Indeed! Has Nature not proven that we have that right, by bestowing upon us the strength needed to bend women to our will?

This was a writer that Joe would have approved of. He'd seen the logic of this immediately. Had he read de Sade? Or had he simply extrapolated from Clausewitz? For it was the same argument. And then there was the matter of murder and violence:

Of all the offenses man may commit against his fellows, murder is without question the cruelest, since it deprives man of the single asset he has received from Nature, and its loss is irreparable. (But) What is man? and what difference is there between him and other plants, between him and all the other animals in the world?... he is born like them; like them, he reproduces, rises, and falls; like them he arrives at old age and sinks like them into nothingness at the close of the life span... Since the parallels are so exact that the enquiring eye of philosophy is absolutely unable to perceive any grounds for discrimination, there is then just as much evil in killing animals as men, or just as little...

If there is no God then we are just like animals. The logic is taut and hard to fault. There are no souls, just fleshy matter. The natural order is a cycle of life and death: death being as natural and as necessary as life. The writer waxes lyrical:

> Now, once we observe that destruction is so useful to her (Nature) that she absolutely cannot dispense with it, and that she cannot achieve her creations without drawing from the store of destruction which death prepares for her. From this moment onward the idea of annihilation which we attach to death ceases to be real...what we call the end of the living animal is... but a simple transformation, a transmutation of matter.

Life and death are just moments in the transformations of matter? Hard to dispute. And so, summing up, he tells us that violence is natural and since nature intends it, we should not pit ourselves against nature:

> Now if she [nature] incites us to murderous acts, she has need of them; that once grasped, how may we suppose ourselves guilty... when we do nothing more than obey her intentions.

Dangerous stuff. War and violence are natural. They're necessary, inevitable, even good! I tried to imagine Carl von Clausewitz writing *On Sex*. De Sade was merely applying the same logic. Violence arms itself indeed. If it's OK for Governments and states then why should it not be OK for individual men and women? That's what he was saying. Joe said it too. We praise Clausewitz for his pragmatism and revile de Sade for his perversion. But their message was the same. Only the context was different.

War is murder. Murder is violence. Violence is Nature. Nature is the absolute basis for being. Everything that follows from Nature cannot be denied. It must be accepted, even affirmed. This is a coherent and rationally based philosophy. It satisfies the beast in man. It is the philosophy of the rampant dick. Cock-logic. It is the philosophy of the insatiable stomach that craves food, more and more food. But, (surely?) there is more to man than the cock and stomach. He has a heart. He has a mind. And perhaps, just maybe, he has a soul. Joe, what happened to your heart and mind? What happened to your soul?

But Joe, perhaps, you would argue that you are merely a reflection of society, that you – as an individual – have the right to base your actions on the same moral basis that the society in which you live bases its actions? If society is rapacious then you can be rapacious? If society is proud and arrogant then you can be proud and arrogant? If society follows a policy that omits the heart and mind that you too have that right? Lust, the power urge, the desire for domination – all this is right, always has been right and always will be right. Everything else is error. If society blames you for this, it is being hypocritical. That's the crux. Can man be more moral than the society in which he lives? Can we argue that he should be? War, after all, is waged by individual men. Can we really expect them to unlearn their lessons when they return home in times of peace?

But, Joe, in one sense you are right. In my dark heart I too find myself drawn to stories of rape. Yes. There is a certain excitement, a certain delicious tension. The heart beats a little faster. Yes, there is something in me that in other circumstances might lead me to rape. This is true. It's not easy for me to say this but yes, it is true. But...But... I also know it's wrong. If I am purely the product of Nature how can I go against Nature? Everything I do or feel is also a product of Nature. Every action serves Nature. If I feel things with my heart, if I think things with my mind, all these too serve Nature. Nature is not just the beast in us. It is the entire being. The entire cosmos even. Nature is the flow of all realized and realizable possibilities. Isn't it strange how far reason can lead us away from our humanity? And isn't it strange also that we have a word – humanity – that seems to suggest that we believe, deep down in our very essence, that we have a moral quality that is fundamentally benevolent? Where did that idea come from? We are a vessel for that idea. And that vessel was created by Nature.

CHAPTER 14

R is for rice cakes.
'This poem uses a Vietnamese dessert as a metaphor,' Le
tells me. 'It consists of small dumplings made of sticky rice and
stuffed with green bean paste. It's served in a sweet soup. She likens
herself to these dumplings.'

Rice Cakes in Sweet Soup
My body is white and round
Sometimes it floats, at times it has sunk
Drowning in the soup of life
Many hands have kneaded this flesh
Some have made me hard and strong
Others have made me so soft I crumble
But know this, inside I am unchanged
I am still pure. My heart is true.
I am still good to eat.

*

I was ready now. My cock was as hard as iron. I stroked it until I knew it wouldn't let me down and then I nudged it into place. Alice moaned. Slowly, my fingers opened her up and I slipped in. And then I was on top of her, inside her, all over her and her warmth flooded through me and when I came it was like a wave running up a long beach. It was only then I saw the blood. I had it on my hands and across my belly and it was smeared across the sheets.

Alice was awake now and her expression was sour.

'I was hoping my period would be late.'

I had my face in my hands and could hardly force myself to meet her gaze.

'I'm sorry, I'm so ashamed...'

'What's going on here?'

'I... I...' How could I explain it? The words refused to form.

'Well, I guess you fucked me,' she chuckled, low, throaty, relaxed. I could feel my face burning with shame and embarrassment. She reached over and kissed me.

'Isn't that what we both wanted? A little honest raw sex? And wow! Was it good for you too?'

I nodded again.

'Sorry about the blood.'

I got so confused between nodding and shaking my head that it wobbled in a dozen directions.

'If you'd asked, I guess I'd have said no. But,' she laughed. 'Since you didn't...' She couldn't stop herself from grinning. 'The fact is you can't spend your life asking for permission. Act now, ask questions later. That's my motto. You ready for some coffee?'

*

S is for Snail.

> The Snail
> *It takes a father and a mother to create a snail*
> *Each day the snail goes about in the stinking grass*
> *If you love this snail you can peel me open*
> *But when you poke please don't choke this small hole.*

*

S is for snakes. Cobras, kraits, emerald green vipers. We stopped at a snake farm in the Mekong delta lands. The snakes slithered lazily in concrete pits. The green vipers wrapped themselves in knots around the bushes of a shrub. I couldn't see them at first until I realized the whole shrub was covered in snakes. The boy showing us around lifted one on a twig and tapped its head. He wasn't worried. The venom had been extracted he told us. Still I kept my distance. 'If this bite you, you dead in five minutes,' he said. I had my doubts about the speed of it. No point in having snakebite antidotes if no-one lives long enough to get to hospital. The cobras were thick-bodied and muddy brown. Their hoods partly inflated, the rocked back and forwards. The farm bred the snakes in cages. Not for the venom obviously.

'For restaurants,' the boy said. Green viper stew, I thought. The stomach heaved slightly. I had thought I would eye the snakes with a cool detached eye, but I couldn't. I thought of the snakes out there in the wild, sliding through the rice paddies, gliding down trees. I shivered.

Later I stopped the car at the side of the road and stepped out. The sun blazed down on the red swathe of the dirt road. But the vegetation started, deep dark green, at the verge. In there it was cool and shaded. I could barely make out a matshed house fifty yards in. Beyond that there was another house and beyond that there was just the darkness of the jungle. I wanted to walk to that house and stop and close my eyes and sink into the atmosphere of that place. But I thought of the snakes gliding in the bushes that I would have to brush against. My guts tightened with fear. It was a different place in there, a different medium. I imagined bulldozers driving in, tearing the place up. Laying down concrete. Then I could walk in without fear. But for this fat American to step in among the trees seemed almost as earth shattering as that first step on the moon. I could not imagine that I could insinuate myself without damage, without risk. I hesitated, daring myself. Then, just as I had summoned up the courage, something brushed against my hair. I leapt back and tried frantically to brush whatever it was away: snake? scorpion? spider? All the sibilant esses. Then I saw it. A caterpillar suspended on a single thread from the tree. It dangled a foot off the ground. Soon it would transform itself into a butterfly. It had that magic ability to transmutate. Then I saw a girl on a bicycle glide out of the shadows, the white skirts of the ao dai flowed around her. This was another world. I could not step out of mine into this other world. The girl was coming towards me like an avenging women warrior, a ghost from the past. She saw me standing there and faltered. She stopped. I saw her uncertainty and felt embarrassed, ashamed. I stepped back hurriedly, turned and got back into the car. She was still there in the shadows as we drove off leaving a cloud of dust to mark our passage. Was it just a dream? Dreams of snakes, writhing hooded cobras, still plague my sleep.

*

T is for Thanh Hoa Cave.

'To understand this you must know that when a Buddhist monk is chanting prayers he keeps time by striking a gong or a wooden clapper,' Ho Nguyen tells me. 'Thanh Hoa is the name of one of the provinces.' I enjoy working with Ho Nguyen. His English is not so good as Le's or Anh's and we progress more slowly but I am more certain of what the actual words say when I work with him. Le and Anh proceed too quickly so that I am often uncertain if I have been given a gloss or a literal translation.

> Thanh Hoa Cave
> *God who made this cave must be most skilled*
> *The entrance folds out nicely round and wrinkled*
> *Bushy grass grows on the stony hillside*
> *Moisture trickles in the oozing stream*
> *The bald bonze seated at the shrine beats out his rhythm*
> *Two round-backed little bonzes worship with him*
> *All who've been here know the beauties of the cave.*
> *Even though their knees are tired they still crave it.*

Ho Nguyen is concerned that I might have missed the metaphor.

'This is about the female organ,' he says.

*

V is for Vietnam. We've almost forgotten what this word means. For us it is not a country, it's an experience, a state of mind (Nam! Nam!). To talk of Vietnam without mentioning napalm, fire-fights, Vietcong or the Ho Chi Minh trail seems absurd. Yet Vietnam exists out there beyond the framework of our associations. Isn't that strange? It's just a place that goes about its business in its own way. We need to understand that. Vietnam. Not an event. A place. Here. Real. Was Joe ever here? Really here? Or was he just inhabiting a state of mind, letting himself be carried along by a train of events? I find I am continuously asking myself this question. Certainly he was never here in this Vietnam that I have experienced. His Vietnam was a moment. A series of moments. Moments in which he never really left America. Yankee Doodle was all around him. Vietnam was that place where the enemy was on the other side of the mirror of what he was seeing. Just round the edge of the glass. There. Easily visible. If only he could get up and move and change position. Look at it from a different angle. But, if he tried, (Would he have tried? I want it to be so but I guess I know better), the object of his enquiry too would shift staying just fractionally beyond the line of vision. But it was there. He knew it was there. Everyone could see it. Everyone except America.

It took us a long time to see it. Too long. Even now, can we really see it? Clearly? The inevitability of our defeat, their victory. Why could we not see it earlier? An impossible question perhaps. We cannot say what it is we know today that we didn't know yesterday. Because now that we know it, it seems that we always did know it. We cannot think back to how it was with us before we knew it. We can see now there never was any point in fighting. At least this truth seems to me to be unassailable. Time sieves out all desires, all reasons. Yet still we cannot seem to acknowledge this error. It's still a closed book. Perhaps we're hoping it will just go away.

But for me, here, now, (writing this in my notebook in Oxford Virginia, I can remember that long ago moment, can remember stamping my foot in the dirt for reassurance), Vietnam is a place. There is no threat. If anything, too much welcome. 'Why do you smile at me?' I find myself asking (but not aloud.) 'We raped your women, killed your babies, napalmed your grandmothers, Agent Oranged your banana groves and rice fields. Goddamn it! You should hate us.' But I don't feel any hate. 'We were the enemy remember?' but of course, for many, we were the friend who let them down, who handed them over to their enemies. But still no reproach. That is the past. Everyone here lives in the present, this present Vietnam which is struggling still to recover from the stupidities of the past. This present Vietnam that we still have not forgiven for beating us. Oh Joe! I came here to try to find you. How absurd. (How Jesus fucking absurd! I can hear you say.) I didn't realize this absurdity immediately. It crept up on me slowly. But once absurdity is evident, you can never go back and reclaim high seriousness.

Vietnam. The sound of the word is like an incantation that has resonated over the years. Nam! Nam! A kind of abracadabra. It seems that each moment in Vietnam should be charged with the ghosts of the past. But that's not how it is. And now here I am in this other country, visiting among the Gooks. Go on. Spit the word out as Joe did. Fucking Gooks! He did it to horrify and it did horrify. My liberal conscience cringed. And then, a long time later, here I too was – just a few days short of three weeks in a foreign country: a country so foreign that when we try to write its history, we fail. Instead we write a history of ourselves, a history of our political manipulations, the heave and swell of power cliques. The 60,000 Americans who died, the two million Vietnamese, just footnotes. Gooks? I didn't meet any Gooks.

Know your enemy, Joe! Confront the enigmas of truth. Who was your enemy Joe? It's a good question. Was it the Gooks? Was it fate? Or genes? Or Uncle Sam? Or the spirit of the times? Or Mom and Dad? Or Wash? Or the whole human species? Who can we lay the blame on? Or was the enemy just you yourself, Joe, for whatever dark cosmic reason nestling in the adamantine depths of your soul?

Jesus! The soul of a man! That flawed and fractured crystal of pure specific being. Oh God! What can we know of that? And whatever we say about your soul, Joe, will stay said because you are not here to unsay it, to deny it.

How can I tell this story? It's not something I can tell from start to finish. Wherever I look there are two worlds: outside and inside, America and Vietnam, then and now, the living and the dead, me and you.

Once, long ago, I tried to record the details of this Vietnam that I traversed, for a short time, so very short. That's all it was – not quite three weeks in a foreign country. Eighteen days as a tourist in another country. There is no narrative. It was a series of random events and serendipitous impressions. It's not something I can tell from start to finish. How can I reach out to you? How can I tell you how it was? I grappled with this problem. I could only see one way. I had to alphabetize the experience.

A is for apple, B is for banana... and W is for war. It seems so long ago and it seems like yesterday.

*

X is for Xuyen. She is a sorrowful woman. I am drawn to women like her like a bee to a blossom. Such women give me my role. I can befriend them with my pity and compassion. She sees me with my book of poems.

'You read this?'

I smile and shake my head.

'Do you like her poems?' I ask.

Xuyen looks at me quizzically. We are leaning on the counter of the souvenirs that she is guarding.

'Ho Xuan Huong? Her poems? Do you like them?'

Her pale, white, tired face pleads incomprehension. She digs out an exercise book for me to write down my question. She studies it briefly and then nods. She understands. Then she nods more vigorously. Yes, she likes them.

'Which is your favorite?'

Once again her eyes look at me questioningly, seeming to hide dark secrets. She is so slim. She seems brittle. I would like to handle her gently. But I understand these women. They are sorrowful because they are victims and they are victims because they acquiesce slowly, resistingly to life, knowing that they do not want this but not knowing what they do want, not knowing how to say 'no'.

I write out the second question. She nods. She looks through the book I have in my hand. Then she finds the poem she is looking for.

> A Woman's Lot
> *Hey! All you women! Do you know this?*
> *On one side is your young son wailing*
> *On the other is your husband's heavy weight.*
> *The son's father crawls to wallow on your belly*
> *The child cries complainingly at your waist*
> *You work to make the best of what you do.*
> *But everything you strive to do turns out a joke*
> *Marriage is a never-ending weight of debt*
> *Hey! All you women! You already know this!*

*

About ten, Alice suddenly got the idea we should go skinny dipping in the pool in the forest.

'It's dark,' I protested. 'We'll get lost.'

'Don't be silly. The moon's out.' And it was, big and bright.

'Come on.'

She led the way down the steps to the road and across it and down the narrow trail. It was a clear night and the stars stood out clear and sharp against the blackness of space. I felt young and naked. Guilty too as if we were doing something wrong, guilty to be having such fun. We didn't need the flashlight that Alice had brought. I was worried about snakes and bears and wolves and anything else that might, well you know...It was pathetic. Here I was, a grown man, and I was jittery about being outdoors in the forest in the dead of night. I could even feel the hairs on the back of my neck bristle. But Alice plunged on ahead and I did my best to keep up with her.

'I reckon the thing to do is to make a racket, let everyone know we're coming so as they can get out of the way.'

It seemed reasonable. I sure didn't want to surprise a rattler or whatever other kind of snake there might be along the way. When we got to the pool Alice peeled off her clothes and waded out into the water before flopping in the shallows on the far side.

'Is it cold?'

She didn't answer except to splash water high into the air, screaming with delight as she did so. I stood and watched her.

'Get your sorry ass in here, pronto.' She called out and reluctantly I started to unbutton my shirt. I wasn't looking forward to this at all. Since taking the pills I'd had a feeling like I had the flu. I piled the clothes where they wouldn't get wet and tentatively dipped my toe in. It was cold. Well, I told myself, I guess you'd better get it over with. I forced myself to surge out into the middle of the pool and flop under the water like Alice had done. Ouch! It was cold. My feet were numb already.

'Jesus Christ!'

Alice laughed as I jumped up and down trying to escape the cold.

'Just relax.'

'What do you mean?'

I was still thrashing about trying to warm up.

'I can't relax. It's too fucking cold.'

'Do it. Just pretend. Just stop shivering and relax.'

Eventually I managed it. And it worked. It didn't feel so cold.

I was wide awake now and my senses were on high alert. The forest around us seemed benign but you never knew who or what might be out there.

'Isn't this fun?' Alice shrieked and waded over to give me a hug as we both flopped together under the water. I was beginning to enjoy myself when I banged my leg.

'Shit!'

I'd scraped my shin on a rock and then a second later stubbed my toe.

'Shit! Shit!' I hopped up and down.

'Are you OK?'

'Yes. No.' This wasn't fun any more. I managed to get to dry land without any further injuries and pulled myself out. But Alice hadn't had enough of splashing and throwing her self flat on the surface of the water causing a ripple of waves to surge away from her in all directions.

'Yowee!'

She was like a child thrilling to the play. I rubbed myself down with my pants before pulling my clothes on again.

'Party pooper!' she yelled at me. She thrashed and splashed for a few minutes while I sat on a tree root and waited.

'I've always wanted to do this.'

'You haven't done it before?'

'No. I couldn't leave Kathy alone in the house.'

When she'd had her fun she stood up straight and started to wade towards me hugging herself and shivering now. It really was cold. I helped pull her out and she wrapped her wet arms around my neck and kissed me with her cold lips.

'I want to tell you something important. Real important.'

'Yeah?'

'Yeah.'

'So, I'm waiting.'

'I know. I just don't know if it's wise.'

'Well, there's only one way to find out.'

'I know.'

She cupped my head in her hand and gave me a light, lingering kiss.

'You're a very tender man.'

'Tender?'

'Yeah. That's a good word isn't it?'

'It's good,' I agreed.

'I love you for it.'

'Love?' I heard my voice say the word hesitantly. I was somewhat fearful of the imposition, of the burden of the word. Alice pulled away from me. I knew she sensed my reserve.

'I'm stupid. I shouldn't have said that.'

'No,' I tried to reassure her. 'No. No.'

'I'll scare you off.'

'No.' I said it more forcefully this time.

'I do love you,' she said again as she pressed her head into my shoulder and for a moment I felt strong and solid again – for a moment I felt I might be worthy of this love. I pressed her to me.

'I think you're wonderful,' I whispered into her ear. 'I feel very lucky.'

'Do you? Me too.'

'How can you be lucky to have someone like me?'

'You just don't know, do you?'

'I don't know anything.'

She gave me a punch, then another. Trying to hammer some truth into me.

'Kiss me.' She said and before I could, she kissed me hard on the mouth.

'We've got to forget the past. Start everything new. Now.'

'The past?' Her mind had leapt forward faster than I could keep up.

'Forget it.'

'Forget the past?'

'Yes. The past has gone. There's only now. Only the future. We've got to let the past go.'

If I only could.

'This is going too fast for me.'

She caressed my cheek and I felt the warmth of her palm burn me. I caught her hand and held it to me.

'Don't worry,' she soothed me. 'I'm here. I'm not going anywhere. There's no hurry. We'll take all the time you need.'

'I'm thinking of Maddie. Maybe she'll come back.'

'You've waited long enough. Let her go.'

Let her go? I didn't know what that meant.

'I made a big mistake once.'

'Yes?'

'When I came here, I thought I'd escaped the past. But I made a mistake. I reached out to the past. I felt I shouldn't lose all contact with the past. I wrote to someone. I thought they were my friend. They told someone I really didn't want to know. You can guess who. Now it's all right. The past is dead and buried. It's finished. But it was close. It shouldn't have happened. And it wouldn't have if I'd had the strength to let it go. Do you understand?'

Did I? Maybe I did.

'Dead and buried?'

She nodded.

'Could you forgive me that?'

Could I? I asked the silence in my heart. It didn't appear to have any objections. There's no sin in defending what's yours. I hugged her to me and we stood still in the moonlight by the pool in the forest. What was I letting myself in for?

Later, back at the house we sat out on the front lawn looking at the moon and the distant stars. Alice spoke her thoughts into the air: 'Thoreau wrote that he got great comfort from the stars. He found them companionable.'

They didn't seem companionable to me. Just cold and infinitely remote.

'When you think about it... The vast distances... The enormous numbers of suns and planetary systems...' I ran out of anything interesting to say about them. Even the words 'vast' and 'enormous' seemed utterly inadequate when compared with the dimensions of the universe.

'Yes,' she smiled and squeezed my hand. 'It makes our concerns seem so very small.'

Later we went to bed and slept but it was a restless night. I was buzzing. I guess I did doze off a while but I was awake at first light. I put my hand in my groin and I felt the stiffness of my cock, a warm memory of happier times, of youth. I was a man again! Shout it from the roofs! How long had it been? And I was suddenly overwhelmed with memories, recalling with sudden vividness the beauty of Maddie's dark flesh, her lithe, firm flesh. Goddamn you girl!

Alice lay sprawled, still asleep, soft and vulnerable, across the bed. I thought of our game last night. I thought of tying her up, blindfolding her and... all the rest of it. Just the thought of it dissolved the anger, made me laugh. Sex games? I didn't think I was the sex game type. Maybe. If I worked at it. Anyway, this was our last morning together. I took the last of the blue pills and lay back on the pillows to wait for it to take effect. Then I must have fallen asleep again and I was back up at the cabin, up there in the mountains. For some reason I was back there with Maddie and Benjy. Why on earth…? Something to do with Tina. Paying our respects. I had a strong sense of foreboding. I wanted to go, leave the mountains, get back to safety. Wash was still there. He'd never been caught. What on earth were we doing there?

'Let's go,' I called out.

'Just one more minute.' She said and everything seemed sticky. Nothing was happening as fast as it should. That was when I heard him, the sound of wood snapping. I whirled round. He had a sour mocking grin across his face. He threw away the two halves of the branch and took hold of his gun, pointing it straight at me.

'Well, now, look what we got ourselves here.' His voice was gravelly and just as mean as I remembered it. The last five years had not been easy on him. He was looking pale and drawn, his skin an ashy yellow. Then I realized it couldn't have been five years, it was three more like. Benjy was still little more than a toddler. This was in the past sometime, something I'd forgotten about. This explained why Maddie had gone away.

'And who's this little fella?'

Maddie had stood up, her hands almost covering her face with the shock of seeing him again.

'Who do you think he is?'

'Is that why you came?'

'What now?' Maddie's voice almost squeaked.

'You ran out on me.'

'And you?' looking at me. 'You was damn near to killing me.'

'No, I...'

But he wouldn't let me finish.

'Shut your dirty mouth, brother Jack. I got some considering to do.'

'Who's that man?' Benjy asked.

'That's your father,' Maddie told him. 'Your big brave daddy who...'

'Shut it.' Wash jerked the gun barrel in her direction.

'Are you goin' to shoot us?' Maddie was gaining courage with every second. 'You goin' to kill your own flesh and blood?'

'I got to think about this.'

'Why don't you just let us go?' I said softly. 'Won't make any difference. The cops know you're up here.'

'I said shut it.' His face was dark with anger now. So, we stood there, the three of us, in the wood buzzing silence of that early afternoon.

'You,' he said finally, looking at Maddie. 'You made a big mistake coming back up here.'

'I know it.' The words came out as a despairing whisper.

'Maybe I should kill you and be done with it.'

'Kill the mother of your son?'

He nodded at me.

'And you!'

But Maddie was obstinate in her scorn: 'Jack's brought up your son and cared for him as if he was his own.'

Wash ignored Maddie. He just looked hard at us, looking at one then the other and back again. I said nothing. I expected to be shot out of hand. But he still looked thoughtful, indecisive. What was he scheming for us? Could he kill his own baby just as he and Joe had killed those Vietnamese babies so many years ago?

Finally he waved to us to sit down on the ground.

'What's his name?' he asked

'Benjy. Benjamin.'

'Hey Benjy?' he called. 'You want to give your dad a big hug?'

Benjy turned to me and threw his hands round my neck. I rocked him gently.

'Do you want to go and say hello to this man?' I asked. Benjy shook his head emphatically and turned his head away burying his face in the skin of my neck. Wash sat cross-legged with the gun laid across his lap. Eventually, I managed to coax Benjy off me and I turned him round towards Wash. It seemed to me our lives depended on it.

'Show him how well you can walk!'

And he started to walk towards Wash who couldn't help himself. I saw the grin of sheer delight blossom across his face.

'This here is my boy! My little baby boy.' He could not disguise the pride in his voice.

For an endless time we sat there, playing all kinds of games, and slowly letting the threat of death dissolve. I kept half an eye out for an opportunity to catch Wash off guard but he was wise to that and even though he lay his gun aside I knew I'd never make it. And then, when we'd somehow exhausted the possibilities of play, it was decision time. He looked at me a long time and I wondered which way the dice would fall.

'OK,' he finally drawled. 'You can go. Take my kid. Bring him up right.'

I could see the immense relief on Maddie's unbelieving face.

'Thank you, Wash,' she said. 'Thank you.'

He turned to her and shook his head.

'Not you girl. Just brother Jack and my boy. A boy needs a father. For a while there, I thought maybe we could all live here in the forest and my cave. But it wouldn't be good. I know that.' He shook his head in bemusement: 'Just think! A son! A son I never knew I had.'

'Let Maddie go too,' I pleaded.

'That's the way it's going to be or...' he waved the gun menacingly.

Maddie looked at me.

'I'm sorry, Jack. You were right. I am a fool. We never should've come. Come here Benjy, give mummy a big hug. There now. You be a big strong boy. You go home with daddy and I'll see you in a bit, OK?'

But Benjy didn't want to leave his mummy behind and it was all we could do to strap him into his seat. He was crying and screaming.

'Get the hell out of here,' Wash yelled, annoyed suddenly, brandishing his gun.

I couldn't get out of there fast enough. I ground the gears and jerked the gas pedal as I pulled away up the track to the dirt road. Benjy screamed. Hell was just starting. The gates were open, the dark heat was rising and I began the long slow fall. Then I woke. The sweat was pouring off me. Alice was holding me.

'Are you OK?'

I looked around me wildly, wondering where I was. And slowly all the pieces fell into place. It was OK. I was safe. Benjy was safe. Maddie? Was gone somewhere, who knows where? Wash? That part of the dream was true. He'd never been caught. He was still up there in the hills, hiding out in his cave. Or he'd gone on somewhere. Couldn't stay up there forever. Yes, it was just a dream. A bad dream.

'Are you OK?' Alice asked again.

I tried to say something but the words stuck in my throat so I just put my arms around her and buried my head in her bosom. It felt warm and safe and good. And then a new thought struck me. We had a gun to get rid of.

JONATHAN CHAMBERLAIN has lived most of his life in Asia. His other works include:

Fiction
  Whitebait & Tofu

Non-fiction
  Wordjazz for Stevie
  King Hui: The Man Who Owned all the Opium in Hong Kong
  Chinese Gods
  Cancer: The Complete Recovery Guide

If you enjoyed this book, please tell three friends*

*We are a small publisher so word of mouth is very important to us.

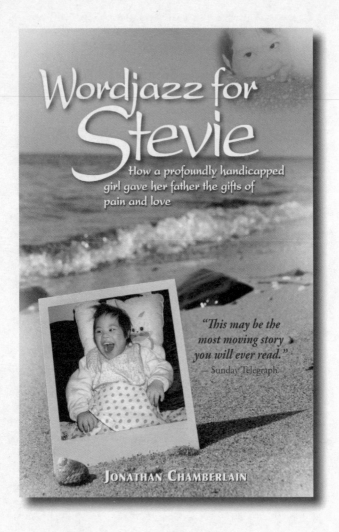

Wordjazz for Stevie

How a profoundly handicapped girl gave her father the gifts of pain and love

"This may be the most moving story you will ever read."
— Sunday Telegraph

JONATHAN CHAMBERLAIN

Also by Jonathan Chamberlain

"This may be the most moving story you will ever read."
— *Sunday Telegraph*

EXPLORE ASIA WITH BLACKSMITH BOOKS

From retailers around the world or from *www.blacksmithbooks.com*